HORSE AND PISTOL

Book 1 in the English Mercenary Series

By

Griff Hosker

Horse and Pistol

Published by Griff Hosker 2024
Copyright ©Griff Hosker

A CIP catalogue record for this title is available from the British Library.

Contents

Real People in the Book

Protestant Leaders

King Frederick V of Bohemia
King James 1st of England and Scotland
King Christian IVth of Denmark - King James' brother-in-law
General Hohenlohe - Bohemian General
Georg Friedrich - Margrave of Baden-Durlach
Christian the Younger of Brunswick
Sir Horace Vere - King James' commander in the Palatinate
Ernst von Mansfield - Mercenary leader
Prince Maurice of Nassau
Prince Frederick of Nassau
Prince Philip William
George Villiers - Duke of Buckingham

Catholic leaders

Johannes Tserklaes, Count of Tilly - Commander of the Catholic League armies
Emperor Ferdinand II, King of Spain and Holy Roman Emperor
Albrecht von Waldstein - Imperial General
Charles Bonaventure de Longueval, 2nd Count of Bucquoy - Imperial General
Colonel Dodo zu Innhausen und Knyphausen - German mercenary
Tommaso Caracciolo, Count of Roccarainola - Spanish mercenary

Others

Sir Richard Young - aide to King James
Sir Théodore de Mayerne - King James' Physician
Edward Zouch - Knight Marshal
John Felton - soldier
Prince Charles of England
Princess Henrietta of France

Prologue

My name is James Bretherton and I know that I was born lucky. I knew it from the first for I had the life of a rich young gentleman. Later, when I became a soldier, my pampered childhood became even clearer to me. I had a mother who was Huguenot French and had brought her father's fortune when she fled to England from the persecution of the French. She had lost her own family but arrived in England as a rich woman. I had a father who, whilst not a noble himself, was descended on his mother's side from Sir Thomas Wyndham, the man who had been King Henry's admiral at the Battle of Flodden. He had an easy life and had the time to teach me to be a gentleman, for I did not see him having to do anything else. He had a bailiff to oversee the lands and was so smitten by my mother that he spent every moment that he could with her.

I was an only child; my birth had taxed my mother and that meant that I was indulged. I had a tutor who taught me mathematics as well as introducing me to books. I was already a fluent speaker of French, thanks to my mother, and my tutor, who was German, also gave me that language. I was taught to ride by my father, who was a superb horseman. I learned to fence, of course, but my father was a progressively minded man and he liked firearms. He showed me how to load and fire a pistol. The pistol had been my grandfather's and it was a precious memory of my mother's father. Each time I loaded and fired it I felt a connection to the Huguenot grandfather killed for his religion. As I grew older my father taught me to use the fowling piece and we hunted game birds along the Tees. The first ten years of my life were, quite simply, the best that a boy could enjoy in Elizabethan England. Queen Elizabeth had outwitted the Spanish and the Catholics who sought to usurp her, and our navy kept our waters clear of enemies.

My world, our world, ended when the Queen died, childless. Part of my education had been in the politics of our land and I knew that this meant a change for England. That change was a new king and a Scottish one at that. The Scots, until the Battle of Flodden, had always been a threat and in the north of England there was certainly suspicion of our nearest neighbours. We lived on the River Tees and the Scots had raided there. My father had friends who visited, for he was a generous host with a fine table. I was often privy to their conversations and understood more than most ten-year-olds. The new king shared my name, James, and, for some inexplicable reason that made me like him from the off. My father was also hopeful about the new ruler. He liked to fish on the river that ran through our land and he took me to catch some trout. It was as we fished that he spoke to me.

"The age of Elizabeth was a glorious one, James, but we have barely a handhold in the New World. The land to the west is rich. Look at the Spanish. Would they have been able to amass such a huge armada without their South American gold? We have a toehold in Virginia. King James brings hope that a younger king will support those of us who wish to benefit from these new lands we have discovered."

"We would move to these new lands, father?"

He laughed, "Move to a place where life can be so parlous? I think not, James. Your mother's health is not up to it and I like my comfort." He began to reel in a brown trout. "No, men like me use our money. We pay others to travel there and to gain lands in our name. When the land yields profit we enjoy the money."

"Are we poor, Father? Do we need to do that?"

"We are not poor but your mother's fortune diminishes each year and the land here, on the Tees, does not bring the income that we need for the life we live. Do not worry. When I finally fit out a ship and send men to the New World, it will yield a great profit for us and you shall inherit all our wealth."

That was my father. He was the most optimistic man I knew. When we returned to the hall and I had cleaned up I spoke with my mother. She rarely left the hall but liked to sit and look at the grounds from her window. I would often sit and talk with her.

"You caught some fish?"

"Yes, Maman," I often spoke French to her. It seemed to give her comfort and made her smile. When she spoke English, it was with an accent and made her sound like a foreigner. When she spoke French, her words flowed. "We shall dine on fresh fish this night."

"Good." She smiled, "You are growing so much. You will soon need new boots. My little boy will be a man." She looked sad.

I knelt next to her and took her hand in mine. I kissed it, "I will always be your little boy and I will always be here for you."

She squeezed my fingers, "You are a good boy. I wonder if I had borne other children they would have been as good as you. I shall never know." She sighed. My mother tired easily.

"Do you need anything? I can fetch it."

"No, James, this is the best medicine that I could have. You this close to me and the view from this window."

I knew, from my visits with my father to other's houses, that we had the luxury of glass in our windows and those windows were large. Most people lived in houses that were illuminated, even during the day, by candles or tallow wax. I knew I was lucky.

My eleventh birthday was celebrated with a dinner in the hall to which I was invited. My mother attended and it was rare for her to do so. I was her reason for living and I was happy that she was there. The other guests were also men with money. They came from up and down the river and arrived on fine horses. It was, for me, a sign that I was about to enter a different world. My tutor had been dismissed the previous year. It was partly that he had taught me all that he knew but mainly because of his dalliances with the servants. It had begun to cause trouble. Now there was talk of my going to university. I was not sure that I wished for that to happen. There were just two in England, Oxford and Cambridge and they were far to the south. I know that the two places of learning had blocked any attempt by those who wished to start new ones. The talk around the table was of the University of St Andrews, in Scotland. Now that we were, in theory, one nation, I could study there and, for some reason, the thought of travelling north was preferable to attending one to the south.

I listened at the table. My mother had taught me that skill. She said little but heard all and it had made her a wise woman. She also taught me to hide my feelings. When she was insulted, and, because she was Huguenot French that happened more than any of us liked, she smiled and pretended she had not heard the insult. I did the same. Some of my father's friends were unpleasant men. They were overweight and reeked of sweat. Their swetebags clearly failed to function. Some of them ate as though it was their last meal and they tore into food. My father was a pragmatic man. These men were important local men. One, Sir Giles Wyndham, was a distant, very distant relative, who was a magistrate further north. As such he was a man to be courted. My mother used the word endured for Sir Giles. He was also a man who was so full of his own self-importance that he tended to hog, not only the food and wine, but also the bulk of the conversation. His view was that there was only one opinion that mattered and that was his.

He was on a particularly high horse that night, "Mark my words, gentlemen," there were women around the table but Sir Giles never referred to them. His wife was dead and he had failed to sire sons. He had only daughters. He sloshed some wine into his mouth and continued, "Our new king comes from the land of Presbyterians. They do not abide Papists. Look what his lords did to that Italian who served his mother. No, the day of the Catholic in this land is about to finally come to a close. There is a movement in Europe that will see the power of Rome eradicated."

I saw my mother ostensibly wipe her mouth but I knew that it was to cover her distress. She had been the only one of her family to escape from Nantes when the French there decided to massacre the Protestant Huguenots. She often told me that she would have exchanged the chests of gold she brought back for her parents and brother to be alive still. She understood, far better than the pompous Sir Giles, the problems of being a Protestant in a Catholic country.

My father was an astute man and he saw my mother's distress. He deftly and subtly changed the subject, "And that is where the New World holds hope, my friends. I hear that in Virginia they have Catholics and Protestants living cheek-by-jowl with no dissension. They have no mighty cathedrals that drain the local people. That is the future."

Sir Giles snorted, "And it is filled with savages and every creature known to man that bites, stings or devours. I would not set foot there."

"Nor would I, Sir Giles, but I would profit from that land. From the stories that I have heard, the land is so vast that no one has any idea of its size. When Drake sailed to its west coast he took half a year to return. Imagine a country that size. What treasure lies beneath its soil? The men who get there first will make a fortune."

Roger Manning was another of my father's friends, his best friend, in fact, and, unlike Sir Giles, a most reasonable man. I liked him. "You have plans, William, to finance an expedition? I know that you are a wealthy man but the risks…"

"The risks are worth taking. We live in an enlightened age, Roger. Queen Elizabeth made it a golden one and now, with a new king, we can profit. The Spanish now look to Europe to increase their power. Thanks to the late Queen's sailors we now control the seas. The voyage is not as perilous as it once was. Aye, I intend to travel to Bristol and equip an expedition."

I saw, again, my mother's reaction and she did not like my father's ideas. Her hand came across the table to squeeze mine. I wondered if he had bothered to even tell her.

Sir Giles harrumphed, "Throwing good money away, William. Invest your gold here, in England."

My father smiled, "The sheep trade was the way to make money but that has now passed. I have flocks of sheep and we barely make a penny from them."

"Muskets and pikes. There will always be war. We may be at peace now but Europe is the place that will devour any kind of weapon. Invest in weapons and you will never be poor."

My father caught my mother's eye, "My wife knows how weapons can end lives in the blink of an eye. I will do many things, Sir Giles, but being a trader in arms is not one of them."

That was my first adult conversation and I heeded every word that passed over my head. When they had left, after the last morsel had been devoured and the last bottle emptied, my mother spoke to me before retiring for the night, "I fear for your future, James. Your father is a good man but he seeks more than we need. We are comfortable, are we not?"

"We are, Mother, but how can this harm us? He equips but one expedition."

"I am not sure but I fear this decision is ill-judged." I wondered if my mother's illness, which was growing worse each day, made her so low in spirits.

It was a month later that my father left us to meet with his agent at the port. The time we spent together saw my mother and I grow closer as she began to deteriorate. We had a doctor who visited but I did not regard him as anything but a leech. His remedy for all my mother's ailments was either to bleed her or give her a purgative. To my mind, they made her weaker. She spent the last three weeks of my father's absence bedbound and I was with her during her waking hours. Often, I would read to her. The books we had were, largely, in French. She enjoyed the language of her birth and it seemed to give her more comfort than any of the remedies given to her by the leeches.

When my father returned he was distraught at the change in my mother. He truly loved her and he took over as her nurse. He was so consumed with her care that he did not speak of the expedition. When, after a month in his care, my mother died, it was as though part of him had died too. He shrank before my eyes. Part of it was that he did not eat as well as he should have done.

The funeral was well attended but that was largely because of the lavish feast my father put on. He also had a tomb built for her. It was made from marble and I knew, from what others said, that it had cost him a fortune. After the funeral, his so-called friends showed their true colours. With the exception of Roger Manning, they stopped visiting. The reason was clear for my father changed after my mother's death. He drank more, and that was not like him. He neglected our lands. He had never been a true agriculturalist but he had in the past at least spoken to the ten or so men we employed. Now he stayed in the house and the farms began to deteriorate. It was not a sudden crash but it was an inevitable slide down a slippery slope.

Then we heard of the dissension in London. It had been some years since the Catholic plotters had tried to blow up Parliament but their grisly deaths had not deterred others. People gathered in London and complained about the king.

"Now you see why the colony I have financed in the New World is so important. There will be no dissension there. The colonists will be too busy exploring to worry about religion."

"Is the colony thriving, Father?"

"I have not heard but I take no news as good news. When your mother died, I wrote a letter to ask Robert, my captain, to name the settlement after your mother. He should have received it by now. When it is established then you and I shall visit. This house reminds me too much of your mother and there is pain each time I enter the parlour and see her empty chair."

The letter, when it arrived, had taken three months to reach us from the colonies and had travelled all the way north from Bristol. My father eagerly tore the seal and then read it. I saw the colour drain from his face and he reread it. He put his face close to it almost as though he was trying to see the Americas. He tossed it aside. It floated to sit on my mother's chair and, before I could speak with him, he left the room. I picked up the letter. It was from his agent in Bristol. The people in his colony, it seemed, had been almost wiped out. A mixture of disease and starvation had killed many of them. When Captain Robert had tried to return to England, his voyage with the handful of survivors had ended in disaster. A storm had sunk his ship and there was only one survivor, a boy called Herrick, who lived long enough to tell his rescuers of the disaster. The agent concluded by including his bill for twenty pounds. I went to my father and found that the wreck of a man had sunk even further. He was already half drunk by the time I found him. I could do little to rouse him from his stupor.

I was now a man, albeit a young man and I mounted my horse and rode the few miles to Piercebridge and the house of Robert Manning. He was busy in his fields when I arrived, with his eight-year-old son, Peter. My visit was a rare occurrence and he stopped immediately when I rode up.

"What is the matter, James?" I told him and he nodded, "I will saddle my horse and return with you."

"Can I come, Father?"

"No, Peter, you are not a skilled enough rider and Master James' words fill me with disquiet. Speed is what is needed."

As we rode he said, "You should brace yourself for worse news, James."

"Worse? How can that be?"

He sighed and said, "He used all the money he had to finance this expedition."

I nodded, "I know and that means he will have to rely on the land. We will not live as well as we did but we can survive."

"No, James, you cannot. Your father took out a loan against the house to find the money to pay for your mother's tomb. He gambled that the colony would bring him the money to repay the debt."

My heart sank. I knew that reneging on a debt could result in prison. By the time we reached our home, I was in such a low place that I did not recognise myself. Was this how my father felt? Everything now hung in the balance. The lack of productivity was now important. Would we have enough time to turn things around and make the money to pay off the debt? I was no farmer and knew nothing about growing crops or raising sheep.

Roger did his best but my father was so drunk that within an hour of my return, he had passed out. Roger sat with me in the parlour, "James, it will be up to you and me to save your father. The house and land have too many expenses. You need a cook and a servant but your father employed ten."

"They are good people."

"I know and I will try to secure them all positions in other houses but money is being drained from the estate and it is not a limitless pot. I know not when the debt is to be repaid but as the loan was taken out some time ago I fear that we do not have long."

"I will do all that I can."

My life changed in that instant. Roger spent almost as much time on our farm as I did. We pared the servants and the budget for the food to the bone. We sold all the horses but two and Roger cast his eye over the farms. Their productivity increased but it was all in vain. The bailiffs rode in with a piece of paper signed by Sir Giles Wyndham. The house now belonged to him. He had bought the debt and we had one week to vacate the house. I detested him even more for we were distant relatives. He was a rich man and could have helped us but he chose, instead, to take advantage of us.

Roger tried to help and he approached my father one morning when he was as lucid as he was going to be. "William, you and James shall live with me. These are dark days but I believe that with hard work and, if you can shun the bottle, we can emerge from this darkness."

My father blinked and I wondered if he had heard. He turned to me and grabbed my hands in his, "My son, I have failed you and I am sorry. I planned for a better life for you than the one you will have. Forgive me."

I smiled and hugged him, "Of course, you are my father and Roger is right. The two of us can begin anew."

His eyes brightened, "And thank you, Roger. I know that you will watch over my son." He stood straighter than I had seen him do so for some time, "Well, if we are to leave then I shall have one last walk around my land. If you two would pack for me we shall leave when I return."

Roger and I smiled and watched him leave the house. We set to with a will. That was the moment when I learned to listen to words. It was only later I recalled this last conversation and realised that both Roger and I had heard the words we wished for and not the actual ones.

It was close to dark and he had not returned. We searched the house but could not find him,

"The river! He loved fishing and I know the spot we would use when we fished. He will be there. He went there to watch the river flow to the sea."

We ran. We told the tale that he had fallen in and drowned but the truth was known to Roger and to me. My father had killed himself. His body had caught on a tree brought down in a storm and we fished him out. *'I know that you will watch over my son.'* The words haunted me. He had chosen this path once he knew that his best friend would care for me.

We told all that it had been an accident. We wanted him buried as a Christian. We had my father interred next to my mother in the lavish tomb that had ruined him and I left my home with just two horses, my father's sword, grandfather's pistol and fowling piece as well as my clothes. I was no longer a rich young man. I was someone who had to find a way to earn a living. What did my future hold?

Chapter 1

Roger and his wife, Caroline, were kind. I was asked to teach Peter the skills of riding, fencing and using a fowling piece. Roger knew that I could do those things and I think he was trying to give some shape to my life. I did not mind for Peter was a good student and I enjoyed teaching him. Perhaps I was too good as a teacher for after a couple of years he did not need me. It might have been that having mastered a horse, pistol and sword, he was bored. I never bored of riding. I loved hunting by the river with a fowling piece and, whilst I rarely had the chance to use either the sword or the pistol, I still practised each day and my sword, my father's sword, was always sharp enough to shave with. I felt guilty as I thought I was leeching from my father's friend. I knew that I was an expense. There were two horses that had to be fed and I had a healthy appetite. My clothes needed to be laundered. Roger's wife never complained but I was a guest in her house and I did not enjoy the experience. Time passed and Peter grew. My life had a pattern to it that was, at first, reassuring and comforting. There were no hidden surprises.

I went with Roger and Peter, one day, to the river. It had not been our intention to go to the river. For one thing, it brought back memories of the discovery of my father's body but, after tramping through the woods to forage for mushrooms, we found ourselves by the river, close to the small island that appeared at various times during the year. We sat on the bank and speculated about the island. I had studied history when I had a tutor. I knew that there was a Roman Fort here and there were the remnants of a Roman bridge in addition to the one that now spanned the river.

I pointed to the island, "I wonder if this was here when the Romans were around?"

Roger smiled, "I suppose so, but why does that interest you?"

Peter was quickly bored or perhaps it was me that made him bored and he left us to find stones to skim across the river. I did not mind as talking to Roger was as close as I could come to speaking to my father.

"Oh, it is just that the thought of that connects me to the past and I find it reassuring to think of Romans being here at this very spot."

We were silent for a while. I found it calming to watch the water rushing by to get to the sea.

"What will I do, Roger?" I had called him Uncle Roger for a while but he had insisted that as I was a man I should use his Christian name.

"What do you want to do?"

"Something useful. You have been kind to me but I cannot stay here forever. I am no leech." A fish popped up for air and as a kingfisher swooped, it descended before it could be devoured. "Perhaps I should go to the New World. My father thought it was a land of opportunity." Even as the words slipped out I knew I would not do that. The New World had ended my father's dreams and taken his life. It would be the last place I would begin my life alone.

Roger waited and when I remained silent he said, "Use your skills. You can ride, and use a pistol and a sword. The king may need men like you and I think you would like a martial life. You could enlist in the army."

I smiled, "I am a gentleman and not a noble. His guards have titles."

"There are the Lieutenant of Durham's men or even the militia commanded by Sir Giles." I cocked an eye and he smiled. "I know that they are a source of great amusement but you could be an officer."

"What, and parade when the lieutenant or the bishop wishes to have their reputations enhanced? I think not. Perhaps I could go abroad. If I sold one of my horses I would have enough for a passage."

Roger shook his head, "You need not sell an animal. If that is your wish then I will pay for your passage."

"You have done enough for me. The more I think about it the better the idea sounds. I can speak French and German and I have martial skills."

"But you would be an innocent abroad. Where would you start? The world of a mercenary soldier is not one I know anything about."

Those words put an end to my dream for he was right and we returned to the house and I went back to a life which was barely above the humdrum. Things might have continued in that vein had not another of Roger's friends come, some many months later, to visit. I had been restless since the talk by the river and I could not see a path to my future. I was unhappy.

Captain Robert Woodrow crossed the bridge heading north. He had with him another soldier and a pack horse. Both the captain and the one who seemed to act as a servant had the tanned faces of men who had served abroad and the captain, who was of an age with Roger, had a beard and hair flecked with grey. I was in the yard practising my fencing. Peter had bored of it and I was using a dummy I had made to practise strokes and blows. Roger was speaking with his reeve. Roger still hung on to the term and the position for he believed in the old systems which had worked since the time of the Conqueror.

"Robert, what brings you here to this rural backwater?"

I stopped my practice and sheathed my sword. Robert dismounted and embraced his friend, "I have recently returned from France and I am heading to Scotland to hire men for my company."

"You are still a soldier then?"

"Aye, for my sins. This is Edgar Smithson, my lieutenant. Is there an inn in the town where I can find a pair of beds?"

"You shall stay here for we have rooms and you are an old friend although we have not met since before I was wed. James, show the captain's servant the stables." He put his arm around his friend, "Come, we shall have our table enlivened by tales this night."

"This way, Edgar." I took the reins of the captain's horse. I had a way with horses and the magnificent animal took to me immediately.

Edgar dismounted and led his horse and the packhorse, "I can see that you have a way with animals and, from what I saw when we entered the yard, you can use a sword. Are you Master Roger's son?"

I shook my head, "Master Roger was kind enough to offer me a home when I was orphaned and my name is James Bretherton."

15

As we entered the stable Caesar, my horse, whinnied a welcome. "Your horse?" The soldier went to stroke Caesar's muzzle.

"Aye, the two hackneys are mine. Caesar and Cleopatra."

He laughed, "Noble names. Are they a couple?"

"No, Caesar is a gelding."

I helped him to unsaddle the animals and we put the saddles on the tack table. I took the curry comb and began to groom the captain's horse. Edgar glanced at me, "I like that. You are not afraid of hard work and you are good with horses." He looked at the manger, "I dare say that this will be my bed." He climbed up and said, "Toss me my bedding."

I threw up his blanket and then saw the hessian-covered object, "Do you want this too?"

He climbed down and shook his head, "No, my friend, that is my matchlock musket." He tapped the sword at his side and said, "Along with my sword these are the tools of my trade."

"You are a mercenary?"

"I am. We have just returned from the Netherlands where we were employed to fight the Spanish."

"And where are the others?"

"They were paid off." He leaned in, "Between you and me, they were not very good. Too many foreigners. That is why the captain came back. He has a commission to raise a company of musketeers and pikemen and to return to Germany. He wants Scots to fight alongside him. They are good soldiers and are cheaper to hire than the Flemish and German soldiers we hired last time." We headed out of the stable, "To be honest, they found it too easy to flee back to their homes when things became hard. If we hire Scots and hardy northerners then they are less likely to be able to do so. Life as a mercenary is not always easy but the rewards can be great."

We headed for the kitchen door. Edgar would count as a servant and, as such, not use the main door. He took off his hat as we entered. The cook, Alice, said, "Wipe your feet." Then she saw me, "Sorry Master James."

I smiled, "I have dirty feet too. This is Edgar and he will be sleeping in the stable."

Edgar knuckled his head and said, "That stew smells fine, Mistress."

It was the right thing to say, "Why thank you, Edgar. I dare say you shall be eating with the servants. I will make sure you have a goodly portion."

As we left the kitchen Edgar winked at me, "An old soldier always knows how to butter up a cook. Food on a campaign is often rarer than hen's teeth. When we can, we eat as though it was our last meal. For many it is."

We entered the hall and Edgar waited there while I entered. Captain Woodrow said, "Roger has been telling me your tale, Master James." He saw Edgar, "Are the animals seen to?"

"Aye, Captain and Master James helped me. I have put my sleeping gear in the stable. Do you need me more this night, Captain?"

"No." He smiled and tossed a silver coin, "Go and find the local alehouse. See what you can discover."

"I will, Captain."

He left and Roger said, "See what he can discover? Here in this backwater?"

"He seeks men. This river marks, for me, the north. From here, until we reach Edinburgh, I shall be hiring men to serve with me in Germany. The coin I gave Edgar will be money well spent. Who knows what he might find?"

Roger waved me to a seat, "Sit, James. You are not a servant, you are a guest."

I felt as though I was imposing on Roger by simply being there but I obeyed and he poured me a beaker of wine. I drank but, remembering my father, not to excess. It had taken my father from me.

"Roger says that you are seeking a future, James."

"I am. I feel as though I am leeching on Roger and I like it not."

"I told you many times, James, I am happy to have you living here in my home. I owe it to your father and your mother."

I said nothing but sipped the wine.

"From what I saw you have skills with a sword. What other skills do you have?"

I was a modest man and did not know what to say. Roger laughed, "Hiding your light, eh James? He can ride. He is a good shot with a fowling piece and he can speak German and French."

I saw the captain's demeanour change when Roger gave out that information, "Fluently?" I rattled off a sentence in French and then German and he laughed. "Those are rare skills in an Englishman."

"My mother was French, Captain."

He said nothing more for Roger's wife came in and introductions were made. As we had a guest we spent the hour before we ate catching up on life here in the rural north and the life of a mercenary soldier. I guessed, from the words he used, that he had made the life sound less bloody than it really was. He spoke of it almost as a crusade. He said he was fighting, not men, but misguided Catholics who seemed intent on eradicating Protestantism from the world. That hit the right note for Roger and his wife remembered the danger presented by the Spanish Armada. King Henry had chosen to leave the Catholic church and a few generations later most people approved. The men like Catesby and Fawkes were the stubborn ones who thought that they could change history through violence.

When we ate the conversation shifted, although Roger was keen to know the captain's plans.

"Will you be returning south when you have your men?"

The captain laughed, "A company of mercenaries tramping through England? I think we would put fear in every man's heart. No, we shall take a ship from Leith."

I was curious, "How do you finance this, Captain?" I knew, all too well, the cost of hiring a ship. It had robbed my father of part of his fortune.

"Prince Maurice of Nassau is my backer. He has given me a thousand guilders to hire my men and pay for a ship. That payment buys me and my men for six months. After that…"

Roger asked, "And then you would return home again?"

"No, for this time I will not hire a rag bag of men but those from this island. We now have a king who has united the kingdom and I would exploit that. We have the best of men here and I will choose only those I think will do as I command." He smiled, "A mercenary company is not a democracy, Roger. I rule with a hand that brooks no argument."

That night my dreams were filled with the captain and his future. After my conversation at the river, this seemed like almost divine intervention. I rose early but I was still later than the captain and Edgar who were in the kitchen and eating. That Edgar had made an impression with Alice was clear and she could not help but smile at the grizzled old warrior.

Captain Robert said, "I like that in a man, James. You rise early."

I did not say that my dreams had been the cause and I just smiled and sat opposite him. Alice liked me and my plate was laden. It was another reason for my guilt. I knew that food cost money and I was doing nothing to earn it. We ate in silence until Captain Robert had finished. He wiped his mouth on his napkin, "It would be rude to leave without bidding farewell to my host but we have far to travel."

"Where do you ride today, Captain Robert?"

"Newcastle. The men there are hardy and I hope to recruit some."

I knew that owning firearms was frowned upon by lords; the fowling piece and my pistol were always hidden from view and I asked, "I can see how you could hire swordsmen, pikemen and horsemen but how do you choose musketeers?"

Edgar chuckled, "You can tell a musketeer for they have ingrained powder beneath their fingernails. Great lords hired them for their skills with powder and they provided the matchlocks. Once the danger was over the matchlocks were placed in armouries and the men were dismissed. As you know, for you saw it, I am a musketeer."

Captain Robert allowed a silence to descend as I finished my food and then he said, "James, from your story and from what I have seen, I think that you would be a good addition to my company."

I was shocked at the offer although I had secretly hoped for it, "I am a callow youth with no martial experience whatsoever."

"All the better for me to mould. You have skills. The fact that you know how to load and fire firearms is a good start. You can ride but, most importantly, you can speak in tongues. I can get by in Dutch but that is all and Edgar butchers every language he tries."

Edgar nodded, "Some say that English is one of them."

"I know not what to say."

Alice shook her head, "Master James, you have a safe and comfortable life here. Why would you exchange that?"

I thought about it later on and it was the phrase '*safe and comfortable*' that did it. True I was safe and comfortable now but I felt like a leech and what would happen when Roger died? I could not see Peter or his mother continuing with the burden that was me. "I will come with you but I must speak with Master Roger first, I owe it to him."

The captain nodded and a huge smile spread across his face, "And you have not yet asked how much you will be paid."

"I assume, Captain Robert, that as I have two horses and my own weapons it will be commensurate with that. Added to which as an interpreter I am as such, valuable."

Edgar burst out laughing and clapped me on the back, "You are a born mercenary, Master James. Without knowing it you have used the right words and phrases. I will prepare our horses."

We headed for the main hall for I heard Roger descend. He smiled when he saw us emerge from the kitchen, "I see that you have risen early and dined already."

Captain Robert nodded, "Aye, my friend, we have far to travel this day." He looked at me and I saw Roger's face. "James has something to say to you. I will fetch my gear from my chamber and bid farewell to the lady of the house."

He left us. Roger was a perceptive man, "You are going with him." It was not a question but a statement of fact.

"We both know that I am like a waif and stray taken in by a man who has the most charitable of motives, but I do not need that charity. I can make a living and, yes, I know the dangers that lie ahead but had you not taken me in then who knows what might have been my fate? You have given me the time to get over the death of my father and come to terms with it. He gambled and lost. I suppose I am gambling too but at least I am not relying on other people to make my fortune. That is in my own hands."

He sighed and held his arms out. We hugged. He said, hoarsely in my ear, "Your father was my dearest friend and I have thought, since his death, if I could have done anything to change it. Perhaps by giving you this time, I have done the right thing. Know that there will always be a home for you here and should this not be the life you really want then return here."

"I will and I thank you. My father could not have had a better friend."

Chapter 2

I did not take Cleopatra. It was on Edgar's advice. "It will be too great of a temptation to others, Master James. Take just one horse. When we reach the Netherlands then the captain might acquire horses to carry our war gear but until then…"

I heeded his advice and said goodbye. I found it hard to say farewell to the horse for she was a connection with my home, now long gone, and my family, also gone. It was like losing my family and my home once more. Peter's eyes were wide with wonder. I was going on an adventure and I think he wished to come. Caroline wept as did Alice, the housekeeper. Roger grasped my arm firmly and said, in my ear, "I hope you find that which you seek. Just knowing what it is you want will be a challenge. I pray you return safely for here is your home now." I was too full of emotion to speak and I just nodded.

With my clothes chosen and packed in two bags that hung on either side of Caesar and a water skin that Roger had used when he had been, albeit briefly, a soldier, we headed north for the town of Newcastle. As we headed through the Durham countryside, I rode with Edgar behind a thoughtful Captain Woodrow. I learned in the time that I spent with him and Edgar, that he was a solitary man not given to inconsequential conversations. Edgar, on the other hand, was more than happy to chat. He had someone to share the burden of protecting his master.

"The thing is that Captain Woodrow is not popular in some quarters. He is too conscientious a soldier to suffer fools and he has made enemies. If he is given a bad order he questions it. Some of the generals who command us are young nobles who think that you can read about war in books and become generals. You cannot. In England, he is seen as a sword for hire, but when we are abroad he is seen differently. There he is seen as a leader of men who fights for those who cannot defend themselves. He returned to England reluctantly."

I could understand that. I had learned that nobles, although no longer the knights who led armies on horseback, mounted and mailed, still looked down on what they saw as professional soldiers. Added to that there were enclaves of Catholicism which did not like the mercenaries who fought for the Protestants. I wondered what I had got myself into.

He knew little of the captain's background but he was quite happy to chat away to me about himself, "I come from south of London. My father was, or so I was told, a soldier. My mother brought me up in a tavern where she served. It was like a blacksmith's forge, tempering the steel that I was to become. By the time my mother died, I was old enough to wield a weapon and I became a billman. I learned to use the harquebus and that meant I became valuable. Musketeers are the future. Men no longer train with the long bow and it is my musket that will decide how battles are fought and won."

I absorbed it all. I felt like an apprentice and Edgar was my master. The captain paid me but my teacher was Edgar.

Edgar could not have been kinder. Before we had left, he had acquired a wooden bowl, spoon and knife for me. He had also persuaded the cook to give us a ham hock and a round of cheese. Edgar, despite his grizzled countenance, had a way with women. He explained how the priority was to keep the captain safe. "That done, and believe me, it will not be easy, we look for food and drink. That is our job. Once we are abroad your skill in languages will be of paramount importance. You can hear what the locals say. Often their smiles disguise sinister intent."

The day passed quickly as he imparted as much information and knowledge as he could. I soaked it in. We called in at Durham to enjoy lunch. It cost the captain coins and we had to pay coppers to have the horses watched by an urchin but Edgar explained that it was necessary. There would be men in Durham who might choose to join our company. The inn we chose was close to the market square and the bustling stallholders. Captain Woodrow was paying and so he ordered. It was a simple stew that had more vegetables and liquid than meat but with a loaf to soak up the juices, it filled a hole. The beer was good beer. Edgar drank three of them but I nursed just one. It was strong beer and I was not used to it.

We stayed for an hour and that was longer than we needed to devour the food but we were rewarded when a man approached. He was not as old as Edgar but he had the broken nose of one who had used his fists in a fight. He knuckled his head and then leaned in to speak quietly. "You are Captain Woodrow, the soldier?"

"I am." He gestured to a seat between him and Edgar. It allowed me to study his face and hear his words clearly.

"Are you hiring men?" He almost whispered the words and I saw his eyes flit to the side.

"Do you seek work? Are you a soldier?"

He nodded and held up his hands, "Stephen Fletcher, I was a musketeer." The reason he held up his hands became clear. There were still flecks of ingrained gunpowder beneath his fingernails. Edgar had told me that men found it hard to rid themselves of it.

"Where did you serve?"

"I worked at the castle," he gestured a thumb behind him."

"And gave up such a lucrative post?"

He shook his head, "They decided to save money. When the new king came from Scotland the bishop decided that we did not need musketeers and we were let go. The muskets were stored and we were unemployed."

"The king has been on the throne long enough for you to have found work."

He snorted, "As a labourer? I am a soldier and a good one. I know how to maintain and fire any weapon that uses gunpowder."

"Can you use a sword?"

"Aye, although I have none. When a man is poor he cannot afford the luxury of a sword."

"No horse?" He shook his head. I knew then that he would be hired and wondered at the wisdom of leaving Cleopatra behind.

"I shall hire you. Until we reach the Netherlands then I will bear all the expenses. This is Edgar, my lieutenant, and James who, until you joined us, was our only recruit. He has a horse and you can ride on the back. After we have hired other men then you shall walk with them."

He grinned, "That suits me."

"We leave as soon as Edgar has finished his ale."

He stood, "And I will be back in a trice. I have little enough."

After he had gone Edgar nodded, "That is one."

"But he has no weapons."

"None of the musketeers we hire will have muskets and few will have swords. When we reach Prince Maurice, they will be provided. The pikes will also be provided by our employer."

"How do you know the skills of the men? You are relying on their word."

Edgar downed his ale in one, "The only men who will seek the life of a mercenary are desperate men. These men have skills and they want to use them. If they did not then they would stay in England and take a job that paid each week and did not try to kill them."

I mounted and watched as the newly hired musketeer pushed his way through the crowds to reach us. He had a hessian bag slung over his back. It must have contained all his worldly possessions. There was a mounting step outside the inn and he used that to climb behind me. I hoped that Caesar would not suffer too much.

As the captain led us towards the bridge and the road north, Stephen seemed to sense my fears and said, "Fear not, James, it is not far to Newcastle and your horse is a good one. Are you a gentleman?"

I was not sure. My father had called himself a gentleman but he had lost his fortune. Had I lost the right to that title when he had died? "I honestly do not know, Stephen. I lost my parents and I lost my inheritance, so I am just a young man on a horse about to embark on a trade of which he knows little."

"Fear not James, Captain Woodrow has a good name. I count myself lucky that I was in the market when you arrived. If I had not been then I would have had to continue my life as an occasional labourer who sleeps where he can. This is a better life for me but, for you, well, you will learn things that you would never learn otherwise."

We headed to the bridge over the Tyne and the castle which had defied the Scots over the years. It was, so Edgar and Stephen assured me, a hard place filled with hard men. I wondered, as we crossed the bridge, if my decision had been a wise one. I was used to a quiet, rural life.

Edgar and our new man talked and I listened. "No wife, Stephen?"

"No, but I was wed and had a bairn. The pestilence came and took them. That was when I served in the castle and it was the service that saved me. And you?"

Edgar laughed, "I am the rolling stone that gathers no moss. Oh, I daresay there are many I have sired who will have this ugly visage as they grow for I do like women but, in this profession, you do not tie yourself down." His voice became serious, "You two are new to this life and you have things to learn that have nothing to do with the skills you bring."

Newcastle was a bustling port. The castle dominated the river and there was a wall that stood to protect the north. I learned, in the week we spent in Newcastle, that the locals were still more than suspicious of the Scots. We might have a Scottish king but they did not trust his former subjects.

We found a cheap inn by the river. We were lucky that they had two rooms. The one Stephen and I shared had a bed and a palliasse. Stephen suggested we take turns using the bed. I was new to all of this and I agreed. Being by the river meant the inn had a high turnover of customers. Those who used the river found it convenient. It meant it was cheap and it was basic. The food I had enjoyed in Roger's home was a delicious memory as we ate watery stews packed with cabbage and beans. The beer, however, was good. The men of Newcastle liked their beer and they liked it strong. Edgar was a trencherman who enjoyed beer and he seemed able to consume large quantities of it with few apparent ill effects.

The captain was all business. It was clement weather and he had the innkeeper bring out a table and a pair of chairs. He and Edgar spent each morning seated there to interview prospective soldiers. Stephen soon bored of this and took me to explore the town. Stephen had been to the town once before. He was scathing about it for he was a Durham man. I learned that they felt totally different about themselves despite living just a few miles from Newcastle.

"It is the Saint, you see."

"The Saint?"

"Saint Oswald of course. His bones lie in the cathedral. We men in Durham have a name for ourselves. It is ancient in origin, haliwerfolc. It means the men of the saint. We are the ones who

guard the bones of the saint and when England goes to war then
the banner of St Oswald leads them." He nodded at the town
which was lively, "Still, it is a busy enough place."

We wandered past the castle and the cathedral and found
ourselves in alleys and side streets. It was a bigger place than
Durham and, being a port, seemed to have a variety of
nationalities. At the end of the first afternoon, we headed for the
river and the captain. The table and chairs were not there and we
headed into the inn. The captain was nowhere to be seen but
Edgar was at a table with the inevitable tankard of foaming ale.

"A good day of work. We found six more musketeers. We
need another fourteen and then we can move on."

He caught the eye of the serving wench and she brought over
two tankards. I was getting used to drinking strong beer but I
never forgot my father's cataclysmic fall. I sipped while Stephen
quaffed.

"What about pikemen?" I knew that we sought them too.
They were the protection for the musketeers.

Edgar shook his head, "They have good billmen here." He
chuckled, "They proved that at Flodden but the Scots know how
to use pikes and they are tough men. Every time I fought them it
took at least three wounds to kill them."

Stephen nodded, "That is what you want before you when
you fire your musket. A wall of mad Scotsmen with fifteen-foot
pikes."

"Edgar, what am I doing here?"

"Ah, you are wondering about your skills, eh? Well, I can use
a musket, and a sword and ride a horse. At a pinch, I can use a
pike. You can ride, you can use a sword and you can fire a
musket. It means that we two, along with the captain can add our
firepower to the musketeers, but we can also use our swords to
protect them and, if we have to, then we can fight as cavalry."

Stephen asked, "Do you and the captain have plate?"

I asked, "Plate?"

"Armour, many men wear helmets with breast and
backplates," answered Edgar. He shook his head, "We have used
it before but we sold it before we returned to England. We can
pick it up if we need it. Some of the pikemen we will hire might
have a helmet and a breastplate. Those will be the better

warriors. Still, that won't be until we cross the Tweed and are in Scotland."

Stephen asked as he neared the end of his ale, "Where is the captain?"

"He knows the castellan and has gone to the castle to seek information. We have the night to ourselves. What say we find somewhere with better food than this cesspit?"

He pulled out a small purse of copper coins, "The captain has provided the funds. Let us enjoy his largesse."

If I had been at home or at Roger's I would have washed before we went out to dine. I learned that the men I was with did not. What Edgar did do was to tell me to strap on my sword. "This can be a rough place and the sight of a sword might be enough to put any of the cut purses off trying to relieve us of them."

Stephen patted the top of his boot, "I have a handy little dagger there."

We donned our hats and headed into the bustling town. There were many noisy, boisterous inns and taverns. We were guided in our choice by Edgar's nose. He seemed to sniff out the ones that might serve the best food. He said, "This one." The sign outside had a crude painting of a crown. Edgar nodded approvingly, "Seems as good a place as any." He tapped his nose, "I smell rabbit!"

We entered and found one empty table. The serving girl, who looked to be just a girl of ten or so took our order.

"You have rabbit?"

She nodded and closed her eyes as she reeled off the food, "Rabbit cooked in ale with mustard, carrots and onions. For a penny extra, you can have bread."

Stephen snorted, "You have to pay for bread?"

The girl gave him a look of disdain, "It is good bread."

Edgar waved a hand, "We will have three portions and three loaves, we have healthy appetites. And bring us three beers."

She had a wax tablet and made marks on it. "You pay before you eat."

Shrugging Edgar handed over what she asked. Stephen was clearly put out despite the fact that he was not even paying.

"Typical Newcastle. They are too close to the Scots and are just as mean as they are."

Edgar leaned in, "Now, no more of that. We have to travel through Scotland and if you can't keep a civil tongue in your head then we will let you go. The captain wants no troublemakers. We had enough of those in the Netherlands with the Germans and the Hungarians. You keep your mouth shut and your ideas to yourself. You are now Captain Woodrow's man and you do as he says."

"Sorry, Edgar."

"And that is another thing, when the other men join us I am Lieutenant Edgar and this is Corporal James."

"But he is a boy!"

I found myself colouring. Edgar snapped, "He is a gentleman and his skills will get us out of trouble where your musket can't."

The ale arrived quickly followed by the food. Both were excellent. I learned that Edgar liked his food and I was often guided by him, especially when we crossed the German Sea and had to eat food which looked and tasted strange to me. While my two companions had four tankards of foaming ale I nursed just one and, when Edgar yawned and we left, there was still a quarter of my drink left. It was good beer but it was strong.

The problem came when Edgar and Stephen needed to make water. They found an alley and relieved themselves. I had consumed less and did not need to avail myself of the opportunity. So it was that when four men appeared from nowhere I was ready and they were not. That they intended harm was clear from the cudgels that they carried. I just reacted and drew my sword even as Stephen said "What the..."

Edgar might have been the oldest but he also had quick reactions. As the club came down his left hand came up to block the blow and he punched the man in the ribs with his other hand. I heard one crack. I whipped my sword sideways and it raked across the back of the hand of a man with a club. My sword was sharp. It sliced through to the bone and I saw a finger hanging by a tendon. I had drawn blood. He screamed. At the same time, Stephen was struck a glancing blow to the side of his head. I darted out my right hand and, as the man raised his club to incapacitate him, I stabbed him in the right arm and blood flowed. Edgar had drawn his sword and he held it at the throat of the only man not struck.

"Now, my friends, as you can see, we are not helpless little ducks to be plucked. You came to take our purses and you have failed. The price for your failure is that you will drop your weapons." The man facing Edgar stiffened and Edgar pricked his sword so that blood dripped, "If we take you to the constable then it will be prison. We offer you a way out of that."

The man nodded and they dropped their weapons. Stephen had risen and he punched the man who had clubbed him hard in the mouth. Teeth fell.

Edgar said, "Now drop your purses."

The prick with the sword had worked and the four small purses were dropped. The man whose hand I had raked said, "For the love of God let me find a healer. I am bleeding to death."

Edgar snorted, "No you are not but you can go."

They fled and Edgar picked up the purses, "Stephen, grab their weapons. We will drop the cudgels and clubs into the river but the knives will come in handy." He nodded to me, "And now you see why young James is important, Stephen. He just saved your life."

Stephen nodded, "Aye, I thought you a sheep now I see the fox masquerading as one."

Once we had dropped the weapons in the river we headed for the inn. "I will speak with the captain. From now on we shall eat here. It is not good food but it is safer food." He shared the coins and the knives. I learned that this was the way of the mercenary. You shared the dangers and the profits. I know my mother would not have approved for I had clearly crippled a man, but I had chosen this particular bed and I had to learn to lie in it.

We stayed another four days and the captain found, in total, nineteen musketeers. Edgar had told him of the incident and the captain spoke to me about it, "You have cut your first man. How did it feel?"

I shook my head, "It happened so quickly that I had no time to think."

"Yet you did, for instead of killing the man who would have clubbed Stephen you wounded him. When we go to war you must strike to kill. A wounded man can kill you. The attack was not the time for your first kill but that day will come and you must prepare yourself for it. If you cannot do that then when we reach Leith and board the ship we shall part and you can return to the Tees. I will not think the worse of you if you do so. Killing a man is not an easy thing but after the first, it gets easier." His words were in my head all the way through Scotland. Could I kill?

As we headed to Scotland, with a line of men behind us, each carrying their belongings, I was largely silent as my mind wrestled with the decision. We no longer used inns, at least not to sleep. There were too many of us. Instead, we bought food and drink and made hovels in the fields of farmers. The towns and villages through which we passed could not wait to get rid of us. We were too large a company to be treated with disdain but they did not like us. By the time we reached Leith, two weeks after leaving Newcastle, we had twenty pikemen. The captain decided we had enough. He left us at the quay while he went to arrange our passage. He found us a ship but it was unloading. We had twelve hours to wait on the stone quay and the weather was wet. I was lucky for I had an oiled cloak which had belonged to my father. I made a tent beneath which Stephen and I sheltered.

It was as we sheltered that we saw four men approach the captain. They were clearly soldiers for they had swords about their waists, helmets, and bucklers on their backs. One had a breastplate.

The captain waved over Edgar and me. Poor Stephen lost his shelter. He said to me, "I do not speak the language of these men. From their English, I think that they wish to serve with us but I would know more before we do. James, try to speak to them."

I tried French. One of them seemed to understand my words but could not speak French well enough for me to understand him. All I could garner was that they were swordsmen. I switched to German and the man with the breastplate grinned, "I can speak German." It turned out that they were Swedes. They had been hired to protect a Scottish lord but he had failed to pay them. They wanted to get back across the German Sea.

I told the captain and he nodded. He spoke a little German, although mine was far better. I was ready to help him, "If you join us then you sign agreements. The rest of my men are Scots and English. I do not trust Germans and I do not know Swedes."

The leader, Erik Hand, said, "We are happy to join you. Your pikemen will need men to stand before them and defend them. We have shields and we know our business.

I saw the captain glance at Edgar who smiled and nodded. Edgar had a sense about these sorts of things as I began to discover the longer I served with him. "Then the four of you can join. This is Lieutenant Edgar and that is Corporal James. I would suggest you have lessons in English from my linguist, eh?"

The Swede grinned, and said, in English, "Aye, Captain." He pointed to each of the men as he gave their names, "Galmr Longstride." Galmr was the tallest man I ever met and towered over all of us. "Lars the Swede." With a shock of blond hair and a beard to match, Lars could have been nothing else. "Drogo Drogosson." He then turned to me, "And we will begin our lessons now, my friend. We do not want confusion in battle because we do not understand a command."

By the time we had boarded the ship the four Swedes could speak a few phrases of English and understand even more. It was the loading of the three horses that took the longest time but eventually, they were boarded and safely tethered. The ship headed down the Forth towards the German Sea. I was leaving England. Would I ever return?

Griff 2023

100 Miles

Chapter 3

I think it was my mother's language skills I had inherited that helped me for I began to learn Swedish as quickly as they learned English. By the time we reached Rotterdam, I could hold conversations with Swedes in both languages. That was the easy part of the voyage for, as the ship tossed and turned on the German Sea, so tempers became frayed amongst the rest of the company and fist fights broke out. The captain had a cabin in the bow castle and seemed oblivious to them. When I spoke of them to Edgar he seemed unconcerned. "It is just establishing a pecking order. Until knives are drawn then I will just watch." He was proved to be correct. After four days the fights ceased. Men sported bloody knuckles and broken noses. Some had lost teeth but there was apparent harmony.

Edgar spent more time with the Swedes. He had great respect for them as soldiers. Once the four had mastered a little English we would speak, after we had eaten the cold food that was our diet for the week, about campaigns in which they had fought. Erik's English was the best and it was he who spoke with Edgar and me.

"We have fought in the war between Spain and the Dutch Republic. They are both good fighters."

Edgar nodded, "We have fought too. The Spanish seem to think that they have a God-given right to rule the world." He chuckled, "We showed them they were wrong when they sent their Armada."

Erik nodded to the knot of musketeers who were lounging in the shelter of the bow castle, "The Spanish pike has had its day and it is the day of the matchlock."

Edgar nodded to me, "Young James here has a pistol, a wheel lock."

My most prized possession was hidden amongst my clothes. It had been my father's favourite toy for it fired a ball without the need for a lit match. The wheel spun and sparked the powder in the pan. The range was laughable. If the target was more than twenty paces away you could not guarantee to hit it.

Erik was impressed, "I should like to have one but I fear they are too expensive."

As we neared the mouth of the harbour and we gathered on the deck, I asked Edgar and Erik why we had hired the four Swedes. "I am not being rude, Erik, but you have no muskets and your swords are outranged by the pikes."

He looked at Edgar for although he understood my words his English was not yet good enough to give me an answer. Edgar smiled. "When enemy pikes approach ours, Erik and his men will use their bucklers to fend off the pikes and then hack the ends from the pikes. Once that is done they will fall back and protect the musketeers. That is why Erik has a breastplate. It cannot stop a musket ball but a pike will not penetrate. If we are attacked by horses then they will stay with the musketeers. Finding these four Swedes was something the captain could not have planned but having found them, they give us an edge."

The harbour was crowded. Rotterdam was the gateway to the Dutch Republic. They were still fighting against the Spanish. Despite the peace, the Spanish wanted their land returned. They ruled the southern half of what had been the Spanish Netherlands but there the people were largely Catholic. The Protestants in the north, like their fellow Protestants in Germany, wanted to be freed from the shackles of Rome. The Holy Roman Empire and Spain were the ones who wished to stamp out Protestantism. This would be a holy war.

Edgar pointed at the flags hanging from the ships in the harbour. They represented every country with a Protestant population, "A big war is coming, James. Spain is a powerful country and she has ambitions. The Emperor also wants to keep his Empire Catholic." He rubbed his hands, "For us, that means employment and pay, good pay."

"I thought that there was a truce between the Dutch and the Spanish." I had used another of my mother's skills, I listened and listened well.

Edgar nodded, "That means nothing. It just means that there are not huge battles but Prince Maurice uses men like us to poke holes in the Spanish defences. He knows that once the truce ends, and it will, we will have gained land. We will not fight major battles, James, but that does not mean that life will be safe. You will see men die and for that, you should be ready."

I wondered if I was. The attack in Newcastle was still fresh in my memory. When we had been attacked I had just reacted. How would I fare, standing in a battle line and knowing that an enemy was coming for me? Would I stand or would I run? If I stood then could I kill? I suddenly wondered at my decision to leave the safety of Roger's home.

The three horses did not cooperate when it came to unloading them. Edgar was philosophical about it, "Horses do not like boats. They will complain but give them the chance to graze and fresh air and you will see a change in them." He nodded to my saddlebags, "We are no longer in England, James. You can now wear your weapons more openly." I frowned and he said, "Hang your pistol around your neck and keep powder and ball handy. Your weapon is, possibly, the most valuable thing you possess. It has a short range but when an enemy closes and the matchlocks have fired then you can fire your wheel lock. It will come as a shock and even if you take out only one man the flash, the bang and the death will make an enemy slow."

We had seen little of Captain Woodrow on the voyage. Edgar had said that was his way but once ashore he dressed for war. He carried his sword and dagger. He wore the helmet he had bought in Leith and he had Edgar order the men to march as we headed for the fortress of Utrecht and a meeting with Prince Maurice. Edgar and Erik had prepared me for the Netherlands. It was a flat country and prone to flooding. It suited small units like ours as we could use the land to hold off greater numbers by using the dykes the people had made to drain the land. As we rode north and east Edgar explained that the prince liked to employ mercenaries so that the people could continue to work and produce food. I was learning that war costs money. He had rich backers; they were Protestants who wanted nothing to do with the church of Rome. As we passed through the recently freed Dutch Republic we saw whole families toiling in the fields. The fact that it was low-lying and prone to flooding also meant that the fields produced good crops. It also explained why Spain wanted them back.

Although the capital was The Hague and the centre of power, Prince Maurice used Utrecht. Utrecht had a good fortress. Redesigned since the days of knights and medieval armies, it had walls intended to deflect the balls sent by artillery. There were angles and glacis that would make assault hard. It was almost a labyrinth to get inside. While the men were left in what had been the outer bailey in times past, the three of us were admitted into the fortress itself and a meeting with Prince Maurice. While Captain Woodrow had little German, his Dutch was better and his skills took us to a meeting with Prince Maurice and Prince Philip William. That the captain was known was clear from the smiles and the welcome.

Edgar and I stood like spare parts while the three of them chattered away in Dutch. The similarity to German meant that I picked up the odd word and gained a general flavour of the conversation but that was all. After a short meeting, we were dismissed. Captain Woodrow seemed well pleased with the way it had gone.

As we headed back to the men he said, "The men will be housed in the fortress for tonight. The pikes and matchlocks, along with the powder will arrive tomorrow. We have a week to get the men used to the new firearms and then we head south for the border. We are to cause mischief around Breda."

I had picked most of that up from the meeting but not the part about Breda. "Breda, Captain?"

He nodded, "Aye, one of the prince's rare failures. He lost the fortress in a siege. There is a truce and so he cannot besiege it again but there is nothing wrong with us raiding the land around it. We are not Dutch."

"It sounds like we are being used as bandits, Captain."

He smiled, "We are called many things, James, but we know that we are fighting to prevent the snake of Rome from denying people the chance to worship the way that they want to." He shrugged, "It is what we do."

Edgar nodded, "And we add to the pay that the prince pays us. If we have to fight soldiers then we will be better than any fortress garrison. This is our chance to get more weapons for our men and to lift a few purses."

I was about to become a true mercenary.

The weapons arrived the next day. The musketeers already had their bandoliers from which would hang the charges but the matchlocks would be new to them all. These were all Dutch made and that meant they fired Dutch ammunition. As the men examined their new weapons, muskettengabel, powder and ball, Edgar gave me a lesson in the matchlock musket. "In England, we use a ball that is heavier than the Dutch. There are eight balls to the pound. These are Dutch-made weapons and they use a lighter ball, twelve to the pound. It will make a difference when the lads become familiar with them. We will spend a week getting used to them and practising our formations and then we are off to war."

I patted my wheel lock. It fired an English ball and was heavier. "What about balls for my wheel lock? I have just ten."

He nodded, "We can probably find some heavier balls but you can use the smaller balls if we have to. Remember, James, your weapon will be used in an emergency. When the matchlocks all fire at once you won't fire at the same time. You have never seen twenty muskets simultaneously. When they do they make a fog as thick as you might see on a winter's day back home. While the men are reloading, they are vulnerable. Our job will be to deal with anything that comes through that fog. Your wheel lock means that you can fire it, drop it to its lanyard and draw your sword to help the captain and me."

I felt the weight of responsibility on my shoulders, but I also understood the reason for my inclusion in the company. I took the opportunity to fill up my powder flask and take three or four of the smaller balls. The men all had charges hanging from their bandoliers but my wheel lock required me to measure out each charge carefully. It precluded reloading in the heat of battle, I knew that without being told. If I drew and fired my pistol it would be a one off and then it would be down to my sword.

I watched the men, professionals all, as they examined their new weapons. The pikemen sharpened the heads of their weapons. Protected by a collar of steel the heads were interchangeable. Edgar told me that some of the men had a different head that could be used against men wearing plate armour. He shook his head, "Fewer men are wearing plate now. Even these Dutch balls can punch a hole in plate. Horsemen like plate armour because it stops sword cuts which is why we still have pikes. A horse will not charge a hedgehog."

The four Swedes were not given any weapons. They all had their own already but they had an interest in the ones used by our company now known as Woodrow's men. Once we reached Utrecht the captain and Edgar had procured orange sashes. It marked us as one company and was also a way of honouring Prince Maurice who was from the House of Orange. As Edgar explained, the use of a sash meant that if we found ourselves in trouble, we could hide the sash and pretend to be other than we were. Mercenary honour, it seemed, was like morning mist. There one moment and disappeared the next.

We left the fortress to find some open land on which to practise. There was precious little and the only patch we found was a boggy barren patch close to the river. We had left the horses in the fortress and marched. My feet were not used to it and they complained.

I noticed that the musketeers all wore wide-brimmed hats. Stephen had explained why, "It keeps the match and the powder dry." He nodded to the pikemen. Some had small helmets while others had woollen hats or caps. "The pikes need clear vision and the hats are there to keep their heads dry. If they are able, they will get pot helmets. We don't need them."

I looked at Edgar and the captain. Both wore wide-brimmed hats. The captain's one had a feather in it. I still wore the beaver skin hat I had used to go hunting with my father. I resolved to buy myself a hat when I had the funds. Thus far we had not been paid. I was not concerned about my food and bed being paid for and what else did I need? I knew how much the pikes, muskets and the Swedes were paid as I had been privy to that discussion. My remuneration was still to be confirmed. The captain had promised a payday before we left for Breda. Some of the men had already earmarked the money for ale and a whorehouse.

The pay came the day before we left for Breda. I was pleasantly surprised to see a gold florin amongst the coins. Captain Woodrow ensured that each man was seen individually. A soldier would not know how much another was paid unless he asked him. It was the Scottish pikemen who chose to spend their money on women and ale. The musketeers and Swedes did go to the inns but they drank sparingly. I was included with the Swedes who saw me as a sort of mascot and I was able to translate for the English who came with us.

"We have a long march ahead of us. Those who are sensible will want clear heads and bodies that do not wish to relieve themselves of the excess they consumed this night. There is always time for celebration when the campaign is over."

I was curious, "But, Erik, we are asked to harass the men near Breda. That sounds to me like an open-ended task. When will it be finished?"

"Either we will be driven off or the truce will end, and war will recommence. The truce was not popular for apart from the siege of Breda the Dutch were successful." He gave me a curious look, "You tire of this already?"

I shook my head, "No, but it seems such an uncertain world I have entered. How do you know if you have won?"

Lars laughed, "You will be alive and looking for another war to occupy you."

When we headed down the road we only rode the three horses until we had left the city. We then dismounted. The horses were too valuable to exhaust and we were marching at the speed of the slowest. The musketeers had the heaviest weapons and, with their bandoliers of charges and balls not to mention their other equipment, trudged rather than marched. I could see why they had not partaken of more ale. I also saw why they shunned plates and helmets. They were just too heavy. The pikemen, however, were the ones who needed to stop the most. Although mainly it was to relieve themselves, some had clearly drunk and eaten too much and left piles of vomit for the first few miles out of Utrecht. I saw Edgar studying those men. Our company numbers were not set in stone. We could hire other pikemen. They just needed courage.

As we walked I spoke to the lieutenant and he told me how, in the fullness of time, we would employ a drummer and the captain would have a standard made. "The drum and the standard become rallying points. We are too few in number at the moment for such refinements but when the bigger war comes along then we shall need them."

"You mean the company will grow in size?"

"Of course. We will quadruple our numbers when this little skirmish escalates into war." He studied me, "Call this your apprenticeship. You can learn to be a warrior. I am not getting any younger and one day the captain will need you to take my place."

"Me? But I know nothing."

"But you have learned quickly and the captain likes you."

"He barely knows me. If we have exchanged more than twenty words since we left Piercebridge I would be surprised."

"He watches and he listens. Do not underestimate the captain. He is one of the foremost leaders of Protestant mercenaries. When you decide to leave this life, if you decide to leave this life, you could be a rich man."

We were marching in the lands wrested from the Spanish and, as such, we were welcomed. Often, we were fetched ale and food. Shelter at night was provided and stabling was found for our horses. Erik knew that would change once we crossed the border.

If I thought we were a solitary company I soon discovered otherwise. We met up with two other companies. One was a Dutch one and the other a mixed one of Germans and Hungarians. They had ten or so more men each than we did. Edgar and the captain got on well with the Dutchmen but there were bad feelings immediately with the German-Hungarian one. It did not bode well. However, as the Dutch captain preferred the company of Captain Woodrow, it did not seem to matter.

We reached the fortress of Geertruidenberg. It had been captured by Prince Maurice more than ten years earlier and had been the place where he had sought refuge when he had lost Breda. It had a Dutch garrison and would be the base for our raids. While we found beds in the barracks the three captains met with the commander of the region. There were enough rooms in the barracks for us to keep apart from the Germans and the Hungarians. It was then that I began to add Dutch to my list of languages. The captain could speak it well and Edgar had a smattering but I seemed to have a natural ear inherited from my mother. She could speak French, English, German and Dutch. Her family had travelled. She had regretted her father's decision to finally settle in France for it sealed his fate and that of her family, my family.

Three days after we had arrived we were given our orders and we marched south. We did not march under the Dutch banner and our orders were simple. We were to cause as much trouble as we could in the hope that the Spanish would react. The Dutch knew the area and they were the ones who scouted ahead of us. It was they who found the enemy. There was a patrol of twenty horsemen heading down the road and the three captains quickly gave their orders. The three companies, minus their horsemen, were secreted down one side of the road that led from Breda. The pikes were on the flanks and the muskets formed the centre. We, the seven horsemen, would wait in the middle of the road and draw their attention. We hoped that the Spanish horsemen would see us and decide to chase us hence. The Dutch scouts reported that they wore helmets and breastplates. We seven filled the road and I found myself on the extreme right. I was petrified. I had not even seen the horsemen but the thought of a soldier wearing a breastplate and a helmet who would make mincemeat of me made me shake.

Edgar leaned over and said, "Draw your pistol. You have a good horse and if you can back him down the road you have an advantage." He nodded at the drainage ditch that ran to my right. "When they are close enough so that you can guarantee a hit then shoot. Drop your weapon and draw your sword. If you back off, then I can use my sword. Have faith in the captain. He saw a soldier in you."

I was not sure but the point was a moot one; I did as he said and cocked the weapon. I knew the effective range was the length of a pike or a lance. If these were lancers who came down the road then my military career would be a short one. When the horses clattered in the road and I finally saw them I was relieved to see that they just had swords. When they spied us they did not hesitate but charged.

Edgar had explained that in an ambush you only put men on one side for fear of hitting your own when their muskets fired. Our men lined the road to our left. As the horsemen passed the matchlocks, the musketeers all opened fire. I would say at once but it was more ragged than that. The rate was determined by a number of factors; the speed of the match, the reactions of the musketeer, and the powder charge. This was not a science but an art. Even so, the smoke that filled the air and the noise from the muskets made confusion reign. We could see nothing but we heard the shouts and the screams as men and horses were hit. I knew that it took minutes to reload a matchlock and that, while the musketeers were safe as they had pikes to protect them, we seven were not.

Amazingly four men and their horses had survived. As they came down our side of the road I suspect that the ones on their right had taken the hits and protected them. One of the Dutch officers had a pistol and he fired at one of the four Spaniards. Even though the Spaniard was wearing a breastplate the heavy ball punched a hole in it and the man fell backwards over his horse. Two of the remaining four rode directly at the three captains. Their better horses marked them as leaders but one came for Edgar and me. I heard Edgar mumble, "Come on then, you Papist bastard. Let us see what you are made of."

I raised my weapon and I leaned my forearm on the saddle. I sensed Edgar raising his sword but I also saw the eyes of the Spaniard and they were fixed on me. Caesar stood his ground. I saw the long, straight Spanish cavalry sword raised and I fired. I had fired the wheel lock before but then it had been in the woods when I had practised. Had I not supported the barrel then I know not where the ball would have gone. In the event, it struck the man in the centre of his face. I had been aiming at his middle and the weapon had lifted. It was a lesson. Had I aimed at his head then I would have missed. The man's head disappeared from my sight in a cloud of smoke and when it cleared he was down and his horse was pawing the ground. The other two Spaniards had been outnumbered and slain. We could not afford prisoners and this was not the time for medieval chivalry.

There was a cheer as the pikemen and musketeers left their places to plunder the bodies. Edgar nodded to me, "You can have what you find on his body. I shall have his horse." It was a command and, in any case, I did not need another horse. I dismounted and it was as I did so I realised that I had not heeded my orders. My sword was still in its scabbard. There was little left of the man's face. My ball had obliterated it. I suppose I could have had his helmet but the thought of scooping out the blood and gore appalled me. Instead, I unfastened his breastplate and took his sword and scabbard. He also had a purse and I took that. I contemplated taking his boots and then saw that his feet were smaller than mine.

I turned and said, "I have what I want."

Just then Stephen ran up. He said, "Any objection to me having what is left?"

Edgar had the reins of the horse and he shook his head, "It was the corporal's kill."

"If there is aught left then it is yours," I said.

He took the helmet from the head. I saw that there was a hole at the rear. Stephen seemed unconcerned and he rinsed out the gore in the drainage ditch. He also took the boots as well as the leather jerkin the man had worn beneath his breastplate. He managed to find a dagger too as well as a locket and a ring. I realised then that my scavenging skills were lacking but I was happy with what I had taken. What I found hard was to look at the body and know that I had taken a life. We had killed them all and by the time we had finished scavenging, most of the bodies were naked. They were thrown into the ditch and we headed back towards Geertruidenberg. We would not return to the fortress but the three captains had spied a deserted farmhouse. We would use that.

As we rode back Captain Woodrow placed his horse next to mine, "A baptism of fire, James, and you emerged unscathed. That first kill is always the hardest. You know that if you had missed then you might be dead?"

I nodded, "I know that Edgar said he would take him and while he might have, the blow that was coming my way would have ended my life."

"Each day will bring you more lessons but I am happy now that I have brought you. Erik Hand is a good judge of men and he sees a warrior in you." He tossed me the hat from the dead leader. "I have a good hat. It is time that you looked the part." The hat was a fine one and well-made with a wide brim. It also had a red feather in it. I wondered if I should remove it, but vanity got the better of me and I left it in.

I felt myself growing as we approached the farmhouse. It was not the victory that did so but the fact that two seasoned warriors saw potential in me. Perhaps I was meant to be a soldier. Certainly, I felt more useful around my new comrades and I also felt comfortable. I was not sure if either of my parents would approve but their deaths and my father's ill-advised decisions had made this almost inevitable.

Chapter 4

Our duty was the second one. I was given command of six of our men and as one of them was Stephen I was happy. We had the watch from dusk until midnight. I knew that it was an easier watch than others would endure. We would, at least, not be woken from our slumbers. With my wheel lock reloaded once more, I led my six musketeers to the road and the track that led to the farm. Edgar had given me instructions and I divided the men into pairs and positioned them to watch both the road and the track. They seemed to accept my authority. I suspect the fact that I had held my nerve and killed the Spaniard helped.

Stephen, when I spoke to him, was extremely happy. "I now have a helmet thanks to you, Corporal. I can hammer the hole at the rear. Being a musketeer it is the top of your head that is in danger. I can hammer out the front and make this into a secrete."

"A secrete?"

"Aye, it is a secret helmet worn, hidden, beneath my hat. It might make a sword strike at my head and not somewhere more vulnerable. The boots I can sell or swap and the jerkin is a good one. I thank you for your generosity." He gave me a sly look, "And if you wish to sell me a sword, I will give you a good price."

To be truthful it was a better sword than my father's but I was loath to give away the heirloom. I shook my head, "The next sword I take will be yours, as a gift."

He laughed, "You have the face of a boy but the mind of a killer."

The land of the Catholics was close enough for us to hear the bells of their holy houses. They were in the distance but it helped me to choose the moment when I sent Stephen to fetch Edgar and our relief. It had not been a long duty but having commanded six men for a few hours made me feel more like a soldier. I thought I had earned my sleep that night and I slept well.

The three captains had not been idle. They had not been asked to stand a watch but they had sat and planned the next course of action. One section of Dutch musketeers had not been designated for duty and they were sent down the road as scouts. They would secrete themselves and watch for the enemy's reaction to our attack. They did not take their muskets. Being Dutch it was hoped that they might be able to escape undetected. Meanwhile, we made the deserted and partially wrecked farmhouse into a fort. As was usual in this area the farm lay on a slightly raised piece of ground. It suited muskets for the pikemen would be below the level of the muskets. If an enemy attacked then the pikemen would simply kneel to allow the muskets to fire while still protecting them with their pikes.

It was late afternoon when the sentry scouts scurried back. The commander in Breda had reacted and sent a mixed force to find out what had happened to his cavalry. The coins we had taken from the dead men had shown us that the horsemen were well-paid and therefore considered something of an elite unit. With Erik and his Swedes as a tiny barrier before the pikes, the muskets formed up in a single line. Their muskettengabel were rammed into the ground and the matchlocks loaded. Each man had his own lighted match and they glowed, ready to be used. Edgar, the captain and I were at the rear of our men. Edgar had his own matchlock. This was an English one and fired a heavier ball. His muskettengabel was also of English design. Edgar looked comfortable with the weapon. I wondered if the Spanish soldiers might be confused for two of the Swedes wore the Spanish helmet, the morion.

The first we knew of the advance was when we saw the upper bodies of the horsemen and the standards. Edgar said, "I estimate two hundred men, Captain."

"Do you see any artillery?"

I could only see horsemen and pikes. How could Edgar estimate the numbers and how could he possibly know if there was any artillery?

"I can only see cavalry. If they had artillery, Captain, then they would need drivers to draw them." He seemed to sense my unspoken question and said, "I count the pikes we can see and add the same number for musketeers."

I was learning valuable lessons each and every day.

The Spanish stopped at the end of the track that led to the farm. Edgar was proved right in every respect. They had no artillery. There were eighty pikes and eighty muskets, the Spanish used the harquebus. The other forty men were cavalry. Our defensive position meant that they had no choice but to make a frontal attack. The drainage ditches that crisscrossed the farmland left them no other option. I now saw the reason for the captain's question. If they had enjoyed the benefit of artillery then they could simply have blasted us out of existence. As we clearly had no horsemen, they moved forward with their musketeers. I wondered at the wisdom of leaving our pikemen and the four Swedes to be blasted by musket fire. Edgar and the Captain did not look unhappy and they just waited. I had realised, when we had ambushed the Spaniards, that it took time to set up the muskets. More importantly, you knew exactly when they were going to open fire when they raised their lighted matches. You could see their right hands as they opened their pan cover and when they touched the serpentine then the weapon would fire. As there was a delay between the lighting and the ball being sent, a professional soldier could prepare. The enemy could not see our muskets and when the Dutch Captain shouted, "Down!" every pikeman and the four Swedes threw themselves to the ground.

Captain Woodrow shouted, "Fire!" and our muskets belched forth a heartbeat before the Spanish. The delay meant that more of our balls struck the enemy than hit our musketeers.

When the Dutch captain shouted, "Pikes rise!" I saw that ten Spanish musketeers had been hit. The survivors were busy reloading. As they were just sixty paces from the pikemen, when the Dutch Captain shouted, "Pikes, charge!" it took the Spanish completely by surprise. Their pikes were at the rear and to the side. The pikes marched purposefully. I could see the panic on the faces of the Spanish musketeers and half of them simply ran. The few who stood were skewered. Erik and his swordsmen had an easy time when a few of the Spanish pikes came at them. Captain Woodrow shouted, "Musketeers, draw swords and after them."

The Dutch and our men understood and obeyed but the Germans did not. I ran, with my sword drawn, towards the confused melee that was developing. The slight slope and the four swordsmen gave an advantage to our pikes and when the

Spanish commander ordered a belated charge by his horsemen it was simply too late. Half of his force were either dead or fled and with the musketeers acting as swordsmen the Spanish pikes were outnumbered. When they joined the rout the skirmish was over. I reached the fight too late to join but the musketeers showed no mercy. The wounded were killed and by the time the captains shouted, "Hold!" it was too late. There were no prisoners and we had slain more than fifty Spaniards. Five of our men had been lost. One unlucky English musketeer, one Dutch pikeman, two German musketeers and a Hungarian pikeman. It was a clear victory by any standards. The bodies were pillaged, purses were lifted and Stephen found his sword. I had done nothing and took nothing. The bodies were left and, the next morning, when we left to return to Geertruidenberg, they were placed in the farmhouse which was set alight. No one tried to stop us as we marched back.

"Is that it, Edgar? It seems little enough. An ambush and a skirmish do not seem enough to warrant the pay we have received from Prince Maurice."

Captain Woodrow had heard and he said, "Explain to our apprentice the realities of war while I go and speak to the other two captains." He spurred his horse to join the other two leaders at the fore of the column.

"We were tasked with upsetting the wasps' nest. We have done that and more. We have accounted for too many Spaniards for the Duke of Parma to ignore it. He will have to do something. If he brings an army then we are too small to face it. If he makes a diplomatic complaint then we can do little about that. There is no point in sitting here some miles from safety for no reason. Prince Maurice may well have another task for us but he wanted the fuse lit and we have more than done that." He saw my confused face, "You have a new hat, a fine sword and a purse with gold." I looked at him in surprise. He shrugged, "I did not look at it if that is what you think but I took a purse from a second and it contained gold. Yours did too?" I nodded, "Then all is good. These have been good days and it may well be that, in the days to come, they are not so good. That is the life of a mercenary."

Certainly, despite the death of Henry Longbottom, the mood in the company was cheerful. His friends carried his weapons and powder. Such things were valuable and as tentmates, they were entitled to them. There were unspoken rules about such things. Once back in the fortress, the captains went to report and the musketeers took to cleaning their weapons. Erik and the Swedes had done well out of the encounter and there was a buzz of excitement in the barracks. For some reason, I felt detached from it all.

When Captain Woodrow returned it was with a smile on his face. The prince was pleased. We spent a month in the fortress where we continued to train and to recruit. More men arrived from England, Scotland and Ireland, seeking employment. With a Scottish king on the throne, there was less work for soldiers in England. Many others had left England to go to the burgeoning colonies in America but with the hazardous journey and the uncertainty of pay, the Netherlands was seen as the best option. The captain hired the ones he thought were the best. I am not sure what would have happened to me had things stayed the way that they were but an event happened in Prague, Bohemia, that changed not only my world but the rest of Europe too.

The news which began the war was relayed to us by a soldier who came from the east. Count Mattias Thurn and the thirty official guardians of the Protestant rights of Bohemia threw two representatives of King Ferdinand from a seventy-foot tower at the Royal Palace of Hradcany in Prague. King Ferdinand was also the King of Hungary and, as Holy Roman Emperor, ruler of Germany. Imperial forces, aided by Spain, decided to take retribution on Bohemia. We heard all this second hand but the next day we heard the official news from Captain Woodrow. It was the beginning of the formation of battle lines. Count Ernst von Mansfield arrived in Utrecht and with him a large Protestant army. We heard that they were, like us, mercenaries. The Duke of Savoy was a supporter of Bohemia and the rebels. He was financing a mercenary army to support the Bohemians. At the time, I was young and I was naïve. I could not see how the deaths of two diplomats in Prague could affect us. We were paid by Prince Maurice and our war was in the Netherlands.

When Captain Woodrow was summoned to the fortress Edgar showed his skills as a second in command. We had more men already and had acquired some horses. He took me and we went to buy another twenty. "Is this not a waste of the captain's money, Edgar?"

He laughed, "It is speculation, I will agree, but when he returns I am guessing that it will be with more money and a new contract." He shrugged, "We took gold from the Spanish. Let us use the Papist coins to make us stronger eh?"

In the event he was right. When he returned Captain Woodrow had a new title. He was now Colonel Woodrow and Edgar was promoted to captain. We were to join General von Mansfield's army and march to Bohemia where we would aid the rebels. Not only were we to be paid by Prince Maurice, but we also had more money from the Duke of Savoy. The men were delighted and with the extra recruits, our numbers were now one hundred and eighty men. Included in that number were ten horsemen and, to my amazement, I was given command of them. Technically, it was Captain Edgar who commanded but as he had other duties, it soon became clear that I would be the one to give orders. If we were used in battle, then it would be Edgar who led. I was now a lieutenant and yet, six months earlier I had been just a recruit and a year earlier I had just been the trainer of Peter Manning. Events were moving so fast that I had no control over them.

Stephen was suspicious of the new commander, "The count is a Catholic! How can he make war against those who are of his own religion?"

I shrugged for my mind was thinking more about the problems of trying to command the horsemen, "I know not. Perhaps he is like the Colonel and a pragmatist."

"A what?"

"It means he is able to put aside personal feelings for practical reasons."

Stephen was not convinced, "Let us say I will heed the commands of Colonel Woodrow but I will review those made by the general."

When I went, with Edgar, to meet our new horsemen, I found them less intimidating than I had expected. For a start half of them were my age. The older ones did not seem to resent me although that may have been due to the way that Edgar introduced me. He made it sound as though I was more experienced than I was. The other advantage I had was that only half were English or Scots. The rest were a mixture of Dutch and Germans. My skills with languages allowed me to talk to them. None of them was armoured. These were not the soldiers the French and Spanish called carabiniers or carabineers. We were light cavalry and Edgar told me our purpose was to scout and to pose a threat to enemy cavalry.

"But Edgar, the enemy cavalry will be more numerous and better armed. They will simply sweep us from the field."

He nodded, "That is true but the Colonel has plans to arm the others like you. He is seeking wheel locks. Charging horsemen will get a real shock if we draw pistols and fire at close range. Remember how we shredded the Spanish line? It will take a month to reach Prague and he intends to arm us before we reach the city."

It was as we began our ride that my standing rose with the men I had been given. I was a better horseman than they were. My father had taught me well and Roger had maintained the lessons. Caesar was a good horse and I was able to ride and command him with ease. It impressed the men, even the older ones. We all received the same pay but horses necessitated grazing and feed. As we were the scouts it meant that we were often the first ones in a town or village. My skills with words often found us the best beds, grazing and food. Edgar always deferred to me. I was becoming a sword for hire and learning skills that I would not have dreamt of a year or so earlier.

Our route took us through Protestant lands. Those who were Lutherans were tolerated by the Emperor and the Spanish but the Jesuits who advised Ferdinand wanted the Calvinists to be treated harshly. That was reflected in the way we were greeted. The Calvinists saw us as saviours. They were not at war yet for the Spanish would have to overcome the Dutch to do so and, despite our raid, the Dutch and Spanish peace still held. The closer we came to Bohemia the more evidence we saw of preparations for war. By the time we reached Prague, we had acquired seven wheel locks and my standing amongst the men had risen when I was able to demonstrate the weapon. Even the older horsemen did not have the skills that I possessed. It took weeks to reach Prague and I had changed dramatically by the time we rode into the capital of Bohemia.

Our leader went to meet with King Frederick of Bohemia, I learned that he was the son-in-law of King James. The colonels all gathered in an inn to discuss strategy. It seemed there was a small Catholic enclave at Pilsen just sixty miles from Prague. Eager to impress the king the general led us to the small town. We, the scouts, were sent ahead. I was relieved that the walls were not very high and, even better for us, the gates were open. They did not suspect a Bohemian army was on its doorstep. Edgar sent Ned, a young horseman, back with the news. The Colonel returned a short time later with both him and another twenty horsemen.

"We will take advantage of their lassitude. The General is force marching the rest of the army behind us. All that we need to do is to take the gate and hold it. Lieutenant James, I want you and the others with wheel locks to be ready to clear away any muskets that await us."

I swallowed. It was a great responsibility but I saluted and gathered the seven men I would be leading. I made sure that their weapons were loaded and I had them form lines of twos. We would not be the first through the gates. Edgar and the Colonel would have that distinction. When we were ready he gave the command and we burst from the woods and galloped. Our horses had rested and were eager. The men on the gates were tardy to close the gates. Indeed, it took them some fateful minutes to realise that we were a threat. The eight men led by the Colonel and Edgar used their swords to sweep away the opposition and then we were through. While the two officers remained mounted Edgar designated six men to dismount and to guard the gates.

The defenders soon reacted and ten men formed up with their muskets behind a thin line of pikes. I watched them raise their weapons and I shouted, "On my command fire at the musketeers." The pikes were twenty paces from us and the muskets thirty. The range was a little too long for me but we had no choice. We had to fire before the muskets. I knew that Colonel Woodrow would be preparing to charge once we did. He had few men but they rode horses and that gave them an advantage. I had taught the men with the pistols to use their forearms and the saddles as a rest and that gave us an advantage. We were firing from a height and when I shouted, "Now!", unlike muskets, the wheel locks all fired at once. That the defenders had not expected it was clear. They had not thought we had firearms. The volley sounded before the musketeers had the chance to touch their matches. The balls flew through both pikemen and musketeers. As balls struck heads and helmets they pinged off to strike a second victim. Added to the smoke there was confusion and Colonel Woodrow exploited it.

"Charge!"

There were only a few of us but because of the fog from the muskets, we appeared suddenly before the pikemen and were able to slash and stab them while they were disordered. Even as the musketeers fled the general and his bodyguard clattered into the town. We had taken it and, as I was told many times later on, it was down to me and my wheel locks. The taking of the town had come as a surprise to all and my standing rose. I knew now what to do after a victory. My men and I searched the bodies of the ones we had slain. We gained muskets as well as the purses of men who, as they owned expensive muskets, were richer than most. By the time we left the city, now in the hands of a garrison left by the general, my star had risen and I was accorded great respect. We returned to Prague, lauded as heroes and it was the time to spend a little of my money.

Once back in the city, Edgar and I explored Prague. Here my language skills were of little use as I did not speak the language. However, we found that my German sufficed. There was an air of optimism in the city. After all, it was far from Spain and Emperor Ferdinand and two thousand men, mainly Dutch, had come to their aid. Even Edgar seemed to have been seduced by the distance we lay from Spain. One advantage of my German tutor was that he had been a clever man. He had never been a pleasant man for he was arrogant but I could not fault his knowledge. He had taught me more than mathematics, languages, the classics and the history of the world; he had taught me about the geography of the world and it was more complicated than Edgar realised. I tried to explain it to the two of them as we enjoyed some Bohemian beer.

I used the foam on the table to make an improvised map, "The Spanish have half of the Netherlands and there is an army there."

"Aye, but Prince Maurice will oppose any attempt to march across his lands."

"The Spanish will not be impeded for Luxembourg is Catholic. The people there would allow an enemy to march across their lands. Their journey would be shorter than ours. Even now they could have an army marching to quash this rebellion."

Edgar was thoughtful. He was that rarity, a veteran who listened to others. Stephen on the other hand was quite bullish, "We have defeated the Spanish before. We were outnumbered when we last met them and yet still sent them packing."

"Because Colonel Woodrow was in command. I do not know this General von Mansfield." The seeds of doubt I had planted in Edgar's mind were beginning to grow. A week after our arrival and before our presence could become a problem for the Bohemians, we set off south to march the one hundred and forty miles to Vienna. It was Hapsburg and therefore Spanish. General von Mansfield had been ordered by the king to take it. This time the doubts were also in the mind of Colonel Woodrow. I was too junior for him to confide in me but Edgar and he were old friends.

"A siege is not the work for us. We should be preparing to meet the army that they will send against us. The other mercenary leaders agree but the general..." he waved a hand, "has been persuaded by King Frederick that this is a good idea. I fear that the money paid by Prince Maurice is wasted."

We had all been paid before we left. Men like Edgar and me still had full purses but some of the other men had spent their pay. They were the ones hoping to be let loose on Catholic lands where they could replenish their supply of coins. Despite the noble cause of protecting Protestants, it was a sad fact of life that we were mercenaries and, perforce, many were driven by less noble motives. I was taking the money but my mother and her experience had made me a hater of Papists. She had described her flight from France and the way her family had been butchered. The reality had haunted her and her description had given me nightmares. I would have served even without pay.

An army on foot does not move quickly. General von Waldstein, the enemy leader in the area, had apparently fled Moravia with the treasury. It was another reason for the choice of Vienna for our attack. The king wanted back much-needed gold taken from his province. Our slow approach meant that von Waldstein had plenty of time to prepare for a siege. Edgar said that it did not bode well.

When we reached the city the walls were manned. The city had endured attacks from the Ottomans for years and knew well how to defend. The River Danube gave them both water and defence and their walls were high. While the pikes and musketeers dug trenches, Edgar and I took our horsemen to raid the lands around the city. Most of the villages we found were empty. Their occupants had fled to Vienna. We found the odd fowl but that was all and we had to venture further afield. Edgar took the decision to camp rather than return to the siege and it proved to be prescient. We ate the fowl we had taken and rose early to raid south of the Danube. It was a wise move. There was grazing and the people thought themselves safe from attack. I found it hard to ride, sword drawn, into peaceful villages to take their food but Edgar pointed out that these were the enemy. They were not soldiers but they supported the emperor. In the event, my sword remained free from blood. Horsemen galloping down the road could be heard and the people simply fled. They left empty houses and animals for us to take. That day we took three small villages and with three captured wagons we carried back much-needed supplies for our army. The men also knew where to look for coins. I was intrigued the first time I saw men remove tables from the kitchens and look beneath the floorboards. They offered to share their cache with me but I declined. Edgar said that I was soft.

By the time we returned to the siege, the trenches were complete. We delivered two of the wagons to the general but Edgar kept the third for us. We now had two extra horses and whilst they were draught animals, who knew when they would come in handy? I expected a lengthy and protracted siege.

Indeed, having been taught by my tutor about such things I was interested to see one first hand. I was in for a disappointment. After a month the general decided that he did not have enough men and, with his tail between his legs, we returned to Prague. There was a mood of dissent amongst most of the men. They had endured a siege but had nothing to show for it. Our horsemen wisely kept silent about their bulging purses. Once more we trudged through a land we had already raided. The people suffered and we were also hungry. It took time for pikes and muskets to march.

As we settled into the city of Prague I wondered if this Bohemian war would simply peter out. The life was not what I had expected.

Chapter 5

It was the need for reinforcements at the siege of Budějovice that made us leave what, for many, was a comfortable billet. General Hohenlohe was besieging the Catholic town that lay many miles to the south. Smaller than Vienna, even Colonel Woodrow thought that we had a chance to succeed. Our two thousand men were reinforced by fifteen hundred Bohemians, and we had a baggage train with equipment to bring about a speedy end to a siege. The mood, as we marched south, was optimistic. Edgar was not so sure. He gestured back at the ragtag army of Bohemians that followed us. They were armed and dressed without any order. Where our pikemen marched with pikes over their shoulders, they marched with neighbours. Their muskets varied from ancient harquebuses to matchlocks. "These have heart, James, but heart is often not enough. You need discipline. If we have to force the walls these will be keen enough but when the enemy repulses them then who knows what the effect might be."

We were ahead of the rest of our company and the colonel did not hear the words. I suspect he would have disapproved.

"But will they have to scale the walls? We bring artillery pieces with us. Will they not batter down the walls and the gates?"

"Aye, they will but in any siege it comes down to men forcing a breach. If the enemy have muskets and cannon on the other side then when our men breach the walls they will have a hot welcome waiting for them. I would trust our men to push on but these Bohemians…?"

Our twenty horsemen had become a tightly-knit group. When we had been in Pilsen we had acquired four more wheel locks. Edgar took one for the Colonel had his own and we became a stronger armed body of scouts. When we camped my horsemen, for so I thought of them, were given a duty in the small hours of the night. It was the first one I had endured and I found it challenging. We had a responsibility for more than three and a half thousand men. I know Edgar was with me but it was still harder than I had expected.

The march was gruelling. There was little food for the land had been plundered already. My horsemen and I were lucky for we were normally the first to find food and grazing. Even so, our horses became leaner. The days when we did not lead the column saw us tightening our belts.

We were approaching the village of Záblatí when we were ambushed. We were not at the fore that day. It was not an ambush such as we had conducted against the Spanish, for the army that found us had hunted us and approached in line of battle. They did not wait for us to walk into their web; the Count of Bucquoy and his five thousand men were the hunters and, as we were strung out in line of march, they attacked along the whole length of the column.

Colonel Woodrow was neither a coward nor a fool and he quickly organised our company into two blocks of pikemen guarding the single block of musketeers. Edgar shook his head as he loaded his wheel lock, "We are next to Bohemian peasants, James, and that does not bode well."

We were behind the musketeers. Our job was to react to any breaches in our line. I had never been in a battle before and it was horrific. The blocks of musketeers blazed away at each other. In the case of our company, we inflicted as many casualties as we took but the Bohemians, representing almost half our army, did little damage to the enemy. When the regiment next to us broke it was like the bursting of a dam. Others joined the flight and the Spanish cavalrymen were waiting to pounce. They charged through the fog of musket fire. These were men with breastplates and helmets. They were the best of the Spanish. They had fired their wheel locks already at the Bohemians and that, I think, was what saved us. There were a hundred of them charging at us. Colonel Woodrow shouted, "Right pikes, wheel!" We were well trained and the block of pikes to the right of the musketeers swung their pikes around to face the horsemen. It was well done but the muskets had still to be reloaded. The pikemen did their job and the horsemen were forced to come around the pikes to strike at us.

I believe we might have saved more men but for an attack by a Spanish Tercio. Four companies of two hundred and fifty men each, in files of sixty men, were launched at the mercenary companies that defiantly faced the Spanish. There were fewer of our pikes to face them and the Spanish pikes simply rolled into the musketeers. The few who had buff jackets lasted minutes longer than the others. We had our own problems. We had a hundred horsemen charging at us. I shouted, "Fire!" when they were just thirty paces from us. The fog of gunpowder hid them but gave me the chance to draw my sword and let my pistol drop to its lanyard. We had hurt them but there were still too many of them. In a way, we were lucky that some of them sought to chase after the luckless Bohemians. Had more than half not done so then this tale would not be told. I had my sword pointed at the wall of horsemen as they emerged from the blanket of stinking grey smoke and I was lucky once more; the plated Spaniard rode straight into my sword and my blade found a vulnerable spot. He tumbled from the back of his horse. Around me, others were not so lucky. I saw men I had marched with being chopped and hacked from the backs of their horses. When I glanced to my left I saw that the musketeers and pikemen were either dead or fled. It was then that I saw Colonel Woodrow being hacked to pieces by two sergeants with halberds. The army was in rout and when Edgar shouted, "We are done for, James. We must flee. I do not want to die here!" I just nodded. I saw blood coming from his arm and knew that he was wounded.

Knowing what needed to be done and doing it were two entirely different things. All around us the Spanish cavalry were slashing and stabbing at men who could do little against plated men. I suddenly realised that the horse of the man I had killed was standing next to me and in the holster was the man's second wheel lock. I grabbed the weapon, cocked it and, hoping that it was loaded, fired. The flash and the powder told me it was and the horseman who was raising his sword to end my life died. I replaced the pistol in my own holster and grabbed the reins of the horse. The man I had killed had given me a gap through which we could ride.

"Edgar, follow me!" I knew it was ridiculous for a callow youth to give orders to a veteran but I had spied hope. Through the gap, I saw that there were few enemies. They were all engaged in the business of slaughter. We could ride through their lines and avoid pursuit.

I knew that Edgar was affected by his wound when he nodded and said, "Lead on, James, for my hope is gone."

It was as we rode through the dead musketeers that a hand was raised and a familiar voice said, "For the love of God, help me, James." It was a wounded Stephen. He had a mound of dead Spanish around him but he was clearly in no position to march.

I could not leave him despite our parlous position. I reined in and said, "Climb on this Spanish mount."

Stephen was no horseman. A pikeman loomed up out of the gloom and lunged his pike at me. I used my left hand to grab the head and, as I still had my sword, slashed down at him. He had a breastplate but no gorget and my sword bit into his neck. He dropped the pike as Stephen scrambled onto the back of the horse. I was the one who was without a wound and I led the other two on a mad ride through the enemy lines. We rode towards the rear of the enemy. It was instinctive for me for I reasoned there would be fewer veterans at the rear. I was right. We even passed the enemy general who gave a bemused smile as the three of us galloped through his baggage train. The men there were too surprised to do anything and when we reached, after a short climb, a wood, I stopped and looked back. Behind us, the battle was clearly over. In the distance, I saw the Spanish cavalry as they pursued fleeing men. The Spanish pikes and musketeers had dropped their weapons and were salvaging what they could from the dead. The coins and treasure we had taken at Pilsen were now in Spanish hands.

Edgar looked in shock. It was not just the wound, it was the death of Colonel Woodrow and all of our men that had shaken him to the core. "Where are you wounded, Edgar?"

He looked at me, dully, "Wounded?"

"I can see blood on your hand. Where has it come from?"

He looked down, "My shoulder, I think." He took out a wad of cloth and rammed it into the wound. "They are all dead."

"But we are not, though we are in a most parlous position." I turned to Stephen. He was already tending to his wound which was to his thigh. "And you?"

He patted his purse, "Unlike our dead comrades I still have my purse and this has decided me. I will return to England.

Mayhap I can find a post with some lord. It may not pay as well as this but a dead man cannot spend gold."

"I meant your wound."

"It was a clean cut. When we can I will use vinegar and honey."

I dismounted and went to his horse. In the saddlebags, I found what I was looking for. There was some grain as well as honey and vinegar. I gave them to him. I also found more ammunition. I transferred the ammunition and powder to mine as well as the two holsters. There was only one pistol but that mattered not. I also found a purse. I left the purse in the saddle bag. Once the wounds were tended, I made the other two eat from the rations we carried with us. I knew they needed it.

"Edgar, do we head for Prague?"

He shook his head. The food had revived him a little, "I think not. The Spanish will head there. Our best bet is to head northwest back to Utrecht. It is a long way and most of the land through which we will pass is Catholic. There is a garrison at Pilsen and we can augment our supplies there."

I knew that Pilsen lay fifty miles away. We would have to sleep in the woods but I doubted that we would be disturbed travelling that way. I led. The battle had done one thing. It had promoted me to leader. I was not sure that I was ready but with two wounded men, I had little choice in the matter.

We were lucky in that my two comrades were tough men. They had dealt with their own wounds and did not complain. The horse I had taken was a good one, better, indeed, than Caesar and was well capable of carrying Stephen. We stopped when darkness came and sought a clearing in the woods close to water. I unsaddled all three horses and examined them for wounds and injuries. They were our only hope of travelling the four hundred and odd miles to safety. They had not even a scratch. I shared the grain between the three of them after they had been watered. It was a cold meal we ate but it was filling. When we had eaten I cleaned and reloaded my two wheel locks and then took my whetstone to my sword. I knew we might need them again.

As we rolled in our blankets, we could not afford a sentry, Edgar said, "I do not know about you, James, but I am of the same mind as Stephen here. I am done with the life of a mercenary, Colonel Woodrow was butchered and he was the finest soldier I ever knew. I shall take my purse and return to England."

"You say that now because the deaths are still too close to ignore. Time will make the memories fade. You are a warrior, Edgar."

"I was a warrior. I am old enough to be your father, James. I have no family and the thought of dying alone here in this land does not appeal. I do not need much and I can earn a living. There are inns in England that need someone with a strong right arm. I could do that." I heard him sigh, "Better a death in a bed in England than in some foreign field."

Stephen said, "All those men...dead."

Edgar's sad voice came from the dark, "We survived. There may be others but the Captain...he is gone." All hope had gone from the man I had thought was a rock. If nothing else it showed me the scale of the defeat.

There was a change in us from that moment on. Stephen had always deferred to me for he thought me a gentleman but now Edgar did too, and it was I who led the three of us. We had ditched the sashes, not that they would attract too much attention, but any who had fought against us would know we had been at the battle and that we needed to avoid. We were not an uncommon sight in Germany. There were many men such as us. They were either seeking employment or returning home. My skills with language came to our aid and as I spoke, I listened not just to the words but the accents and nuances. Both Edgar and Stephen could understand German but it was a mechanical understanding. I was also able to modulate my tone and I received more smiles than scowls when we stopped for directions or to buy food. It took weeks for us to move, slowly and surreptitiously through a land where every village was potentially hostile to us.

We managed to get a few supplies at Pilsen. The news of the disaster made them less generous than they might have been. Each night when we stopped, I examined the wounds. We had taken to camping rather than risking an inn. We did use inns and taverns, where we found them, but we did not seek beds. Towns and villages might have someone who was an enemy and a room trapped us. Our horses could be taken. By camping, we could hobble our horses close to us and choose somewhere off the beaten track. Edgar's old skills came to the fore and he showed us how to make traps around the camp that would warn us of an enemy. We did light fires for hot food helped revive spirits and the fire gave us a little warmth at night.

We had travelled one hundred and five miles when danger reared its head. It was Caesar who warned us. He was usually silent and so, when he whinnied in the dark, I was alert. We had taken to sleeping with weapons close to hand. My pair of wheel locks lay just beyond my blanket and my sword was near to my right hand. I hissed, "Edgar!" and peered into the dark.

I did not move for that would alert our enemies but I did peer into the woods at the edge of the clearing. Four men approached and they had swords in their hands. They meant us harm. They came from the opposite side of our camp to our horses and that helped me. I could fire my wheel locks and know that I would not risk hitting our three animals. The animals were probably the reason the men sought to ambush us. I had no idea if either Edgar or Stephen had heard my hissed warning but I acted as though they had. I threw off the blanket and grabbed both a wheel lock and my sword. As soon as I moved they did too and ran at us. The fire was between us and them and gave me just a moment or two. I raised the wheel lock. It was in my left hand and that was not as strong as my right. The pistol was loaded and cocked. I fired when the first man was just five paces away. I had learned to aim at the middle of a target and the gun exploded like a crack of thunder. The flash half-blinded me and smoke came between us. I dropped the pistol and it was as I reached for the second pistol that a crossbow bolt flew over my head. Had I remained standing I would have been dead. I grabbed the pistol and fired it at the man whose face was just four paces from me. He had a halberd and was almost within touching distance of me. This time the pistol jerked up and the man's head disappeared.

From my right came the sound of another wheel lock. That was Edgar who had fired from a prone position. I heard the cry and saw the crossbowman fall. It was a good shot as the man was twenty paces away. I swashed aside the sword that came at my middle with my own blade. It was just a reaction but the man was no swordsman and I brought the wheel lock around to smash into the side of his head. These men had intended to kill us and as he fell to the ground I stabbed him in the throat. That left one man and Stephen and Edgar caught him before he could flee. Their swords ended his life. The whole attack had taken less than three or four minutes and I think he did not realise he was alone.

"I will check the woods."

The crossbowman had been hidden and I wanted to ensure that there were no others waiting in the dark. I dropped my wheel lock and drew a dagger as I stepped over the bodies. When I reached the crossbowman I saw that Edgar had been more than lucky. His ball had smashed into the wooden crossbow and a huge splinter had been driven into the man's eye. There were no others but I saw the trail that they had used. I deduced that while we had used the road the five men had taken a trail from the village that lay three miles to the south and east.

By the time I reached the camp, the bodies had been stacked and searched. Old habits die hard. We had their weapons and a few coins. They had boots and leather jerkins but nothing worth taking. I said, "We should leave."

Stephen said, "Why, it is still dark?"

Edgar sighed, "We fired three pistols and the sound would carry." He looked at me, "Whence came they?"

I pointed south and east, "From the village. There may be friends or family who know what they intended. It is best not to tarry."

We quickly mounted and left. We made our way back to the road where I waited, in the dark, to listen for movement along the road. There was none and we moved. From now on we would have to keep a sentry at night. That would tire us and I knew the last miles would be hard ones. We were getting close to the border with the Dutch Republic. Luxemburgers did not like the republic and we would have to skirt that land. Close to the south were the Spanish Netherlands. Our little skirmish was a foretaste of what we might expect.

We did the last fifty miles in four days. We were lucky in that our horses were good ones and also that we had no more enemies to deal with. Once we passed into the land of the Dutch Republic we relaxed for the first time. I was new to battle and not wishing to bring us bad luck I had kept a question in my head since our conversation that first night. Now, as we neared the fortress of Utrecht, I asked it. "Edgar. Will there be other survivors?"

He looked at me and gave a sad smile, "Aye, you cannot slaughter three and a half thousand men so easily. Some will be prisoners and whilst most may well be dead, there will be survivors, like us who are fleeing. As we learned in the forests there are human carrion." He sighed, "If this was England then those who survived such a battle could flee home. The Bohemians, God curse their cowardly souls, might well have managed to get to home but those like us, the Dutch and men like Erik, have too far to travel. I have pushed my luck too far, James. Like Stephen, I will go home. The last many days have not changed my mind. Come with us, James. You have had your adventure and you have learned much."

"Aye, James, it would be bad luck to break up the three of us."

"I am not sure. I came here because I wanted something to do. I needed to be useful and not a parasite living off my father's friend. I also came to defend Protestants. I wanted to do something in memory of my mother."

Edgar waited a moment or two and then said, "I did not know your mother, James, but would she want her only son to die here?" He waved a hand at the flat land of the Netherlands.

It was a good question. The only one who could answer it was me and I did not have the answer, yet.

Chapter 6

We were dirty and weary when we rode up to the fortress. The sentries looked at us with suspicion. It had been a long time since we had left the Prince of Nassau's fortress and we did not recognise the sentries.

"What is your business?"

It should have been Edgar who answered but I knew he would not. He and Stephen had been all for heading to the nearest port and seeking a ship to take us home. I spoke, "We are from the command led by General von Mansfield. We are here to tell the prince that the command no longer exists."

That was all that I said but it was enough. The sergeant of the guard was summoned and when he heard the story we were admitted to the fortress. The captain of the guard heard me tell the story for a third time and then I was whisked away to meet with Prince Maurice. Edgar seemed more than happy to sit in the guard room and enjoy beer warmed with a poker, as did Stephen. With hat in hand, I was led through the labyrinth that was Utrecht to the room the prince was using. He was with his brother, Prince Frederich Henry. I was left at the door while the captain spoke urgently to the stadholder. I was waved forward.

"I am told that we have lost an army. I heard that a battle was lost but an army?"

I sighed and retold, for the fourth time, the story. This time, however, I gave more detail and colour. I wanted the prince to know that his colonels had fought bravely and done what they had to. I emphasised that it was the flight of the Bohemians that caused our defeat.

The prince said, "Captain, have this man's companions fed and chambers prepared for the three of them. I would speak further with this man." The door was closed and I was waved to a seat. "You are English, are you not?"

"I am, Prince Maurice."

"You are the one that Colonel Woodrow thought so highly of. You have good language skills." I did not reply for any answer would seem like boasting. "Were you the only officer to escape?"

I shook my head, "Captain Edgar also survived but he was wounded."

"Yet it is you who reports to me and not him."

"He would return to England as would the other survivor."

"And you, would you return too?" I did not answer for I had none to give, yet. "The three of you could simply have gone to a port and taken ship home. Why did you come here?"

"A sense of duty, my lord. We took your pay and I felt honour bound to tell you what occurred."

Prince Maurice smiled at his brother, "Do you see, brother, there is honour amongst mercenaries despite what their detractors say." He turned back to me, "I would have you in my service…what is your name again?"

"James Bretherton, my lord."

"You were a corporal when you were here last."

I smiled, "For the briefest of times I was a lieutenant but such titles now seem immaterial."

"Titles and ranks are to be noted but it is the man beneath the rank that is more important. You are still a young man and yet you led your men through hostile lands safely and that does you credit. We have lost a battle, that is true and, I suspect, Bohemia, but this war that has come is far from over. You should know that your King James has offered his support for the war and there are other Protestant kings and princes who have aligned themselves with me. Would you accept the rank of Captain and stay on my staff? I need someone I can trust to send to England when I have messages for your king, and when we have rebuilt our army, then I will need you to lead a company of Englishmen to war. You are young but I can see that you have grown in the service of the republic. I am looking for positives from this disaster. Who knows, it might spur the Bohemians to defy and confound our enemies."

I nodded, "I will accept, my lord, although I know not how I can help. I owe it to Colonel Woodrow to carry on."

"Good, that is the answer I wished for." He smiled and added, "Leave us now for we have much to discuss. Captain Berghof will show you your quarters. You can have a day or two to recover and to say goodbye to your friends."

When I left the room there was a soldier waiting for me. He spoke to me in Dutch. I realised that my Dutch would need improvement if I was to serve as an aide to Prince Maurice. "The captain asked me to take you to your chamber. Your men have taken your gear there and they await you."

I smiled. I wondered how Edgar would take to being called my man. We headed up some stairs to a small chamber in one of the towers. The man opened the door and said, "We soldiers eat in the refectory. A horn will sound." He grinned, "Your friend is an old soldier, and you can follow his nose."

When I entered the room, I saw a small bed on which were seated Edgar and Stephen. Two palliasses rested against a wall. Edgar said, "The captain asked if we would be staying and I said we would return to England as soon as we could." He nodded to the palliasses, "They will be our beds for the night."

"No, Edgar, you have the bed and I shall have the palliasse."

He sighed, "Things have changed, James. You were the apprentice but the battle and the journey home have shown that it is you who are now the master. It is for one night only. Tomorrow we will ride to Rotterdam and take a ship to England."

I nodded and told them what the prince had planned. For some reason that delighted them both, Edgar most of all, "That is the best news I have heard. You are being accorded honour and you will not be thrown into the fray again. Who knows, I may see you again for I plan on living in London."

"London?"

"You two are northerners and like the quiet rural life. I enjoy inns and company. Where better than London and there will be places I can be employed too. I remember an inn, south of the river, close to the bear pits and playhouses called *'The Saddle'*. I will head for first. I have money in my purse and need not seek employment for six months if I choose. This is good, James. I feared to leave you here alone. Colonel Woodrow and I wondered about plucking you from your home. Now I can see that it was meant to be." Just then we heard the horn and he stood, "Come, that means food and hot food at that. Let us see what the beer is like here in the prince's home."

Edgar had finally regained his smile and I was happy. Word had leaked out that we had been in the battle and the men in the garrison wanted to know more. Edgar had his confidence back and it was he who regaled them with the story of the fight and the flight of the Bohemians. It had not been the prince's men who had fallen, but Dutchmen had died and that angered the men of the garrison. I said little. I was just enjoying, for probably the last time, the company of Edgar and Stephen. Our survival had been because we had depended upon each other and now I was being left alone. It was my choice but that did not seem to help and doubts still assailed me.

We were still eating when Captain Berghof found me, "You will not be needed for four days, Captain Bretherton, but then you will be required to be at the side of the prince. He has much to do."

When he had gone Edgar said, "It took me twenty years to become a captain and you have done it in less than two."

I smiled, "The difference is, Edgar, that I will not be leading men. My rank is one of convenience. I will be advising the prince and translating for him."

"The prince is a generous employer, Colonel Woodrow knew that."

Stephen suddenly asked, "What about the money the colonel was paid for the company? Where is that now?"

Edgar gave a sad smile and shook his head, "I never worried about money for Colonel Woodrow dealt with all of that. I was paid and I was content. I am guessing that it is in Prague. The fact is that he was a private man. I never got to know him other than as a soldier. He gave orders and I obeyed. He handed me money and I gave it to the men. It was a system that worked." He pushed his empty platter away. There were servants who would scoop it up and clean it. "It is another reason for my departure. I have neither captain nor colonel to be my rock and I am too old to begin again." He emptied his beaker of beer, "Come, let us retire and make an early start. I am keen to leave for England."

The journey was not a long one, the Dutch Republic was not a large country. We found the office of the harbourmaster and asked about ships sailing to England. It was I who did the talking and we spoke in Dutch, "Where do you wish to go in England?"

"A ship going anywhere will do."

"And you want transport for your horses?"

We had discussed this already, "No, just two passengers."

He nodded and studied his lists, "There is an English ship due tomorrow. *'The Rose'* will unload and take a cargo of cloth back. I can arrange two berths for you."

We headed for a horse trader. There was always one at a port. Men needed to either hire or buy horses when they landed. We had decided that we would sell Edgar's and the two of them would share the proceeds but I would keep the other, the Spanish horse. We had named him Henry after the king who had defeated the French at Agincourt. The money from the sale of Edgar's horse would pay for a night in an inn and their passage home. Both Stephen and Edgar had full purses. We stabled my two horses and found an inn. It was loud and it was busy but the food was good and old soldiers like Edgar appreciated such things. We were not maudlin but we were reflective and we spoke of the men who had fallen in the battle. By talking about them we seemed to keep their memory alive. The recruitment drive now seemed like a lifetime ago.

"None of us thought that we would die."

Edgar nodded at the simple statement made by Stephen, "No soldier ever does. Each one thinks that they are the one to bear a charmed life."

Stephen was like a man with a piece of meat stuck in his teeth. He persisted as he sought answers, "Could the Colonel have done anything differently, Edgar? Could he have extricated the company?"

Edgar shook his head, "We were lucky. James' decision to ride through their lines saved us. Even if Colonel Woodrow had given the order to retreat we would still have been pursued by the Spanish cavalry and we would have been cut down."

"We could have surrendered."

"We could, Stephen, but that was not the Colonel's way. We will never know. He was cut down. Do not dwell on their deaths but rather rejoice in your life."

It was the end of the discussion for someone began singing in the corner. It was a Dutch song and a lament but most of the men in the inn joined in and it seemed to suit our mood.

I stood and watched as the English ship took the afternoon tide and headed out to sea. Edgar and Stephen waved and I felt very much alone. It was like being the last man at a party. The rest had gone and, as I mounted Caesar, I wondered at my decision. The die was cast and I had to make the best of it. My father's decision to invest in the colonies had made my life what it was and I had to deal with the reality and not the dream. I led Henry.

The ride back was a lonely one. I reached the fortress not long before dark when the gates were closed. Captain Berghof had given me the passwords but it seemed I was known already. I was *'the Englishman'*. I did not mind the appellation. I was not into titles in any case, I was given my rank when addressed but my nickname stuck. I ate alone in the refectory and I did not mind. It allowed me to ponder what my work might entail.

I spent a couple of months following the prince around his land. I was there to learn and I did. He was a popular man. My Dutch improved as I heard a variety of accents and regional dialects as we visited his border forts and the lands close to his enemies. I now had two horses and I was able to alternate them. I did not ride at the side of the prince but I was always close enough to be summoned to consult with him. I was the most senior officer to have survived the battle and he used my knowledge of that battle. We ended the tour at The Hague. It was where the politicians debated and the prince was needed to speak about the next phase of the war. I returned with the other warriors to Utrecht. There I honed my skills with a sword, sparring with others of the prince's retinue.

When the prince returned to the fortress from The Hague, I was summoned along with Captain Berghof and his other senior commanders. I had not wasted my time when I had come back from the tour and I had ordered a buff jacket to be made. It was cowhide and flexible. It would stop a sword slash and slow down a musket ball. The tanner said it would take a week to make. I had also purchased some better clothes. I now had a good doublet and what were termed Spanish breeches. My most expensive purchase was a pair of boots. I had spent half of my treasure but there was promise of more from the prince and he was known to be a generous employer. It was one reason the

colonel had sought him out. I had yet to buy a better hat. I liked
the one I had been given by Colonel Woodrow when we had
ambushed the Spanish, a lifetime ago. The man he had taken it
from was a Spanish officer and, as such, was well-made. It did
not look out of place in my hand as I waited in the antechamber
with the other officers.

When we were admitted I saw that the two brothers were
poring over a map. They looked up when we entered and Prince
Maurice waited until the doors were closed before he began to
speak. "Dire news has come to us from Bohemia." I saw his eyes
alight on me. "The battle that was lost by von Mansfield was just
the beginning, it seems. The Imperial troops fought a battle
against the Bohemians at White Mountain." He paused and I
knew it was for effect. I was learning to read the prince. He was
like an actor performing before an audience. "The Bohemians
lost more than five thousand men and Bohemia is now lost to the
Protestant cause. Their army was hopelessly outnumbered."
Again, he looked at me, "Two thousand English volunteers died,
Captain Bretherton. Your countrymen fought well but against the
Spanish cavalry there was little hope of success."

Captain Berghof asked, "And the king?"

The prince shrugged, "He and his wife escaped. Where they
are I know not. I would hope that they might find their way here.
We are an oasis in a Catholic desert." He allowed that to sink in.
"We will not break the truce with Spain for we cannot take on
the might that is Spain alone. We need allies and we need our
own army to be strengthened. I want all of you to work towards
the day when we can take on Spain and defeat them." We all
nodded. "Captain Bretherton, would you stay when the others
leave? I have a more important mission for you."

The other captains all nodded and smiled at me as they left.
They were envious I could tell. He waved me to a seat and began
to speak, "There are English soldiers spread throughout
Germany. They have volunteered, for pay of course, and they
fight for Protestantism. I want you to travel to England as my
representative and seek an audience with King James. I will have
the necessary authority prepared for you. I hope that the presence
of so many Englishmen in Germany will prompt your king to

commit men to the cause. The English defiance of King Philip inspired many of us here in the Netherlands."

I was not so sure. That had been Queen Elizabeth and she had been an inspirational leader. King James was new.

"Even if he does not commit to sending over the English army, I would hope that he would encourage more men like yourself and Colonel Woodrow to join us. You have three months to do all that you can. I would also have you recruit, on my behalf, more mercenaries. The reports came from other survivors of the Battle of Záblatí. It was the English companies that held the line. They did not falter. Many Dutchmen survived because of their courage and I would have more such men to fight for the republic."

He had a clerk, Johannes, who dealt with such matters and I sat with the almost bald man as he patiently took me through my documents and authority and enlarged upon the details of what I would do. "You will be acting as Prince Maurice's ambassador. In this position, you owe your loyalty to the prince. I realise that this will put you in a difficult position as you are English." He gave an apologetic smile, "You are young and I am sure that you will find a way to deal with this. You have the authority to take passage using any ship of the Dutch Republic. I have a list of Dutchmen who live in London. They will accommodate you and save the expense of an inn. The prince does not expect a formal written undertaking. A verbal one will suffice. It is more important that you eloquently persuade King James to aid the cause. The prince also needs you to encourage more soldiers of fortune to come to the Netherlands. There will be a purse of gilders to enable you to buy food and drink for such men."

The meeting went on for more than an hour and my head was spinning by the time he had finished, but I had a clearer idea of what I needed to do. I had my documents and authority and he gave me a leather satchel to hold them.

"There is a waxed lining that should stop the penetration of seawater. Good luck, Captain Bretherton."

Alone in my room, I began to plan for my visit. I would go afoot. I could sail directly to London and avoid the stabling of my horse. From what I had been told I could do all that was required of me in London. I would, of course, need my best clothes and I knew that I should really hire a servant but I did not want a Dutch one, I needed an Englishman. I put that idea to the back of my mind. While I was recruiting soldiers, I would also seek an Englishman to be a servant. Apart from my sword, I would just take a couple of daggers and, of course, a single pistol. I was not going to war, I was going to find warriors. I sorted out my clothes and decided that I would use leather bags rather than a trunk. I had coins and if I needed more clothes I could simply buy them. I had a chest and I could leave the chest at the fortress. It would be safe. As I lay down to sleep I could not help smiling. I was no longer going to be in danger. The prince had given me a task that was without risks. I would be serving the Protestant cause but not putting myself in harm's way. I had enjoyed a rare stroke of luck and my dreams, that night, were pleasant ones.

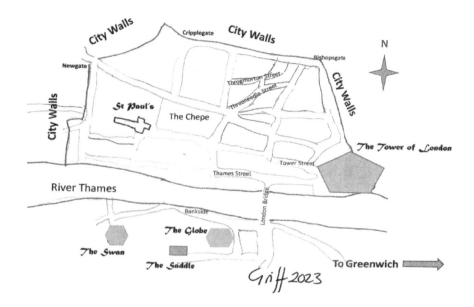

London 1611

Chapter 7

I had never been to London and did not know what to expect. My documents had afforded me courteous treatment on the ship that took me to Tilbury. The captain of the ship even arranged for a hackney to take me into the city. Thus it was that I saw the capital of my country for the first time as I approached from the east. It sprawled out on both sides of the river but it was the magnificent Tower that loomed up before me that drew the eye. The original white stone, now a little grubby, rose above the solid-looking walls of the greatest fortress in England. To enter the city through one of the gates, I was forced to ride around the fortress to the Bishopsgate. It was a clever design feature by whoever had devised it for it showed the power of the king. The famous fortress was no longer a royal palace and, instead, was a place to store ordnance. There was a garrison there and if the populace became rebellious then they would be summoned. I had been told that, instead of the Tower, the king used one of the many royal palaces around London and rather than waste my time seeking him out I rode instead for the house of a Dutch merchant, Pietr van Dyke. When I had been given the name, Johannes had told me that van Dyke was a common surname in Holland but Pietr was the richest with that name. He had a home on Thames Street which lay close to the river and was downstream from London Bridge. He was a merchant and the river was his lifeline. The captain of the ship that had brought me knew the man and often carried his cargo. He had given me directions and I found the house. It was an impressive building with three stories. The warehouse he must have used lay across the narrow street.

I dismounted and approached the door. I used the magnificent lion's head knocker and a liveried footman opened it. His look of disdain changed only slightly when he took in my clothes and my sword. I was not someone coming seeking employment.

"Can I help you?" His look suggested that I had stepped into something in the street.

I nodded, "I am Captain James Bretherton and I serve Prince Maurice of Nassau. I was told that I should speak with your master upon my arrival in London." I had chosen my words carefully to give him just enough information and yet keep my real mission hidden.

He nodded and then said, behind him, "Ned, take this gentleman's horse to the stable."

A second servant darted out, knuckling his forehead as he passed, "What shall I do with his bags, Master Wilkinson?"

"Leave them on the horse until I have spoken with the master."

I hid my smile. The major-domo at the door was not removing all the barriers to his master. I did not mind. The letter I had assured me of a warm welcome. I handed it to him, "If you would see that your master reads this first." I smiled, "The written word cannot harm him, eh?"

Taken inside the house, I saw fine furnishings. They painted a picture of a rich man who knew how to use his money. I knew, before I met her, that he was married for a woman's touch was clear in all that I saw. I was taken to a small antechamber and asked to sit and wait. The door was closed. Master Wilkinson was doing his job and protecting his master. I liked that.

Pietr did not keep me waiting long. I was ushered into what was obviously his office. Ledgers and parchments littered it and the clerk who left, as I entered, carried away with him an armful of such items.

"I am sorry you were kept waiting. An emissary from the prince should have been brought to me immediately." I guessed the major-domo had been chastised.

"It was not a problem." I answered his English in Dutch and I saw his eyes widen.

He spoke in Dutch, "I did not expect that, my friend. You are English are you not?"

"I am but I can speak a number of languages and that is why I think I was chosen for this task."

"And one so young. Intriguing."

I studied the man. He was in his mid-thirties and looked comfortable. He had a waistline that was growing and his hair was receding. He had a neatly trimmed beard which looked to be his only attempt to be fashionable.

I shrugged, "I fought for a mercenary company and while most of my companions were killed, I survived and the prince thought to use me to persuade King James to support his cause."

He nodded and reverted to English. I suspect it was for clarity and I emulated him. "King James has already shown his support by sending men to help his son-in-law King Frederick."

"And now he has been defeated."

He nodded, "The news has recently reached us. King James, so I heard, has gone to Parliament to ask for more funds to continue his support but the Spanish party oppose him."

I knew nothing of English politics and I asked, "Spanish party?"

"The Howards and other Catholic-leaning ministers and diplomats. They oppose aid being sent to Protestants. It is they who have encouraged the proposed marriage of Prince Charles and the Spanish Infanta. You will have a difficult task for while I think the king supports the idea, there are too many in England who wish for a return to a Catholic England. You will have to tread carefully, my young friend, for there are those who will feign friendship and then stab you, quite literally, in the back. Coming to London you have entered a dark and dangerous world."

I sighed and shook my head, "Nonetheless I have accepted the commission. Where will I find the king?"

"At this time of year, he likes to use Eltham Palace. I will go with you there on the morrow." He nodded to the parchments, "They are useful passports but I know some of his courtiers. There are those who have Catholic sympathies and I can direct you to the ones whom you can trust." He smiled, "This is your homeland and you are a soldier but you will find life here more dangerous than on a battlefield. There your enemies are all before you." He stood, "Now let me find you your chamber and introduce you to my wife. She too is English."

He led me from the room and we went down a short corridor to a sitting room with furnishings that were functional but comfortable. Soft seats with cushions were the order of the day and with a fine hearth and chimney the room was both warm and welcoming. His wife was just a few years older than I was. I spied a toddler playing close by her chair.

"My dear, may I introduce Captain James Bretherton who is acting as an ambassador for Prince Maurice." I bowed, "This is my wife, Elizabeth, and the boy you can see getting dirty on the floor is my son, Robert." He smiled, "We named him after my wife's father."

"I am pleased to meet you, Mistress van Dyke."

"Will you be staying with us, Captain?"

My host nodded, "I will have Master Wilkinson make up the guest room."

She said, "I will tell him to put a heated stone in the bed for it has been two months since my parents used it."

"I am a soldier and do not wish for any to be put out on my behalf."

"Nonsense, you are our guest and it is only servants who will be inconvenienced. I am honoured that the prince would choose me to host his emissary."

Elizabeth said, "Would you like to freshen up, Captain?"

I was suddenly aware that I stank of horse sweat and the dampness of the ship in which I had sailed for two days. "Thank you. I have travelled for some days to reach here."

I had eaten food in the Netherlands, Bohemia and Germany for the past many months and the taste of English food was like manna from heaven and I devoured it all.

Elizabeth smiled, "I like a man with a healthy appetite, Captain."

I felt embarrassed, "I am sorry, Mistress, but good food like this is rare in the life of a soldier."

"Oh, do not apologise, Captain, for you do the cook great honour by wiping your platter clean with a piece of bread."

"I pray you call me James. The title of Captain is a new one. It serves to impress servants but I still feel like James, the boy from the far north."

Pietr leaned back in his chair. He, too, had used bread to clean his platter, "Now while our meal digests and we await the pudding that will complete the meal, tell us your story for you have us both intrigued."

I had long ago decided that the story of my father's ill-advised investment should not be hidden but told as a warning to others. I began with my family's descent into poverty and ended with my flight after the battle that had cost the colonel his life. The pudding arrived just as I had finished and Pietr said, solemnly, "Before we enjoy this food let us say a prayer for your parents, James, and the brave men who died in that battle."

We prayed and it seemed to be the right thing to do and brought the three of us together. I liked them both and would be lying if I said I was not attracted to the beautiful Elizabeth. However, I was not an animal and I controlled my feelings. My mother had taught me that it was best to hide your feelings beneath the mask of a smile. Now that I was about to enter the murky world of politics it seemed a good strategy.

The next day I rode with Pietr and my wax-lined satchel to Eltham Palace. We were both dressed appropriately for court and I had been provided with a bath by Master Wilkinson. With bags of rosemary beneath my doublet, I did not smell as rank as when I had arrived. What I noticed, as we rode towards the palace, was that my hat and sword marked me as a soldier. The wide brim was distinctive and while many men carried swords, they were not as fine as the Spanish one I bore. As we rode I also realised that I rode with the easy grace of a soldier while the merchant next to me rolled around like a sack of oats.

There were guards at the entrance to the palace but my parchment from the prince afforded us entry. Our horses were taken from us and stabled and we went to a huge antechamber. The king was holding court and we would be seen, we were told, in the fullness of time. As Pietr had warned me, we needed patience. I took the opportunity to look at the others who waited. Some were clearly there to seek a favour. I saw them clutching parchments and their eager looks when the next person was invited for his audience. There were others whose motives were harder to determine. They had confident looks and were, generally, in pairs. I took the opportunity to speak in Dutch to Pietr and ask him about those men.

"Ah," he said, "you have seen those who come to trade information for position. There are Catholics who will try to undermine the position of Protestants and Protestants who will inform on Catholics and their plots."

"What about the nervous-looking fellows?"

"They are men who seek commissions to colonise the New World. It is a dangerous undertaking. Not only is the voyage hazardous but as Walter Raleigh discovered to his cost, if you upset Spain then it could result in the loss of your head."

"But I thought that the king supported the Protestants over the Catholics."

"So he does but he needs to marry the prince to the Infanta." He shrugged, "Politics are never simple."

Our use of Dutch had made many around us pay closer attention to us. That attention was magnified when the door opened and an equerry said, "Captain James Bretherton and Master Pietr van Dyke, the King will be pleased to see you now."

We entered the Great Hall. There were sentries in the room but after a brief scrutiny of our faces, they stayed close by the wall affording us and the king, privacy. As well as the equerry also present was George Villiers, the Marquis of Buckingham and Lord High Admiral. A clerk was seated close to them with a wax tablet. My first thought was that the room reeked of perfume. I had rosemary swetebags but I felt as though I stank of a field in comparison to the two men. The other thing was that they were seated unnaturally close to each other. As we bowed, I glanced at Pietr who gave a subtle shake of his head. I would discover more later.

King James had a slightly high-pitched voice which verged on the effeminate. I knew that he had fathered seven children but it was anomalous. "Captain James, we have read the missive from Prince Maurice. Firstly, can I thank you for your service to my son-in-law? I am just grateful that he is now in The Hague and safe from the emperor."

"I was pleased to serve, King James."

"However, you should know that it is impossible for me to join an alliance against Spain and the Emperor." He turned to the Marquis of Buckingham, "Until we have a Parliament that will heed the request of their rightful king, we will have to behave in a manner which we find unacceptable."

The Marquis had a silky voice which made me dislike him immediately, "My liege, we just need to be patient. Your decision to suspend Parliament will ensure that we win in the end."

"I know not how you can say that for my hands are tied. I cannot afford to put an army in the field and we have to rely on men like Captain James here to fight for Protestantism under the flag of a mercenary. I would rather we sent men to fight under the flag of St George."

The king was clearly speaking that which the marquis did not wish him to. An irritated look flickered across the face of the marquis, "We can discuss that at our leisure, my liege, our two guests need to know what we plan to do."

I do not know if Pietr picked up on the word, but I did. He had said we as though they were equals. I would need to walk warily around the marquis.

"You are quite right, George. You may tell Prince Maurice that I do support him as well as my son-in-law. That support, however, will be moral rather than military. However, we are happy to supply pikes and muskets from our arsenal. So long as they are sent discreetly then all will be well."

Pietr said, "I can arrange that, King James."

"And as for this request to hire English soldiers..." he looked at the marquis who shrugged, "I cannot see that it will be a problem. You have my permission to raise companies. Return in a week and we shall have ready all the necessary authorisations."

It was clear that we were dismissed and, after backing our way to the door, we left. I was keenly aware of the stares from the waiting supplicants. We had attracted their interest and my name was known. Had I wanted any secrecy that opportunity was lost. I waited until we were on the road before I said, "The Marquis of Buckingham?"

He smiled and leaned over to speak quietly to me although the clip-clop of our horses' hooves disguised the words, "Let us say the two men are close and the marquis is the most important noble in the land. He is the king's favourite... in every way. He has links with Spain but I do not think he undermines the king's support of Protestantism. He is an enigma but, on the positive side, you seem to have impressed them both and we have weapons for the prince. I can arrange their shipment. You have the harder task of finding men."

I nodded, "At least I have a place to start."

He looked intrigued, "How so, for you know not London?"

"True but I know of an inn, south of the river, *'The Saddle'*. It is a starting point." I remembered that Edgar was heading there. Even if he was not at the inn then he might be remembered. It was all that I had to go on.

"Be wary, my friend, for south of the river is a dangerous place."

"I know but I am prepared."

I did not know exactly where the inn lay nor even if Edgar had gone there. It had been some months since he had returned to England and his plans could have changed but it would be a start. If he was not there then they might know where he had gone. Pietr was right, south of the river was a different world. It lay beyond what was London proper. There was no watch here as there was north of the river. There were more bawdy houses and places of entertainment; the places they showed plays, baited bulls and held cock fights were here. I knew, from my short time with Pietr and his wife, that there were Protestants who held firm views about that and they were demanding that the king do something about what they perceived as licentious behaviour. I rode carefully through the streets which seemed, somehow, threatening.

I crossed London Bridge and entered a different London. One thing I had learned was how to spot an ex-soldier and I saw one, clearly disabled from some war or other, leaning on a crutch. He was seeking alms but he had a straight back and did not call out pleadingly as others did. He still had his pride. Ignoring the others, some of whom I knew were faking a wound, I dismounted close to the man. I took out some copper and pressed it into his hand. I said, "You were a soldier?"

He nodded, recognising me as an officer, albeit a relatively junior one, "Sir, I fought in Ireland. A wild bog man hamstrung me." He shrugged, "Others died so I suppose I am lucky."

"I seek *'The Saddle'*."

He said, "Aye, one of the safer places to drink. Head for The Globe and it is on the next corner in the place they call Paris Gardens. If you reach The Swan Theatre then you have gone too far. There is no play at either playhouse today so it will be quiet." He chuckled, "Except for the actors who spend what little money they earn in the inns there."

"Thank you." I walked my horse to the playhouse which was an enormous, whitewashed building close to the river and I heard the noise from the inn before I saw it. There was a water trough and a hitching post outside and I tied the hackney to it. I wondered if it was safe to leave my horse there. I did not see Edgar, not at first but when a shadow moved from the side of the inn I did.

His familiar voice and outstretched arm were both welcome. "James, what brings you here? Have you left the service of the prince?"

I smiled with relief, "Not really. I need to talk. Is it safe to leave my hackney here?"

In answer, he whistled and a youth, not quite needing to shave, emerged from within, "Hob, watch the captain's horse and be wary around him. He is ridden by a soldier."

Knuckling his forehead, "He shall be as safe as any in my charge and mayhap the good Captain will see fit to reward me appropriately."

Edgar clipped him about the head, "This is a friend of mine and you do this for free. Come, James, let us enter this darkened den."

The old soldier I had met was right, it was full of actors and those who aspired to be actors. Their voices were loud but what gave them away were their elaborate hand gestures and poses that they struck. Edgar rolled his eyes as we passed one wearing rouge on his cheeks who was mimicking a young maiden.

"When they are not acting they come here to rehearse. There are others who wish to be actors although for the life of me, I cannot understand why. Here is my table." He led me to a table which nestled in the corner with a serving bar on one side and a wall on the other. I let him take his seat and was not surprised when it was the corner one affording him a view of the whole room. He held two fingers up to the serving wench and then said, "We will toast the dead before we talk and see if I can spy any problems."

"I am in your hands. I am just pleased that you have found a position."

He leaned over to speak but never took his eyes from the room, "More than that, I am a partner. I own half of the inn."

I was surprised, "You had enough money for that? I knew you had a full purse but…"

"It had fallen on hard times. My money kept it afloat while I helped the widow to make it a going concern again." The beer arrived and Edgar winked at the serving wench, "Alice here is the widow's daughter, aren't you?"

She giggled, "That I am and who is this handsome young gentleman, uncle?"

"He is Captain James. You keep your hands off him, hear?"

She continued giggling as she headed off.

"Uncle?"

He shrugged, "Let us say it makes the arrangement I have with her mother a little easier to explain." He lifted his pewter tankard, "Here's to the dead. Life cannot hurt them more."

"To the dead."

We both drank deeply and said nothing for a moment or two. We were honouring the colonel and all the others who had fallen. I suspected we would be the only ones who remembered them.

After a suitable time had elapsed, I said, "You were talking about the widow."

He smiled, "Aye, Mags. She is younger than I am and her husband had pissed away the profits from this place. He made the mistake of borrowing money from a hard man when he couldn't repay the loan." He drew his finger across his throat. "The gang thought to take over the place. Fortune favoured Mags for I arrived that very day and when they came back to recover their debt I was able to pay it off."

"I bet they weren't happy about that."

He chuckled, "They weren't but they learned that I have not only a sword and dagger but the skills to use them. One lost his fingers and another an eye. They have chosen to move further west. Mags was grateful and I find her comfortable."

"You are married?"

Shaking his head he said, "There is no need. We are south of the river and we need not worry about such things. So, what brings you here?" I told him of my promotion and my task. We were on our second ale when I finished. "That is a Herculean task, James." He waved a hand around the inn, "I can find you any number of swordsmen, pikemen and musketeers. Many work here occasionally. The company needs men with martial skills. We have enough prancing ponies to speak the words but they have skills that make the plays seem real. However, you need captains." He rubbed his beard. I noticed that it was now trimmed and oiled. Mags had begun to change him. It was then I noticed that his clothes were of better quality. He still had his sword and dagger and I spied a leather sack filled with sand, they were the tools of his trade, but he certainly dressed better.

I emptied the second tankard and waved over to Alice, "Is there anywhere I could seek such leaders?"

As the beers were deposited and I put coins on the table he said, "I could ask around. There are places where such men congregate. They are low places."

Alice gratefully scooped up the coins and planted a kiss on my cheek, "Thank you, Captain. For a silver coin, you may have more than a kiss."

"Away with you, you trollop! Leave my friend his innocence." He was grinning as he said it. He turned back to me, "Give me a week. The prince is paying?" I nodded. "Then it is known he pays well and as you have the king's blessing then they can gather and then march to take ship. You will need to arrange transport."

"That is the least of my problems. I have another month to complete my task."

"Do not worry, we shall manage it."

"One thing more, I need a servant. I would be happier with someone watching my back."

He thought about it for barely a moment and then said, "Hob. The youth holding your horse. He is clever and quick-witted. He can handle himself in a fight but he has the innocent look of a bairn. I have little enough work for him here and he has expressed a desire to better himself. You are that opportunity. I can think of no other man I would entrust him to and vice versa. I think that the two of you are made for each other."

"What is his story?"

He leaned back, "No different to many others. A chance encounter between a sailor and a serving wench. The wench dies of the pox and the child has to fend for itself. Mags found Hob at the age of eight seeking scraps in the hogbog. She took him in and he acted as a servant. The skills he acquired were learned here. I have used him as a horse holder, but he needs more. I think that serving with you will be the making of him. He has seen almost fourteen summers but he still has some growing to do."

I drained my tankard and rose, "I had better get back across the river."

Edgar smiled, "It is more than good to see you. I feared that you might have died at White Mountain. We heard that many Englishmen died there."

"No, I was safe, with the prince."

"And I pray that you stay there. Let others take the coins and risk all on the battlefield. I would have you return to England as often as you can and tell me of life at court."

"It is duller than you think."

"If you mean safer then good. Come, I will walk you out and we can put the proposition to Hob. You do not need him today, do you?"

"No, but soon."

"Mags will want to say goodbye to him as will Alice. He and Alice grew up together. They are close."

Hob was stroking the mane of the horse when we emerged, "A fine horse, Captain."

I nodded, "I have two at home that make this one look as though it is ready for the knacker's yard."

The youth had a hand already out and as I placed some coins in it Edgar said, "The Captain needs a servant and I thought you might do. Before you answer it would mean leaving England, and as the captain is a soldier you might have to fight. What say you?"

He had taken the coins but the grin on his face gave me the answer before he uttered the words, "Do I leave now?"

Laughing, Edgar said, "Mags and Alice would make my life a misery if you did. No, the captain will return in a day or so and then you can leave."

I looked at his feet. He wore clogs. I also noted that his clothes were holed. I took out a gold coin, "See that he has boots, clothes, a cloak and..."

Edgar folded my fingers about the coin. "None of that, James. We owe the boy and I owe you. Now that the owner is not drinking away the profits the inn is doing well. Without fights every night, the actors use it more and when they produce plays we are rammed to the rafters. This is my gift to you for my life."

Hob suddenly stared at Edgar, "Your life?"

Edgar ruffled his hair, "Aye, and that is a tale I will tell before you leave us."

I mounted the hackney, "Farewell, Edgar and this was well met, Hob." I turned the horse and headed back to London Bridge and the grisly sight of the heads of criminals adorning the drawbridge tower. Once, so I had been told, fletchers and bowyers had been found in the houses on the bridge but with the decline of the bow they had been replaced by haberdashers. I found myself looking at the wares on sale. Perhaps I would avail myself of a haberdasher and buy new clothes when next I crossed. It was my inspection of the houses that allowed me to see the man in the shadows watching me. That he was watching me was clear for when he noticed my attention his cowled head disappeared, but I had been watched and I wondered why. The thought haunted my journey back to Thames Street and prevented a good night of sleep.

Chapter 8

I had not spoken, during our meal, of my meeting. It did not seem right to speak of such things before Pietr's wife. However, the next morning I spent some time with him. "That is progress, James, but I shall need time to arrange for the ships to carry the men. It is not an impossible task but there are tides and cargoes to consider. How long will you need to find the men?"

I shook my head, "I confess that I do not know. I set the wheels in motion yesterday, but such things take time. I am not even sure how many men I should hire. The prince just said to get as much help as I could."

He saw my concern and said, "Just do your best, James. Any help you can find for my country will be welcome."

My mind was still distracted by the watcher on the bridge and Pietr, who was an astute man, noticed, "Is there something else, James?"

I nodded, "I was watched."

"That is not a surprise. My visit to the king was not unexpected but you are a young soldier and that drew attention to us. Men will wonder who you are. The Spanish Party will know that you support the Protestant cause and your association with me means that they see you as an enemy."

"Then I am in danger?"

"Of course, as am I but have you not noticed, James, that I rarely venture beyond my little empire? I am a rich man and I use others to take risks for me."

"Does that include me?"

He shook his head, "No, if you wish to stay safe in my home protected by good locks then I would not blame you, but you have been set a task and I do not envy you that."

"I know that I have not given him much time but I will visit with my friend again. If I hire a servant is there room for him here?"

"Of course. We have good servant quarters. I have learned that a happy servant is a loyal servant. I will have Wilkinson arrange it." He smiled, "There is good news too. I have heard, from one of my captains, that Count von Mansfield has returned to the field and commands the army of the Upper Palatinate. He is holding his own so, perhaps, more English soldiers might be the impetus he needs for victory."

"Then time is not on our side. I will leave immediately to see how the search progresses." I rose and paused, "We will visit with King James as soon as I have numbers. Perhaps he will have changed his mind about supporting us."

Pietr shook his head sadly, "I fear not but we shall see." He pointed to my doublet, "That is not enough protection."

"I know but the buff coat is for the battlefield and not the streets of London." I wished I had retained a leather jerkin but I had not. Hindsight was always perfect. Instead of the jerkin I used a heavy, oiled cloak. It had a cowl and meant I could if I had to, afford myself a slight disguise.

Once I left the house to head for the busy bridge I kept a good watch for any who was hunting me. My diligence was rewarded as I was crossing the bridge. I spied the two swarthy-looking men as I was halfway across. They were lurking in the shadows and it was clear that they were waiting for me and that was how I spotted them. The rest of the people on the bridge were going about their business, purposely moving across the packed structure. While it was daylight I was safe, even in Southwark, and I had identified them. Having done so I rode as quickly as the traffic would allow and headed for the inn. Once on the other side, I was able to move quicker. If they followed me then they would have to run. As I turned to pass the Globe I glanced behind and saw them running. It was now clear that they were watching me and that begged the question, were they just watching or did they have murderous intent? I would need to speak to Edgar.

The inn was quieter for it was morning and the actors were still abed. There was a stink of stale ale, pipe tobacco and, outside the inn, piss. I tied my horse to the hitching post and spied the wounded soldier. I waved him over and held out four copper coins, "Watch my horse and I will double this."

He grinned, "Gladly, Captain. It is as near to honest labour as a man can come these days."

I entered the inn and saw that Edgar was absent. Hob was there and he was eating a late breakfast with Alice and Mags.

From the proximity of Alice to Hob I suspected more than friendship between the two.

Mags rose and said, "Edgar is away on your business, Captain. An ale and some breakfast?"

"I have breakfasted already but some of your excellent ale would go down well."

I knew that alewives prided themselves on the quality of their ale and Mags' was well brewed. I had discovered that in London it was not always so.

She beamed and fetched me a foaming flagon. I sat next to her facing Alice and Hob. Nodding to Hob I said, "Are you happy that I will be taking him hence, Mistress Mags?"

She smiled, "He will have a better life but he is like a son to me. I have raised him these last years and he and Alice are close but…" she looked at me earnestly, "you will watch out for him, won't you Captain James?"

"Of course."

Hob swallowed, wiped his mouth and said, "The captain is a hero, Mags. Did Edgar not tell us last night how the captain saved his life? I am confident that this will see me rise and become…" he grinned, "who knows what? It is said that Master Shakespeare began life as a glover's apprentice and became a gentleman. I shall aspire to be one too and then," he squeezed Alice's hand, "I shall return for you."

Alice's reply told me that she had a sensible head on her shoulders and was not carried away by Hob's rhetoric, "Aye, Hob, and that is a nice dream to hold but when you leave we know not what the Fates have in mind for us. You may find a prettier flower to pluck and, who knows, I might find a handsome captain to whisk me off my feet."

Mags laughed and shook her head, "I think that Captain James is bound for something more than a serving wench in a Southwark alehouse."

I was relieved when the door opened and Edgar strode in. He had a happy look on his face, "Well, Captain, I have done the Prince of Nassau such service this day as would need a chest of gold to reward me. I have found you five captains and they are happy to serve." He sat next to me for Mags had vacated her seat to bring him ale and food. Alice began to clear the table. I could see that Hob was torn.

"Hob, I shall not need you awhile. Go and...do whatever you need to. We shall not leave here until after the noon bell from St Paul's."

He nodded gratefully and grabbed some platters to follow Alice into the kitchen.

Edgar waited until he had food, ale and we were alone before we spoke. "The name of Captain Woodrow helped. Three of them had served with me and the captain before. The other two I knew not but one seemed a good soldier, the other..." He waved his hand up and down as though he was undecided. "I told them that they had a fortnight to get their companies together. When they asked about payment I said that it would be forthcoming but would have to wait until they met the prince. I gave my word, James, I pray that I will not be forsworn."

I knew the amount earmarked by the prince and I shook my head, "You will not be made out to be a liar. They will be well paid and the arms that they need will be on the ships that take us there."

"English weapons? That will please them. I have spread the word to pikemen, swordsmen and musketeers that there will be employment." He rubbed his forefinger and thumb together, "Mags and I will profit for they will come here and even those who do not take the Dutch gilder will spend English coins here. All is good."

I hesitated and then said, "There is something else. I was followed, last night and this morning. I would not put Hob's life in jeopardy."

"I would not worry about Hob. He is like a cat and has more senses than a body should have but it is you who are in danger." He leaned over the table, "It is the Catholics. Since the plot to blow up Parliament failed they have gone to ground, and that is dangerous. It was better when they were shouting and ranting, now they lurk and they plot. If they could kill you then that would mean fewer men fighting the Empire and Spain."

"How would they know?"

He looked down, "As soon as I spoke to swords for hire they knew."

"They followed me last night. One was waiting for me on London Bridge."

He took a deep swallow from the tankard, "Then there must be a spy at court for I assume your Dutch host would be close-mouthed." I nodded. "When you return to court watch for those who smile too much. They are the enemies you should fear. I have given Hob my old short sword and he has both a dirk and a dagger. Mags has her women making my old leather jerkin fit. It is a little protection for him."

I nodded and then remembered Stephen, "Have you a secrete? He could wear it beneath his hat."

He grinned, "Aye, I have. I stopped wearing it when my hair thinned but it will do the boy. I will give you my pistol too. Such weapons are frowned upon here and, to speak truthfully, I need just a sword and a club to deal with troublemakers. I do not wish to kill any."

We spent most of the morning going through the names of the captains and the likely numbers they would bring. I now had the information that Pietr needed and if the captains were told the time scale then they could work accordingly. In the afternoon, after we had eaten and while the inn filled up, Hob, Edgar and I packed Hob's gear. Mags had given him a hessian bag and we crammed that with what he would need.

When Edgar gave him the secrete, Hob was surprised. "We are not going to war yet, why should I need it?"

I explained, "Men are following me and there may be danger. Wear your jerkin and keep the hat on your helmet. It may save your life." He nodded. "If you wish to stay here and not risk your life then I would understand."

He smiled, "It is an adventure, Captain James. All will be well. An enemy has to get up early in the morning to put one over on me. Before Mags found me I slept amongst thieves and vagabonds. I am content. I can smell an enemy."

The parting took longer than I wished. It was almost dark when we left and the long lingering kiss shared by Hob and Alice told me that they would miss each other. Hob rode behind me with his hessian sack over his back and his arms around my waist. I knew that I did not need to keep a good watch, Hob would do that.

When we reached Pietr's we went directly to the stable. Hob said, "There were four men, Captain. Two followed us to the bridge and two more were waiting by the dungeon tower. They followed us here. They are waiting at the end of the street."

My first thought was that they now knew where I lived but then I dismissed it. If Edgar was right then as soon as we had left Eltham Palace they had known my destination. We entered the house through the rear entrance. Elizabeth was in the kitchen and took to Hob from the first. "Come with me and I shall show you your room." She noticed a glowering Mr Wilkinson who did not like his ordered life upset. Elizabeth laughed, "Do not mind that curmudgeon. He thinks that this is his house and we are the servants."

The major-domo looked appalled, "Mistress, that is not so and I cannot help my features. God gave me a malodorous expression and I can do nothing about it."

I left them to it and found Pietr. He was in his study and it took an hour to give him all my news. "Do not worry that they know where I live, James. I expect the Catholics to take an interest in my life. What you do not know is that the men who work in my warehouses also double as sentries and watchmen. They are well-paid and discreet. You have not seen them yet and that means neither have our enemies but it is good that you have told me. A fortnight is perfect. I have four ships I can use that week. When next we visit the king I can give him the date and I can arrange for the ships to pick up the cargo from the Tower." He suddenly became serious, "While you are in here then you are safe and I would beg you not to venture forth."

"I will not be a prisoner but I will be careful. Hob and I will need to visit the inn once more, in a week's time, to meet with the captains. It would not be right for them to sail and that was the first time they met me."

"Just be careful then."

What I did not say was that I had purchases to make from the Chepe, the market. Hob and I still needed things that we had to buy. The next morning, I told Pietr of my plans. He understood but he was worried. "It if makes you feel better then I will wear my buff coat and Hob shall don his secrete and his leather jerkin."

He looked relieved, "Good, for Elizabeth has taken to young Hob. He is a most engaging youth."

I felt as though I stood out as I walked into the Chepe wearing the new buff coat. My cloak disguised it a little but it seemed like armour to me. I suppose that was a good thing and it helped me to become accustomed to the protection. We made all the purchases we needed. Hob was a good negotiator and saved us many coins as he haggled down prices. He had learned how to do so when he had been a street urchin living on his wits.

The three of us left for Eltham four days later. Following the visit to the Chepe, we had not ventured forth. Instead, Elizabeth and I took the time to teach Hob those things he had not learned when he had lived on the streets. If he was to be my servant then he needed to know how to address those of higher status, how to eat in public and the right way to dress. He was bemused by it all. I also took the opportunity to begin to teach him some Dutch. When we returned to the Netherlands, he would need to be able to talk to those around him.

Pietr found a sumpter for Hob to ride and he accompanied us. As we neared the palace I said, "You will stay with the horses, Hob. I want you to keep your wits about you and use your eyes and ears."

He seemed to regard it all as a grand adventure and grinned, "Aye, Captain."

When we reached the palace Hob joked with the guards and brought smiles to their faces. Some might have deemed it inappropriate behaviour but I did not. When we left him with the horses he was chattering away to the men and I knew that he would learn things that Pietr and I would not. This time, when we entered the waiting room at court, I knew that we, and especially me, were the objects of close scrutiny. It felt as though every eye was upon us. We did not have long to endure their gaze for within a short time after giving our names to the king's clerk we were summoned in. If nothing else it would make us even more unpopular.

There were another two men with the king and Buckingham. I never knew their names and as they sat slightly apart from the king and his confidante it was hard to work them out.

"So, Captain James, have you managed to acquire men for your venture?" It was the Marquis of Buckingham who spoke and it felt more interrogatory than had the king said it.

"We have, Your Majesty," I pointedly addressed the king. I saw that it annoyed the marquis. "We shall have five companies ready within the fortnight. We shall require, with Your Majesty's permission, the muskets and pikes that were promised."

He nodded, "You should know, Captain, that there are many in my Parliament who think that I should sever my ties with my son-in-law. A man cannot abandon his family, can he?"

Before I could answer Buckingham showed his true colours, "King James, a king has to put the needs of his people before his family."

The king did not like the criticism, "Do not presume to lecture me on the role of the king. I was King of Scotland before I was given England." He smiled, "All will be made ready. Burley, have the necessary papers prepared. Give them to Captain James before he leaves." One of the two men I had not recognised nodded and began to scratch on the parchment. "I doubt that I shall see you before you sail, I leave London at the end of the month. I wish you well and I believe that Prince Maurice has made a good choice in an Englishman as an ambassador."

The Marquis of Buckingham said, "If you would wait without, we have much business to conduct this day."

His tone and the glowering look on his face told me that I had clearly gained an enemy.

Pietr and I said nothing as we waited. We were studied and we, in turn, studied the faces of those we saw. Any of them could be the enemies who were following me. I spotted one who had a Spanish look about him. With olive skin and an oiled moustache and beard, he stood out from the others. There was no way of discovering his name but he would have been one I would have thought was the enemy.

Before any other was admitted the man called Burley came forth with the parchment. I recognised the king's seal. We had our passport to the Tower. We left and I felt men's eyes pricking our backs as we left. They were wondering how we had gained admittance so quickly and been given a commission.

We heard laughter before we reached Hob and the horses. As we mounted one of the sergeants said, "He is a lively one, Captain. I am sure he keeps you entertained with his wit."

I nodded, affably, "Aye, he is a good lad."

We did not speak on the ride back to the city and I waited until we had stabled the horses before I did so. "What do you think, Pietr?"

We headed for the house. Hob was close behind us. "That Buckingham is not our friend and I saw a Spaniard I think I recognised."

"Don Miguel Alvarado, Captain."

We both stopped and stared at Hob, "How on earth...?"

He grinned, "I saw a fine horse in the stables. I learned to distinguish good horses from bad when I worked at the inn. It determined my tips. I asked the guards who owned such a fine horse and they said it belonged to one of the Spanish delegation to the court of King James, Don Miguel Alvarado. He and his brother are often at court."

"You have done well and did you learn anything else?"

"That the king and the Marquis of Buckingham sometimes share a bed."

Pietr laughed, "I have long suspected so but within a few minutes of reaching Eltham your servant has confirmed it. The sergeant was right, James, you should nurture this fine pair of ears."

I was learning much but I still did not know how it would help us. We rode, the next day, to the inn. We had spotted our followers when we had gone to Eltham and they were either lazy or did not care if we knew for it was the same two men who followed us the next day. When we crossed the bridge, I spotted the other two who lounged close to the abutments on the southern end of the crossing. They were making a poor attempt to look as though they were studying a boat on the river. As they were afoot I mischievously spurred my hackney. Poor Hob was like a sack of oats on the back of his sumpter as he tried to keep up.

When we reached the inn Hob dismounted and said, "If we are to do more riding, Captain, then I shall take pains to acquire a cushion."

I smiled as we tied up the animals, "When we reach the Netherlands I shall teach you to ride correctly." I nodded towards the two followers who had run after us, "Keep an eye on them."

Once in the inn Alice spied me and came over, "Hob, Captain?"

"He is outside."

"I shall take him ale. Edgar is upstairs if you would sit at his table." She went to the bar as I sat at the table. As she poured the ale she shouted, "Edgar. It is the Captain."

She plopped a tankard before me before heading outside. Hob would not be lonely. Edgar soon joined me. "Well, Captain James, I have you the captains and they are out finding the men that you need. I do not doubt that there will be five hundred men ready to sail with you. You have the weapons?"

I wiped the foam from my mouth and nodded, "We have the warrant and Pietr is preparing the ships. We just need to coordinate the arrival of the men."

He stood and went to fill his own tankard from the jug on the bar, "I told the five that it would be ten days from yesterday."

As he sat down, I did a calculation in my head and worked out that would be perfect. "I shall need to meet with them."

"They are busy men. Let us say seven days from now, vespers. They are men who prefer the evening."

"Good, that gives me time to make the arrangements with Pietr."

"Where is Hob?"

"Outside with Alice. I cannot thank you enough for the boy. He is perfect and has such sharp eyes and ears."

"Aye, he is a good lad. Mags and I want the best for him and I know he will get that from you. There are not many who are as thoughtful as you, James." I shrugged. "Are your followers still with you?"

"They have two watching the house and two watching the bridge. What I cannot understand is what they are doing."

"They will work for some rich lord. From what you have told me he must be a rich Catholic. To them, you are an enemy."

"I am just a soldier hiring others."

"To fight the Empire, Spain and Catholics. Tread carefully, James. These are men who will stab you in the back without a moment's pause. When next you come, protect yourself." He shook his head, "The five captains care not what they look like, they wear plates fore and aft. One wears a helmet. They are not too proud to look as they do."

"I will take your advice. The captains, who are they?"

He held up his fingers as he named them, "Wilson and McKay are Scottish soldiers. Good men but without an ounce of humour between them. Carter is like you, a northerner from Carlisle. He is a good man and as hard as they come. De Vries comes from a noble family but I am guessing that they lost their money sometime ago. He was brought up to be a knight but they lost their money too soon. He has the airs and graces but lacks the experience of the others."

"It sounds like you do not like him."

"Nor do I but beggars cannot be choosers. He is a captain and he has men. I would trust the others before him."

"And the fifth?"

"Harry Lawrence. He is the one I know best. He served with us in the Netherlands before you joined us. He was our Englishman and when we returned he used his money wisely. He already had twenty men when I sought him out. If you go into battle you could do worse than having Harry and his men close by. He is as close to Colonel Woodrow as I have seen."

I had the names and I knew that we had days at sea to get to know one another, not to mention the ride from Rotterdam to Utrecht.

We left not long after sext. Mags insisted upon feeding us. Edgar came out to bid us farewell. It was not just sentiment. He wanted to identify the watchers. Ostensibly waving us off I knew he was studying the men so that he would recognise them again. I did not worry about the watchers. It was broad daylight and I doubted they would risk the wrath of the guards on the bridge. From there it was a short ride to the house of my Dutch host.

Pietr had already contacted his captains who regularly plied the waters between London and the Netherlands. The coordination of the ships for the transportation of the men and arms would be complex. The days before our return to the inn passed quickly. Hob's lessons continued apace and he was a good learner. Already he had changed and his conversation and social skills were far better than they had been. His Dutch was now almost conversational. When we reached the Netherlands he would need to learn the words that were used in battle.

One evening, as we chatted at the table and Elizabeth put the boy to bed, Hob asked me, "Will we be fighting, Captain James? I only ask because I do not have sword skills yet."

I nodded, "That is remiss of me and tomorrow we will begin your lessons. As for the fighting in battle, I do not know. My task was to procure men to fight for the prince. I have skills and it would be a shame not to use them."

The next day we began lessons. I taught him the way I had learned. I showed him how to use the edge of the blade when necessary but also to use the flat when striking another sword. Keeping a weapon sharp was vital. I gave him the skills to riposte and to use his feet. He was quick on his feet and agile. They were skills that might save him. By the time we were ready to return to the inn, I was confident that he would not freeze if he had to use a sword. I told Pietr and Elizabeth that we would dine in the inn and they should not wait for us. I did not know how long it would take to conduct our business.

It was not yet dark when we crossed the bridge but getting on for evening. I heard the men working on the new buildings to the south of the playhouses. London was beginning to sprawl to the open land to the south. St Paul's, to the north of us, had not yet sounded vespers as we reined in at the inn. Hob knew his task and after watering the animals he sat by the trough to watch them. Alice would tend to his needs.

I entered the inn which was crowded. The Globe had a play on the next day and the actors had retired to the inn after working all day. The fire in the Globe that had destroyed it once meant that they wanted no risk of fire at night through rehearsals. They knew their lines and were celebrating. A new performance meant money in their purses. I wondered if I would be able to hear the captains above the hubbub of the babbling actors. Lines from plays and high-pitched squeals were the backdrops to the normal sounds of the busy inn. Edgar waved me over to a table. He was alone there but there were six chairs waiting.

As I sat, I said, "Busy."

Edgar nodded, "How Mags' husband lost money I shall never know. This is like a gold mine, James. Tomorrow we shall need extra wenches to serve those who will watch the play. That is why there are more buildings going up. Soon we shall have competition but for now, we are the inn that sucks in the actors and the customers."

An ale was placed before me. I had not seen Alice approach but I saw her back as she skilfully wound her way through posturing actors to get to the door and Hob. I had to lean close to Edgar to make myself understood, "Everything is arranged. We go tomorrow to pick up the ordinance and we can sail the day after."

"Good for you do not want to keep soldiers waiting. Remember the problems we had after we took on the Scots." We were both silent as I nodded. Apart from Stephen, we were the only two left from that company. Their lives had been snuffed out.

"I will pay the bill for the food and the ale."

Edgar smiled, "Your credit is good here but I thank you. Who knows I may have enough money to marry Mags."

"You would marry?"

He shrugged, "There is a growing movement of Calvinists who do not approve of man and woman sharing a bed if they are not married. I may well marry her for it would make her happy and me more secure. We shall see."

The debate ended when two of the captains, clearly soldiers by their build and the way they shouldered their way through the throng, approached. "The two Scotsmen, Wilson and McKay," Edgar spoke in my ear and identified the two men.

I smiled as they sat and held out my hand. The handshakes were both firm. "I am Captain Bretherton and, until we reach Utrecht, the one who directs your passage."

Captain Wilson smiled. There were flecks of grey in his hair and beard, "You are young to be a captain."

I decided on honesty, "Aye, and as the greatest number of men I have led is but twenty I know that I do not have the experience of the men I hire, but I am merely a go-between. When we are in the Netherlands you need not be offended by my youth."

Captain McKay laughed, "I am, if anything, jealous of your youth. When I was your age I was a follower. You will be a rich man when you are old."

Captains Carter and Lawrence arrived next and I liked them both from the first. Ale had been brought as soon as the two Scotsmen had sat down. Apart from the two Scotsmen the others did not know each other and the four of them chatted about their trade and the wars in which they had fought.

Mags came over, "The food is ready, Edgar. I would not have my fine cooking spoiled."

He nodded, "If Captain de Vries is tardy then it is his problem. Fetch the food and a platter for our missing man."

The pie, when it was brought, was magnificent and I saw actors looking over enviously as the steaming pie was carried by the man who looked after the beer, Ned. He placed it in the middle of the table while Alice put down the platters and Mags, the bowl of vegetables and beans. "Bread will follow. We do not have more than two hands. Enjoy."

We all watched in anticipation as Edgar cut into the pie. It was a steak and oyster pie cooked, from the smell, in porter. The four soldiers' eyes lit up as Edgar dropped a generous portion on each platter. They helped themselves to the vegetables and then began to eat. I knew that they would save the bread that was placed on the table to mop up juices. It was a good pie. The crust was well made and the bottom of the pie was firm. Mags had made a real effort and whatever price I had to pay it was worth it.

When Captain de Vries appeared, it ended the good humour on the table. He was so late that Captain Carter who appeared to inhale rather than eat his food, had almost finished. De Vries swaggered through the room and had such a look of disdain on his face that even the affected actors looked surprised. The man reeked of perfume. He smelled like the Marquis of Buckingham. He saw the seat waiting for him and sat. Alice brought a tankard of ale.

"Beer? Is there no fine wine?"

Before Edgar could speak Harry Lawrence said, "We are guests and the beer is good. The rest of us are all happy with the food, the ale and, until your arrival, the company." The other three all glared at de Vries.

I smiled, "It is a good pie, Captain de Vries, and had we known you preferred wine then we could have bought some. Next time, eh?" I held out my hand as I had done with the others, "I am Captain James Bretherton."

I saw that he wore gloves and he smiled apologetically, "I am sorry, Captain, I have a skin complaint. You understand?"

"Of course."

While the rest of us cleared our platters, Captain de Vries picked out the pieces of meat in the pie. Oysters were the food of the working man and I saw that the captain thought himself superior, not only to other men but also to the other captains. I wondered if he was a wise choice.

Time was getting on. The numbers in the inn had thinned and we could talk more easily. "I will have the weapons by tomorrow. The day after tomorrow you need to bring your men to Thames Street and the warehouse of Pietr van Dyke. It is just a few hundred paces from the Tower. You will see the ships immediately."

De Vries said, "And the pay?"

"Will be waiting in Utrecht," I glanced at Edgar who nodded, "as you have already been told."

The oily nobleman leaned back, "I am sorry but I know neither of you nor this Dutchman, van Dyke. How can I trust you?"

Once again it was Harry Lawrence who stepped in. I could see that he was a fearless warrior. He would step into any breach, "Then do not come. Tell your men that there is an offer of work but their perfumed captain does not wish to avail himself of it. We four will hire them and if they are English pikemen and musketeers they will trust the word of one who is well known to us, Edgar Smithson."

"You insult me." His hand went to his sword.

Ralph Carter laughed, "You would take on Harry Lawrence? I would pay good money to watch him gut you like a fish." He shook his head, "Edgar, we do not need this prancing pony."

Edgar just smiled and Captain de Vries stood, "Very well, I will bring my company the day after tomorrow but if the ships do not match my standards, I shall not board."

As he stormed out Captain Carter said, "I thought rats left ships when they were sinking."

We all laughed and it eased the embarrassment. Edgar said, "Once you are in the Netherlands then it will be easier."

Harry looked at me, "And where do we fight?"

I shrugged, "I am guessing in Brabant, the Spanish Netherlands. There is a truce at the moment but with events in the Palatinate, I cannot see it lasting. It might be that we have to march to Germany. You captains will be the rock on which Prince Maurice builds his hopes."

"Good, I am satisfied. We have the beating of the Spanish. They wear fine armour and ride good horses but our men are stouter."

We chatted for a little while longer and I gave them as much information as I could and then they left. The inn was now half empty. Drunks sprawled on tables. Edgar would remove them. I took out some gold gilders and slid them over to him. "These are for you."

"The meal and the ale are a fraction of this."

"And the rest is your commission. We both know that I could not have done this without you. It is not my money, but the prince's. Take it."

He nodded, "Thank you, you are a noble fellow. Your parents raised you well."

It was my turn to rise, "Will you come to see us off?"

He nodded, "Aye and a tearful Alice will be with me. He is not yet gone from this land but she misses Hob already."

When we reached the horses, Alice and Hob were in an amorous embrace. Edgar snorted, "Enough of that."

Hob was not put out, "Edgar, I am just showing Alice what she will miss when I am abroad."

Alice burst into tears and raced back into the inn. Edgar shook his head, "Hob, there are times when I despair of you. That was the wrong thing to say."

Hob looked distraught and said, "I will go and apologise."

I mounted my horse, "That will have to wait until she comes to say goodbye. It is late and I would not be out after the watch has been set."

He mounted and I reached down to grasp Edgar's hand, "Until the day after tomorrow."

The streets were empty as we passed the looming shadow of The Globe. A few actors were staggering their way to their mean lodgings but other than that all was quiet. As we turned towards Bankside and the bridge I caught a movement and my instincts took over. I drew my sword and hissed, "Ware, Hob!"

The men who ran at us were bandits and thieves but there were too many of them for us to deal with. I counted ten dark shadows and saw bladed weapons glistening. Had I been alone I would have spurred my horse, swashed my sword and relied on speed to escape. However, I had Hob and his sumpter would not keep up with me. I might escape but he would fall and I could not allow that. This was not Caesar. The hackney had no martial skills and I had to use my left hand to guide him. The first man made the mistake of coming to my right. That may have been because Hob was to my left but his decision cost him his life. As he pulled back the short sword to stab upwards at me I slashed down with my sword at his unprotected head. I could not afford mercy. The young man who had first drawn his sword in Newcastle was now a hardened veteran and knew that mercy might result in my death as well as that of Hob. The spattering blood and pieces of skull showered the man behind. It shocked him and I veered the hackney to ride at him. My slash did not kill him but cracking down on his shoulder I heard a bone break and knew he was out of the fight.

"Captain!"

I whirled and saw that Hob was doing his best and flailing around with his sword but the man with the long sword had the beating of him. Heedless of the other men racing to get at me, I rode at him and leaned from the saddle to skewer him in the arm, just as he brought the sword down to hack off Hob's leg.

"Hob, ride for the bridge and raise the alarm." I knew that the watch was about to be set and there would be armed men there. Even as he dug his heels in I felt the sword slice across my leg. I was lucky that I wore my buff coat. It covered the upper part of my leg but the sword still cut through my hose and into flesh. I ignored the pain and slashed the sword sideways. I was rewarded by a scream as the blade tore through the man's nose and cheek.

Hob had escaped but I was now alone. Four of the ten men were eliminated from the fight but the other six now menacingly circled me. Had I ridden Caesar I would have made him rear. This was a livery hackney and I would have to try to fight all six. I made it hard by circling the horse and looking for a sight of flesh. My wound was not life threatening but it would, eventually, weaken me. I saw one man with a short sword spy his opportunity and he came at my blind side thinking to strike unopposed. I stood in my stirrups, ignoring the pain that coursed up my wounded leg and slashed across his skull. He reeled away and I had halved my enemies.

The voice that gave commands had an accent, a Spanish one. "On my command, we rush him. He cannot fight five of us. His purse to the one who slays him."

I knew then that I was a dead man. Suddenly, another six shadows appeared from behind the men. I recognised Edgar. "Kill the bastards!"

The five men who were attacked died quickly and savagely. The men were all from the inn. Some had been soldiers. One or two wielded swords but their most effective weapons were their clubs and cudgels which broke bones and shattered skulls. By the time that Hob arrived with the watch, it was over.

The sergeant recognised me from my many crossings of the bridge, "Are you hurt?"

"A scratch. Edgar, I am indebted to you and your friends."

The sergeant turned over the eight bodies. Two wounded men had fled. He grunted, "Cutpurses and thieves all. The world is a better place for this. Have their heads taken to the dungeon tower." He reached the one who had commanded and he frowned, "This is a gentleman." He sniffed, "And a perfumed one at that. What is he doing here?"

"I think he was Spanish." As I looked at the body I thought that there was something familiar about it but I could not place where I had seen him.

The body was kicked by the sergeant, "Papist scum. Have his head placed there too." He looked up at me, "You need a healer, sir." He turned to look for Edgar but he and my saviours had melted into the night. I knew that the corpses would have been robbed while the heads were being removed. The sergeant gave me a wry smile, "You are lucky to have such friends, sir. Take my advice. Do not risk this part of Southwark after dark."

I smiled, "Fear not, sergeant. This was my last visit."

We rode across the bridge and the short way to Pietr's. I had been lucky and I knew it.

Chapter 9

Neither Elizabeth nor Pietr would let me stir once the doctor they had summoned had stitched my leg. I was not allowed to go with Pietr to pick up the ordnance and Elizabeth wished for me to spend a week recuperating. Even Pietr knew that was impossible. The wound was irritating more than painful. There were just eight stitches. The doctor advised me to have them removed in a fortnight. There was a good doctor at the fortress in Utrecht and that did not worry me. Hob never left my side. He kept thanking me for saving his life. He could not know that I did it as much for me as anything. I had not wanted his death on my conscience.

Pietr arranged for the hackney to be returned to Tilbury. The horse had been a good servant but I now saw that a horse like Caesar could save my life. I had been lucky and Fate is a precocious mistress who can desert you at a moment's notice. The parting from Elizabeth was touching. Hob and I had come into her life and she had found joy. I knew that was largely due to the lively Hob but I, too, had tried to do as my mother had taught me and be a good guest. There were tears and hugs as we left. I think Hob found the parting hard. Alice and Mags were wonderful women but they were not ladies. The genteel Elizabeth had been a revelation.

We walked to the ships, or rather the other two walked and I limped. My bags were carried for me but I avoided using a stick. I set my teeth and ignored the pain. There was a squeal when we neared the river for Alice was waiting there. She hurled herself at Hob who could do nothing about it as he had his arms laden. She smothered him with kisses and the musketeers, swordsmen and pikemen who were boarding paused to cheer and catcall. I saw Edgar shaking his head. The captains were too busy marshalling their men aboard the ships to notice. One ship bore a pennant and I knew that she was the flagship. Pietr had told me of the ships that would transport us and their captains. She had Pietr's best captain, Christian van Hooft. Hob and I had berths aboard her. I was relieved to see that it was Harry Lawrence's company who were aboard and not the nasty de Vries. I would have found it hard to endure his company.

Edgar allowed Alice a few moments to assault Hob and then said, "Alice, you have said goodbye now time and tide wait for no man. Let Hob board the ship."

She pulled back, "Will I ever see you again? Do not say no for that would break my heart."

He looked at me for help. I said, "Prince Maurice has said he will use me as an ambassador, of sorts, so aye, we will be back but I cannot say when. It could be six months or it could be a year or more."

She nodded, "So long as you come back and when you do, then, if you wish it, I shall be your wife. I do not mind being a camp follower. It can't be any less dangerous than serving ale in a Southwark inn."

"And I swear that I will come back. The captain has promised he will teach me to write. Edgar can read and he shall read my letters aloud."

Pietr said, "You need to board or else you shall miss the tide."

I put my hand out to Edgar, "Thank you, old friend."

"Thank you, James. I have now got soldiering out of my blood and I can marry Mags and become a fat old innkeeper."

I turned to Pietr, "And I know that I shall be seeing you again. Thank you for doing more for me than was needed. Come Hob. The others are boarded."

It was then that I spied a face I knew. Edgar should have recognised him too but he was busy comforting Alice. "Stephen, is that you?"

The sergeant wearing the livery of the garrison stepped forward, "Aye, James, it is."

I heard the First Mate shout, in Dutch, "All aboard. The tide is on the turn."

I had to board but I needed to greet my old comrade, "You found employment?"

"Aye, my skills, it seems, are still needed. I saw you boarding and left my post to speak with you."

I nodded to Edgar, "Edgar has an inn. I will seek you out when I return." He nodded and leaned on his halberd.

The gangplank was empty and, with Edgar restraining Alice, the two of us climbed the gangplank. Stephen walked over to Edgar. The soldiers lined the side, grinning at Hob. The First Mate stood waiting at the gangplank. Already the other four ships had cast off. As the flagship and the largest ship in the flotilla, we were to lead them out. He spoke in Dutch, "If you wait at the bow castle, Captain James, I will show you to your quarters when we are in the main channel. It will not be a long wait."

"Do not worry about us. You have a job to do."

The gangplank was hauled aboard and the hawsers that had tied us to the land were loosened then dragged back. The orders were given and the sails were loosed. The tide was already dragging us to the sea and the slight breeze, being from the northwest, made the movement more pronounced. I knew, from my words with Pietr, that we would not race down the narrow and twisting river. There was a palace at Greenwich and many smaller ships used it. There were ferries and wherries that crossed the river and Tilbury was a busy port. The captain and his crew would need their wits about them until we reached the mouth of the estuary. I stared at the Tower and wondered at the events that had led Stephen to become a sergeant of the guard. He had done well, Edgar had a happy life and I was returning to the maelstrom of war and politics. More, I was dragging a youth with me. Was this the right decision?

Hob had deposited the bags by the bow castle and stood with me waving at Edgar and Alice. She was weeping and it touched Hob, "I am torn, Captain. This adventure will be the making of me but Alice, well, she is the love of my life."

I was going to laugh but knew it would be wrong of me. "You are young, Hob. How do you know?"

He turned to look at me and asked, "Have you never fallen in love, Captain?"

It hit me hard. I had never held a lady's hand with amorous intent. I was much older than Hob and yet he had kissed and been kissed back. Perhaps he had enjoyed even more than just a kiss. My life with my family had been sheltered and my time since then given over to the pursuit of war. I had felt attracted to Elizabeth but there were rules and I had observed them. More than that I had been brought up well by my parents. I was saved from having to answer when a seaman said, "This is your cabin, Captain."

He opened the door to the bow castle and we entered a narrow walkway. There were four low and narrow doors and he took me to the one on the port side and closest to the bow. It was small but there were two hammocks hanging there. He opened a shutter and air rushed in, "This will afford you light but, at sea, it can mean a dousing." He shrugged, "It is your choice. Above us is the bow castle and there is the place where you make water and empty your bowels." He grinned, "You have used one before, I think."

"I have and I will instruct Hob."

"The First Mate said that you are to eat with the captain and the other senior soldier along with the officers in the stern cabin. You will be fetched when it is time."

Hob looked at the hammock as though it was an instrument of torture. "Do not worry, Hob, you shall enjoy a good night of sleep in one of those. I fear that while I am wined and dined you will have to make do with the food and ale that Mistress Elizabeth provided."

"And as she gave enough for two then I shall be content."

We returned to the deck. We would spend enough time in the tiny cabin when we were at sea. Harry Lawrence came over, "I hear that cutpurses set upon you. Are you well?"

I patted the leg, "It aches and soon it will itch but such are the problems that a soldier can expect."

"Just so."

I lowered my voice, "But I do not think they were merely cutpurses. I think that they were men hired to kill me." His eyes widened but he said nothing. "There was a Spaniard leading. I believe that the Catholics in England wish me dead."

"But why?"

"I am the conduit between the prince and the king. If I am dead, then that link is severed and the Catholics have a victory."

He nodded, "And they are winning at the moment. The Battle of the White Mountain lost Bohemia."

"I think that this war has a long way to run. There are many Protestant kingdoms who resent the way the Catholic Church is going about its business. Denmark and Sweden are lands which border the Baltic and Spain is stretched."

He changed the subject a little, "I hear that you can speak many languages."

There was little point in false modesty and I nodded, "French, German, Dutch and a little Swedish." I remembered Erik Hand and his Swedes. They had been not just good warriors but great warriors and now their butchered bodies lay in Germany.

"I know that it is a short voyage but some Dutch might help. If you could spare the time and have the patience then I would learn some Dutch."

And so as we wound along the serpentine Thames, I began to give Harry lessons in Dutch. The meeting with Stephen had been important. He lived and was employed. He had not joined the detritus of old soldiers who littered London streets. I needed to give Hob the same chance, to gain skills that would keep him employed. Hob showed that he had heeded his lessons and helped me while I taught Harry. It passed the time. By the time darkness came, the sea was still some miles away and lanterns had been hung from our stern as we sailed along a half-deserted river. The captain, as senior captain in the flotilla, would have to wait until all five ships were safely at sea before he ate. Harry and I would have to endure the sharp pangs of hunger.

"Hob, you have food, eat. I shall not need you."

The alacrity with which he sped off told me that he was starving and had been staying out of politeness.

"He seems a good lad."

"He is and he is like a sponge. He absorbs all that I tell him and he is a quick learner. He has natural skills that cannot be taught. He survived on London streets as an urchin."

"Aye, London can be a cruel place. My wife and child lived there and when the plague ripped through the city, they were two victims. I was fighting in Ireland else I might have joined them. I am always happy to be leaving."

We felt the swell of the sea not long before a servant came and said, in Dutch, "The Captain apologises for the delay but there is now food."

The low cabin was lit by lanterns and seemed warming and welcoming. I saw that the table could accommodate eight men if they squeezed in but there were just four places. The captain had with him another officer and there were two places for us.

Captain van Hooft was a jolly man and he enjoyed his food. The table was laden and he smiled, "I take advantage of fresh food whenever we are in port. The voyage may only take four days or so but I like to dine well." We nodded although I am not sure how much of the Dutch Harry had understood. "I should introduce you, gentlemen. This is Captain Bretherton, Prince Maurice's ambassador and Captain Lawrence who commands the company we carry." The man nodded. "This is my friend, Doctor Hofsted. He has just spent a month in England consulting with other doctors."

Frederick Hofsted was a clever man and I liked him from the first, "A doctor needs to learn as much as he can. I am lucky to have a friend like Christian here. He gave me a free passage."

The captain had already begun to eat and he shook his head, "Not free, Frederick, I have a doctor for the voyage. It is you who is doing me the favour. Come, gentlemen, eat. You make me feel like a glutton."

The food was delicious and well-cooked. Most sea captains had good wine, for whenever they visited a vinous country they stocked up and Christian van Hooft was no exception. The conversation was lively. The doctor quickly realised that Harry spoke little Dutch and switched to English. That suited the captain who was able to give his full attention to the food laid before us. We had begun to eat late and I found the motion of the sea, added to the huge meal I had eaten made me sleepy. I was relieved when the cabin boys cleared the table and I was able to depart.

Poor Hob was still awake and waiting for me, looking warily at the hammock, "I did not know how to get into this...thing, Captain."

I smiled, "It is easy. Have you made water?"

"I have."

"Good then watch me." I undressed to my underwear and, holding my blanket in my left hand, sat on the hammock which, as I had expected, sagged alarmingly. Then I flipped up my legs, ignoring the pain from the wound, and as my weight spread

along the hammock, it lifted. I tucked my blanket around me.
"There. Now you."

He was a quick learner and he beamed when he managed it,
"Now it is I who feels like Tom Fool, Captain. It is easy."

"Goodnight." I was so tired that almost as soon as I closed
my eyes I was asleep. The problem I had was that my bladder
had not been emptied and, while I might normally have slept
through the need to pass water, I must have turned and scraped
my wound. It woke me and once awake I had little choice but to
leave my hammock, don my cloak and pad my way to the bow
castle. Hob, sleeping on his back, snored away.

The cold sea air hit me as I left the cabin and then climbed the
ladder to the bow castle. I went to the leeward side and lowering
my breeches, passed water. I had just finished when I noticed the
lookout who was perched precariously on the bowsprit.

"I did not see you there."

He did not turn but said, "I have the sea to watch."

"For what? The land is many leagues to the east."

"The sea is not the only danger. There are privateers and
pirates. We are the flagship and I am the eyes of the flotilla."

I made my way back to the cabin. The cloak had been a wise
choice. The spray had soaked it. I rolled into my hammock and
slipped the still-warm blanket over me. This time I did not fall
asleep as quickly. I had thought that any danger lay in England
but I had forgotten the threat posed by privateers. Pirates would
not risk five ships but a privateer had a warrant from a king,
duke or emperor. He was allowed to make war and take cargo.
Drake had been one such privateer and made himself rich during
the reign of Queen Elizabeth. The five ships represented a threat
to Spain not to mention the Empire. I hoped that we were well-
armed.

I rose early. The meeting with the lookout had disturbed my
sleep. When I had dressed, emptied my bowels and made water I
went on deck where a cabin boy approached, "There is food laid
out in the captain's cabin, Captain. The other Englishman is there
already."

As I walked down the ship I saw that we were, indeed, armed.
There were four falcons and falconets spread out on both sides.
The Dutch called them drakes but I had seen them on English

ships when we had left Leith and was told they were called falcons and falconets. They were old-fashioned weapons and had no wheels to facilitate their movement, but they were a defence.

There was just Harry in the cabin and the table was laid with bread, butter, ham and cheese. He chuckled when I entered, "Some of the men have never sailed before and found the movement, shall we say, disconcerting. The next days will prove to be interesting."

"I slept well enough. Hob is still sound asleep." I tapped my leg, "This wound is annoying. The sooner it begins to itch the better."

The doctor had entered while I was speaking and said, "You have a wound?"

"I was cut a few days ago and there are stitches."

He nodded, "When I have eaten, I will apply a salve to ease the wound. It will help you to sleep."

I knew how much doctors charged and I said, warily, "Thank you, doctor, but you need not trouble yourself."

"No trouble and call it repayment for those interesting stories you told last night."

The salve, when he applied it, was nothing short of miraculous. He gave me a small phial of it and told me to apply it at night. That done, and when Hob joined us, we took a turn around the deck.

At the sterncastle, the captain waved a thumb behind us, "Not all the captains are as skilled as I am. See how some of them do not keep station."

We peered aft and saw what he meant. One was within the required two lengths of us but the one at the rear was lagging four lengths behind the nearest ship and that, in turn, was three lengths behind the next.

The captain sighed, "It means that we shall have to shorten sail. It may delay our entry into the harbour by up to a day."

Harry said, somewhat surprised, "A day?"

"We have been at sea a short time and already ships are falling behind. We have to stay together for a myriad of reasons. Losing time like this means that we might have to wait for another tide to enter the harbour. Time is money to a sailor. Still, gentlemen, it won't affect you. A day or two cannot harm you."

It was towards dusk that trouble came. We had reefed sails four times and yet *'Orange Maiden'* was still lagging behind. Our captain blamed weed on her hull. A sharp-eyed lookout on the mainmast called down, "Captain, there are ships astern of Maiden. I like not the look of them."

Captain van Hooft was a decisive man, "Order all men on deck. Beat to quarters."

There was a cabin boy who grabbed the drum and began to rattle out the alarm.

I said, "Trouble?"

"It might be. Sunset is coming," he pointed to the darkening sky ahead, "These may be pirates or privateers coming to cut out Maiden." He picked up his speaking trumpet and shouted to the next ship in line, "Call Captain Loften, I would speak with him." A few minutes later a young man reached the bows. Captain van Hooft shouted, "There may be trouble at the stern. Take the lead and I will be the sheepdog that rounds up the stray." The other captain waved his acknowledgement. Captain van Hooft then turned to us and said, "It may be nothing but I would arm your men. Keep them out of the way," He pointed to the bow castle, "You are free to shelter there."

Already the men assigned to the eight cannons were fetching powder and ball. The ancient guns would be better than nothing but I guessed that if these were pirates or privateers then they would be well-armed. While Harry went to see to his men, Hob and I went to the cabin. I donned my buff coat and Hob his jerkin.

"Will we have to fight, Captain?"

I shrugged, "I know not but let us be prepared. The ships that follow may be harmless. I know from my last voyage that sailors like company but our captain is a prudent man. Arm yourself." I tapped his head, "And wear your secrete."

I donned my hat and with a pistol hanging from my belt and my sword from my waist, I was ready. We were now sailing into the wind and the captain was having to tack to and fro. There was a lookout at the bow and I said, "Do we know if the ships are a threat?"

He pointed aft and said, "I cannot tell yet but I have an itch at the back of my neck that says they are privateers. They have the look of greyhounds and Richard here says he swears he saw light glinting off a morion."

A morion, especially at sea, would suggest a Spaniard.

Another sailor scoffed, "Richard has been drinking bad ale again. It is nothing."

Harry had brought out some of his muskets. If nothing else it would give his men the chance to fire them. They had cleaned them already but there had been no opportunity to fire them. The men with pikes had their pikes laid close to the mainmast where they could be easily reached. Harry wore his helmet and breastplate.

I smiled, "Iron, at sea?"

"If we are doomed to sink then it will just hasten my end...I cannot swim." I saw that he had a good sword as well as a brace of wheel locks like me.

We had passed the third of our ships and there were just two left, *'Sunrise'* and *'Orange Maiden'*. Both laboured and I guessed that our captain had been right and they had too much weed on their hulls. I also saw that the two Scottish captains had armed their men. The two ships had just two guns on each side.

The lookout said simply, "Privateers, four of them." He turned and cupped his hands, "Four privateers, Captain."

Captain van Hooft raised his hand in acknowledgement. He shouted, "Load with double shot."

I knew, from our conversation the night before, that loading with double shot was potentially dangerous but firing a double load in the first encounter might just swing the outcome in our favour.

Harry called, "Muskets load."

Hob had never seen muskets before although Edgar had described them to him. He was fascinated by the complex actions. There were many manoeuvres but these men were veterans and each did it his own way. They had rests but the gunwale on the ship was as good a support as any.

"Harry, perhaps if you hid your musketeers it might come as a surprise to the privateers?"

He looked ahead and then nodded, "Lay on the decks and keep your weapons hidden." There was grumbling but the men obeyed.

Ahead I saw that the setting sun was illuminating the four privateers. Compared with the lumbering merchantmen they lay lower in the water and, to me, had the look of hunting dogs. I looked aft and saw how close was the night. I could barely see Captain Loften's ship and I guessed that the privateers might not see us at all as we approached from the dark.

When the two guns at the front of the leading privateer fired it made me jump. I saw the flashes as the cannons fired and then there was a crack. Harry said, "We know now, eh, James." He said to his men, "Prepare to rise but only on my command."

I saw the gunners at the side of our ship blowing on their linstocks. Approaching as slowly as we were would give them a more stable platform to fire but if the privateers had already boarded then there was little that they could do about it. I made sure my pistol was loaded. I would not need that unless it was close combat but, as I had discovered, that one shot could be the difference between life and death.

The captain of the *'Orange Maiden'* might have had a weed-covered ship but he was no coward. I heard the pop of muskets and his two guns as he tried to take on the two privateers that were rapidly approaching the two sides of his ship. Christian was also no coward and when he put the helm over to close with the nearest privateer the extra wind made us race.

"Stand and prepare to fire."

I would not dream of advising Harry how to command his men but I knew he had to wait until the last moment. From what I had heard privateers packed their ships with men and a volley at close range might just tear the heart from them.

The First Mate shouted, "The first shot is our best chance lads and he can't see us coming from the dark. Wait until I give the command and then clear the enemy decks."

Harry shouted, "Pick up your pikes. When we have fired, one of the others might try to board."

I drew my sword. It was more for something to do than anything. Hob emulated me. The two privateers had now closed with the stricken ship and they fired their cannons to clear the decks. We could do nothing about the starboard side but when the First Mate shouted fire, the four cannons erupted and scythed through the nearest privateer. I saw at least one of the cannons upended and heard the screams as men were hit with double-shotted balls. Then I saw a wall of fire from the *'Orange Maiden'* as her musketeers rose from beneath the gunwale to open fire. From my lofty position on the bow castle, I saw the carnage in the well of the ship. Captain van Hooft had not yet finished and he continued to sail and pass the stern of the privateer. It was the most vulnerable part of the ship. Our cannons might have been old but the First Mate knew his business. He had reloaded the guns and he personally fired each one as we passed the stern. The balls and grapeshot drove unopposed through the ship. If any were left alive they would be able to do little.

The second privateer had boarded and I saw the pikes of Captain McKay's men as they gave the privateers a rude shock. More men were waiting in the well of the privateer and even as our cannons were reloaded, prior to firing, Harry shouted, "Musketeers, fire."

We were above the privateer and each musketeer with a matchlock had a clear view. The volley was ragged because of the differences in the matches but, even so, the screams were a good reward. When the four cannons fired at point-blank range, they hit the ship and the main mast which fell to smash into the steering board.

The cheers from our men were premature for a third privateer had raced from the dark and was approaching our stern quarter. The First Mate ran to the, as yet, unfired larboard guns and he fired each one in succession. It was an acute angle but he hit, with his first shot, the side of the ship which had their bow chaser. The splintering wood was a savage weapon. Shards of wood embedded themselves in men's faces, bodies and hands. The second one cut through waiting men. Then the ship ground next to ours and grappling hooks were thrown.

Harry had his sword in his hand, "Now, I think, we earn our passage." He leapt from the bow castle to join his waiting pikemen. Our crew had each grabbed a weapon. Privateers and pirates showed little mercy. With my pistol in one hand and sword in another, I stood to the right of Harry.

"Hob, stand behind me and watch my back."

The privateers had been savaged but that had merely made them angry and they swarmed over the side like angry wasps with stings as nasty as any flying creature. Even as he swashed his sword at the foolish Spaniard who leapt across from the privateer, Harry was shouting, "Musketeers, reload and clear their stern!" It was the right move for the captain and helmsmen were key targets.

After that, we had no time to think as the Spanish privateers, cursing and screaming, boarded us. The first two I slew were simple kills. Until they established a foothold the privateers had to descend from our gunwale. I hacked through the legs of one, severing his right leg and slicing through to the bone of his left. With blood pumping away he fell to his death. I fired the pistol at a range of no more than four feet and threw a second Spaniard to fall back and disrupt those who were following. I dropped the now useless pistol to its lanyard and fended off the halberd wielded by a giant of a Spaniard. He made it to our deck and he advanced towards me, punching with the spike and axe head of his halberd. I did not want to blunt my sword and so I did the unexpected. I had quick hands and my left hand darted out and, avoiding the axe head, grabbed the langet, the metal protection just behind the head. I pulled to my left as I drove at him with my sword. He did not let go of the halberd and was impaled on my blade. He was a big man and I pulled out my sword and stabbed him again to make sure he was dead.

We were holding them but numbers were on their side. We were saved because one of the captains had decided to follow us and as the ship with Captain Carter aboard had also turned, it meant we had three ships against two. The Dutch cannons wreaked havoc and the musketeers aboard the ships had live practice. As the first ship we had attacked slipped beneath the waves, the other three all turned tail and ran. One of them, at least, was a floating charnel house while a third had lost half of its crew.

As they fled into the night our men cheered. I looked down and saw that one of the Spaniards was still alive. I kicked his weapon away from him. He reached up and, finding his cross, he kissed it. It was only then that I recognised him. He had been one of the men who had first followed me to the 'Saddle'. He had not taken part in the ambush but he was clearly an enemy. He gave me a lopsided grin and said, in English, "Don Miguel Alvarado will have his vengeance, Englishman. Your days are numbered." Then he expired.

Hob had heard and he too had recognised the man. "Who is this Don Miguel Alvarado, Captain?"

"A Spaniard and I saw him at the court of King James. At least now we know who is behind this and who is my enemy."

Hob shook his head, "Life will be anything but dull with you, Captain." He then sheathed his sword and began to search the dead men for treasure.

I stood and turned to Harry, "Any casualties?"

"Three men wounded but nothing serious and at least we have a doctor to tend to them. I am not sure about Captain McKay's men though."

They had been boarded and it meant we had fewer men for the prince. It could not be helped and at least I now had a name to give to him. If I saw him again, I would know him. The most seriously wounded were brought aboard our ship. Minor wounds, cuts and the like could be dealt with by the men left aboard the *'Orange Maiden'*. I saw as we headed east to catch up with the other ships, the skill of the doctor. The light was not the best and the motion of the ship conspired against him but he patched up all the wounded and did not lose a single man. Hob and I gave what assistance we could. In my case, it was to learn a little from the doctor. By the time we tumbled into our hammocks, we were exhausted, and I did not bother to undress.

Horse and Pistol

Chapter 10

When we rose we saw the damage from the battle. The wood on the gunwale had been splintered and shattered in places. The ship's carpenter was already repairing them. Some rigging had been weakened and sailors swarmed up ratlines to make repairs. The captain had ordered *'Orange Maiden'* to sail close to us and we could hear as well as see the work that was needed to repair her. We also saw the bodies that were buried at sea as dawn broke. It was a sombre sight.

I stood with Harry and Hob at the waist, looking aft. Hob was a bright youth and he showed that he was a thinker, "I do not think that Captain McKay will have a full company. Will he be able to fulfil the contract?"

I nodded, "There are men in the Netherlands who will serve. Prince Maurice was keen for English and Scottish captains as well as English and Scottish soldiers for they have done well for him. He will be able to hire more."

Harry pointed forrard to the two ships which now led us, "Had they come back with us we might have saved more."

I shook my head, "I heard the orders that were given. Captain Loften was told to take command and sail on."

Harry chuckled, "Ralph Carter would not have liked that. He enjoys a good fight."

"You have fought alongside him before?"

"Aye, and he is a good man. He is as tenacious as a terrier. Give him a place to defend and it will be yours come hell or high water. Ask him to attack and you shall need to have men ready to support him when he succeeds. His fault is that he never knows when to quit and that is sometimes necessary."

I had little experience in battle but I knew that he was right.

The battle and the repairs added two days to our passage. It was fortunate that I had been eating with the captain or else our food would have run out, therefore Hob did not starve. Elizabeth had provided well. By the time we reached the quay, the first two ships were already tied up and their passengers were disgorging. The men who had been wounded were, in the main, mobile but there were two who would need either to ride or I would need a wagon to carry them. I decided that when we landed, I would use my authority from the prince to commandeer a wagon.

Because of all that I needed to do, my parting from both the captain and the doctor was briefer than I would have wished. Thanks to the attack we had not been able to enjoy as much of each other's company as I might have hoped. The doctor was travelling to The Hague and assured me that we would meet again. I hoped so for I liked him.

The captain gave my hand a hearty handshake, "And when I next see the master of these ships I shall tell him of the steel that is in the one I thought so young. I will carry you anywhere, Captain James."

As we descended the gangplank I could not help but feel guilty. I had been the scent that had led the privateers to attack us. I had been watched for a reason and the attack had been to prevent me from fulfilling my contract. I would be warier in future.

I left Harry to organise the men and I went with Hob to the stables where I had left my horses. Caesar welcomed me as always. The Spanish horse I had captured at the battle seemed to me to have a haughty look. Stephen had been afraid of the animal and because of his black coat and fiery eyes had called him Black Henry, even though I had named him Henry after the English king. Stephen's reaction told me that the horse might frighten another such as Hob. Of course, the animal had been raised with a Spanish name and we could not possibly have known what that name was. When Hob saw the horses and, especially Henry, he was intimidated. I smiled, "This brown one is Caesar. He is a good horse. Saddle him first. That is my tack above his stall. The other is a Spanish warhorse called Henry. You can leave him to me but one day you will have to saddle him and, who knows, ride him."

Leaving a terrified Hob to walk warily around the warhorse, I sought the owner of the stable. I had used my authority from the prince for the stabling and when I used the same authority to requisition a wagon and horses to pull it, his face adopted an expression as though I had slapped him. "You will drive me to an alms-house, Captain."

I felt sorry for him and I had not spent all my expenses. I slipped him a golden gilder, "Here is for your trouble."

His expression lifted immediately.

By the time I returned, Hob had succeeded in saddling Caesar. "We have a long ride ahead. You can ride Caesar. I know you are still learning so walk him around the yard and let him grow accustomed to your voice."

Henry snorted as I began to saddle him. I used a firm tone as I addressed him, "Do not get stroppy with me. This is all your fault. When your master fell you chose me. Had I left you on the battlefield then who knows where you might have ended up. You have eaten oats and you have been groomed, now behave yourself or you will be put in the traces of a wagon." I do not know if he understood a single word but he seemed calmer somehow. Perhaps it was my voice that did it. I realised that I would need to learn Spanish as well as the other languages. They were our enemies and even a few basic phrases might help. I resolved to find someone to teach me.

With the horses saddled we left the stables and I waved over Captain McKay. He had suffered a cut along his cheek and that just made him look angrier. "I have a wagon for your wounded, Captain. I will let you appoint a driver."

We had not had the opportunity to speak since the attack and now he drew me to one side, "You should know that I am in your debt, Captain. I thought we were doomed when the two privateers boarded us. You saved me and my men."

"It was Captain van Hooft who came back to save the ship."

"But Harry told me that it was your decisions that ensured victory. All bodes well for our time here in the Dutch Republic."

"I may not be assigned to you."

His face fell, "I thought you would." I shook my head. "Harry says I can replace the dead with men here in the Netherlands."

"Aye, there will be both English and Scots. The men who survived the battles we lost make their way here like lost sheep. When we reach Utrecht you should find them."

Captain de Vries apart, the other captains were quite happy to walk with their men. As Harry laughingly said, it would take a good walk to become accustomed to the land once more. I think what galled de Vries was that my servant rode a horse while he walked.

Hob said, "Let the captain have my horse, Captain. I do not mind walking."

I was firm, "Hob, the other captains are walking. Perhaps it will make the arrogant captain humbler."

I knew that there was even more bad feeling between de Vries and the other captains for we had learned that the captain of his vessel had suggested turning during the fight, to aid, *'Orange Maiden'*. De Vries had refused. Captain McKay was all for offering to fight de Vries but wiser heads convinced him to bide his time. As we headed up the road I wondered if the prince would think that I had done all that I could have done. I had not brought as many men as he had wished and the Spanish were aware of what we were doing. Perhaps my commission would be a short one.

As Hob and I were riding, we left the wagon and the men five miles from Utrecht so that I could warn the castellan of the arrival of the men. They would need to be fed and housed. I was recognised this time and while Hob tended to the horses, I was taken to Captain Berghof. He beamed when I met him, "A timely arrival." I frowned, "Count von Mansfield is marching south to join an army marching north led by the Margrave of Baden-Durlach. We have a chance to avenge the defeat of the White Mountain. You and the men you bring will march south as soon as is practicable. The count is heading towards Düren and if you take that road you should meet up with him."

I was still hazy on the geography of Germany but I guessed we were talking about hundreds of miles rather than a few.

"Captain, we were attacked by Spanish privateers. Men were lost."

He frowned as though I had suddenly showered him with icy water. "The Spanish?"

I told him of my adventures in London and he nodded, "I know this Alvarado. He is a spymaster. You were lucky. There are men who can make up the numbers and the prince has five hundred Dutchmen who will march with you. I am to command those. Do not worry, Captain James. The tide in this war is about to change."

"But the truce."

"Is ended. All pretence is gone." He smiled, "I will arrange for the accommodation and food. I will let the prince know and payment will be forthcoming. I know that it is best to keep mercenaries sweet. The money comes from King Frederick. The prince offered to fund you but King Frederick wishes his country back. When the Palatinate is safe from the Catholics then your contract will be over."

I took Hob to my chamber. It was a little too small for two of us but we would only be there for one night and I did not want to make a fuss. Hob's Dutch was still a little rough but at least he could understand most of what was said to him and answer in halting Dutch. That, and his happy smile, endeared him to those he met. After depositing our bags, I went down to greet the captains as they arrived. When I told them of the orders they all reacted as I had expected them to. Four were philosophical about it while de Vries grew angry.

I had endured enough of his tantrums and I gave him an ultimatum, "The pay is coming from the prince and as he is paying for the men then they are his to command. If you do not wish to go, and I am sure that all of us here would be happy for that to be the case, then I will take over the men until a replacement can be found."

"You cannot do that."

I smiled, "I think I can. What is your answer, Captain de Vries? If I am to command the men you brought then I need to get to know them."

He was angry but he was also defeated and he knew it. He was a bully who normally got his way through bluster and threat. I had met the threat with my own and he eventually nodded, "Very well, but I am unhappy."

I laughed, "In the short time I have known you I have never even seen you smile, so I look forward to that rare event." The other four all laughed and it compounded his discomfort.

The prince and Captain Berghof arrived. To the obvious chagrin of de Vries, the prince greeted me warmly. I doubt that de Vries would have understood the Dutch but the sentiment was clear, "Captain James, you have come at a most judicious time and endured, so Captain Berghof tells me, the wrath of our enemies. Your fortitude does you great credit. If you and your officers would dine with me this night I can add to the detail of the campaign."

After he left, I told them that we would be dining with the prince. Harry said, "I do not know about the others but, for my part, I am keen to learn some Dutch. We made a start on the ship but the attack…"

"Then let us continue where we left off now as I take you to your quarters."

I had begun with a basic vocabulary. Some of the words were familiar. I knew that they would massacre the words at first but the time spent marching to meet with von Mansfield would improve their skills.

Captain de Vries did not smile but I could tell, from his expression, that the feast laid on by the prince met with his approval. He was even politer to me for the next few days as he sought to improve his Dutch. I knew that the reason was pragmatic. He wanted to be able to insinuate himself into the prince's good graces.

Before the meal I had sought out Johannes, the clerk, and he had provided me with maps. I recognised his hand on them. He had copied them, anticipating my request. He was as invaluable to the prince as the whole army. It meant that while we ate I was able to give waypoints to the captains to help them plan. We would be accompanied by Dutchmen and a baggage train but I would be the one coordinating the largest element of the column, the English and the Scots. I had come far in a relatively short space of time. Now I was a quartermaster.

Captain Berghof spent some time, just before I retired, explaining his plan for the march. "It is just short of one hundred and ten miles to Düren and I do not want an exhausted army. We will just march thirty miles a day. We have no artillery, that is with Count Mansfield, and so we can keep up a good speed. The roads are well made and the land is flat."

"Will you and the Dutchmen lead?"

"We will. We need a good commander for the rearguard. While we have no artillery to drag we have wagons and if we lose those…"

I nodded, "Captain Lawrence is reliable and does not panic."

Captain Berghof nodded towards the captains, "They seem a good lot except for one."

"Captain de Vries."

"Aye, he keeps apart from the others and... well there is something about him I do not like."

"He is not likeable but he has a good reputation. I did not have long to gather your army."

"Do not apologise. The prince and I think that you have performed wonders. The real test is when we meet the Imperial Army."

"Not the Spanish?"

"Not yet. Count Tilly and the condottiero, Ambrogio Spinola Doria, are the two leaders. The margrave and the count are trying to join each other to prevent the enemy from joining forces. When the margrave and the count join up they will command fifteen thousand men. Our company will take it to sixteen. The Imperialists, when they join up, will field fifteen thousand so you can see how important we are. We may be the soldiers who swing the battle in the favour of the Protestants. We need a victory to wash away the taste of defeat."

We loaded our bags in the wagons with the spare weapons, powder and ball. The men would march with sloped pikes and muskets. The exception was Harry's company which were the baggage train guards. They had the wagons that they could use and if we were attacked then they would be fresher. We had with us twenty horsemen. I was not convinced of their quality. They were young Dutch nobles. They dressed flamboyantly and talked as though they were all veritable Alexanders. However, as Captain Berghof pointed out, we needed eyes and ears ahead of us. Like me, he did not trust them. Captain Berghof was a professional soldier and the young nobles were clearly amateurs playing at being soldiers.

Behind the horses came the sword and buckler men. They were not Swedes like Erik Hand and his men but they were equally good soldiers. Half came from Swabia while the other half were a mixture of Germans and Italians. The only banners we had were with the Dutch regiments. The one used by Colonel Woodrow would now be adorning some Spanish nobleman's home. If we lasted more than six months then we would have our own banners. Men liked a rallying point. The boy drummers in each company would have to become the rallying point. The boys were all less than ten summers old. If they survived then when they became men they would join either the pikes or the muskets.

Captain Berghof picked a route to the rendezvous which avoided any potential confrontations. The Catholic and Protestant communities lived apart and we travelled through Protestant settlements. It added to our journey but we were warmly greeted and treated well. I learned much from Captain Berghof. Our scouts soon bored of riding just ahead of us and they ranged further afield. Thus it was that they made contact with the count's rearguard. We were just setting up our camp and lighting our fires when they rode in.

"Captain Berghof, Count Mansfield is but one day away. He has left Düren but we can catch up with him the day after tomorrow. He has artillery and he moves slowly."

It was good news and the food tasted better that night knowing that soon we would no longer be alone.

One problem we had was that we were now the rearguard and behind the count's baggage. It meant we not only travelled more slowly than before but had to endure passing places which had been stripped of all food before we reached them. The captain was forced to send men out to forage along the side roads, seeking isolated communities. We were five miles from Mingolsheim when it became our turn to forage. Hob and I went with four of Harry's musketeers. We commandeered horses to enable us to move more quickly. We found a small village, St Leon. It was Catholic and, at our approach, the villagers fled. We found hams and cheeses as well as bread and beans. It was a veritable treasure trove and with our horses laden we turned to head back to the main column.

The four musketeers were chattering away, buoyed by our finds but I was concentrating on the road ahead. Hob had yet to learn to use his eyes and spot that which was anomalous. I saw the horsemen a mile up the road and I knew that they were the enemy. For one thing, they were coming from the north and we were the rearguard and secondly the light reflected from breastplates. I knew that we had no cuirassiers. This meant that it was an army coming down the road. I suppose I could have risked riding closer to it and ascertaining numbers but getting the news to my superiors was more important.

"We must ride hard, there are Imperial Troops arriving." Their chatter ceased and we galloped. We might have been seen, I did not know but we had to warn the captain and the count. The count was trying to stop Tilly and Gonzalo Fernández de Córdoba from joining forces. A mixture of Imperial and Spanish soldiers was a serious threat to the count and our relatively small army.

The men were looking forward to a camp at Mingolsheim. We could smell the fires lit by the main body already and when we rode in there was a cheer as they saw our laden horses. The joy was short-lived when I shouted, "There is an Imperial Army heading down the road."

Captain Berghof was decisive. He sent two riders to warn the count and then had six of the others ride north to discover the enemy numbers. He began to deploy the musketeers and pikemen while the baggage train lumbered down the road to Mingolsheim.

I saw that he placed the five companies I had brought in the centre. It was a testament to the faith he had in the men I had picked. When just three riders and two riderless horses galloped from the north, I knew that the reckless young nobles had exceeded their orders.

One of them shouted, "There are more than fifteen thousand men coming down the road. We are doomed!" He and the others galloped off.

Harry spat, "Horsemen! Not worth the oats they feed their horses."

I turned to Captain Berghof, "Orders, sir?"

He smiled, "We slow them down and work our way back. This is where we see the training of the musketeers you have brought."

I nodded and knew what he meant. Blocks of musketeers would take it in turns to fire allowing us to retreat down the road in an orderly fashion. It took nerves of steel to fire and then reload. I hoped that my captains had chosen their men wisely. We were about to have a baptism of fire.

Chapter 11

Hob and I remained mounted but we were close to the musketeers of Harry's company. I had my three wheel locks loaded and I had impressed on Hob the need for him to remain behind me. My buff coat would stop a sword thrust but not a ball. Hob's jerkin would not even stop a sword. "I need you behind me so that I can give you orders. It might well be that we need to fall back faster and you will need to ride to the count and warn him." Hob was so nervous that he did not speak his answer but just nodded nervously. I smiled, "All will be well Hob. Keep calm and use those wits of yours." He smiled back at me.

I was relatively new to such battles as the one I was about to fight but when the horsemen came racing down the road I realised that the foolish nobles who had fled had done one thing, they had encouraged the enemy horsemen. They did not expect us to be arrayed in battle order. Captain Berghof timed his command to perfection. As the wall of horsemen approached, he ordered Harry's men to fire and even as the smoke erupted from their muskets, he had shouted for Ralph's men to fire. And so the five companies all fired a rolling barrage which meant that, by the time Captain McKay's men had loosed their volley, Harry's men were reloaded.

The horsemen were disordered and fell back, leaving more than fifty men and horses blocking the passage of their army.

"Musketeers, fall back four hundred paces."

Shouldering their matchlocks and stands, the musketeers marched backwards. The pikemen filled the space they vacated. Captain Berghof, Hob and I were the only mounted men left and we had a good view of the Imperial Army as their general, we learned later that it was Count Tilly, organised his own pikes and muskets to drive us from the road. The result was that we had time to march the pikemen back to join the musketeers. Every matchlock was now reloaded but it would not be as easy as firing at horsemen whose only offensive weapon was a short-ranged pistol. This time we would be exchanging fire with a greater number of muskets. It would be a test of our muskets against Imperial ones.

Unlike the Spanish, Imperial troops did not use massive formations and in that they were similar to us. Blocks of musketeers were protected by large numbers of pikemen. Our one advantage was that while the enemy would have to set up their stands before firing, our men were ready to fire. As soon as the enemy halted, Captain Berghof gave the same order he had given before. This time the effect was greater for the musketeers wore no plate to protect them. By the time our volley had rippled down to Captain McKay, the Imperial musketeers had caught up and poor McKay's men took the same number of hits as the Imperial troops.

It was when Harry's men fired their second volley that we really hurt the enemy. His first volley had decimated the ranks of musketeers and his second effectively destroyed the enemy block. Their pikemen charged.

Both Harry and Captain Berghof were calm and the musketeers of Harry's company shouldered their muskets and moved back the half a mile ordered by the Dutchman. The pikes as well as the sword and buckler men were in position to spar with their opposite numbers. Captain Berghof and I were in a good position to use our pistols as the rest of our musketeers marched down the road. I aimed at a sergeant with a halberd who was rallying and encouraging his pikes. He was thirty paces from me and I aimed at his middle. The pistol bucked up and the sergeant's face disappeared. I heard a cheer from Harry's men. By the time the two of us had emptied our pistols and drawn our swords, we had taken out some of their officers and Captain Berghof gave the command to fall back. The men would have to march backwards, presenting their pikes until they reached the musketeers who would be in a position to blast the enemy once more. As we moved back I saw swordsmen and pikemen's bodies. They would remain in Germany. Like all mercenaries, they had gambled and, in their case, lost.

The last three to move were Hob, Captain Berghof and me. When the sword and buckler man ran at us I was the first to react and it was my Spanish horse that enabled me to do so. He sensed the man and flicked out a hind leg. It did not strike the man but made him step to the side and I was able to sweep my sword at his head. He wore a morion but I had a good blade and it rattled into his helmet, disorientating him. His comrades raced to his side and I decided that discretion was the better part of valour and I let my Spanish steed carry me to safety.

Ahead I saw the first of our pikemen form ranks between the musketeers. The smoking matches were ready to touch the powder. The attack from the sword and buckler man had encouraged others and thirty or so of them raced down the road towards me. Even as I took my horse between the pikes and muskets Harry had shouted, "Fire!"

I was enveloped in the smoke from the muskets and when it cleared and I turned I saw that twenty men lay dead. The enemy soldiers were forming up their pikes and muskets once more. It was then that Count Mansfield and the rest of our army arrived. It was not before time. I doubted that we could have endured another attack. Matchlocks needed to be regularly cleaned. The powder they used quickly fouled the barrels and slowed down the rate of fire. Count Tilly halted his men to form up their ranks. This time our detachment was in the centre of a huge line that spread on both sides of us. Cavalry at the flanks was there to counter the enemy horses who were on their flanks. They had more than we did but as we had more infantry it meant that they could only use their horses when the pikes and muskets had been thinned.

While we waited, I reloaded my pistols. Hob was staring, wide-eyed, at the bodies on the road. Our muskets had swept through the breastplates of the men who wore armour and the ones with buff coats. They had been shredded by the savage fire from matchlocks at close range.

Captain Berghof nudged his horse next to mine, "You brought good musketeers, James. They are steady men and that is what any commander wants."

The count joined us, "How many men do we face?"

Captain Berghof waved a hand ahead of us, "Your estimate is as good as ours, my lord. I would say more than fifteen thousand."

He nodded, "And the margrave is still to the south of us. We will try to join him when this is over."

I saw our artillery pieces being pulled into place. That was another advantage we held. The Imperial guns would be at the rear of their column. In the early exchanges, we would have superiority and that might make the difference. The Imperial line headed towards us. Tilly intended to sweep us from the field. His victory at White Mountain had given him a low opinion of Protestant armies. The Spanish had already defeated Count von Mansfield and this was his chance to drive us from the Palatinate.

The gunners opened fire and their balls swept through pikes and muskets alike. They were brave men and still they came on. It was when the muskets' rolling fire swept through their ranks that they retreated. It was not a rout. The horns from Count Tilly simply ordered a fall back. Our men cheered at the victory.

"We will camp here at this village and see what they plan in the morning." He smiled, "The rearguard did well, Captain Berghof." He seemed to recognise me, "You are the young Englishman who fought with Colonel Woodrow."

"Yes, my lord."

"You and your Englishmen did well today."

I smiled, "And Scots, my lord."

He laughed, "And Scots. Let us see what we can do tomorrow. Perhaps this is the moment when the war swings in our favour."

There was a feeling of victory in the camp. Some of the pikemen had ventured forth to rob the Imperial dead. The booty was shared with the musketeers for the captains had created companies that fought for each other. Hob was also in high spirits. He had been close to the action and whilst his life had not really been in danger, Caesar was too good a horse for that, he had felt as though he had been in his first battle… and survived.

In the camp that night Ralph and Harry ate with me and we spoke of the battle. Harry and I had something in common. We had studied the past and Harry voiced something that had been in my mind, "You know, a little more than a hundred years ago, before we had muskets, the English ruled the battlefield through the longbow. Had we had longbows today and men who could have used them, then the enemy would have been slaughtered when they were two hundred paces away."

I nodded, "I read that a bodkin arrow could pierce plate."

"Aye, I heard that too. Sometimes things that are new are not as good as what we already have." He shook his head, "Aye, well, the carrot is out of the ground and as we no longer train longbowmen we will have to hope that the muskets we have improve."

It was the next morning when the euphoria of victory disappeared like dawn's mist. Tilly had decamped and gone around our lines. He was now free to join up with the Spanish. He was heading to confront the Margrave and the men of Baden. The count refused all requests to follow the Imperial Army. I was privy to that conversation.

"No, gentlemen. Christian of Brunswick is on his way here with an army. When they arrive we shall combine and go to the aid of the margrave."

Instead of marching south, we raided the lands close by for food. As was usual in times of war, it was the ordinary people who suffered the most.

We were kept informed about our allies from horsemen who rode to give us their news. Christian of Brunswick had a long journey to reach us and we did not expect him for almost a month. The margrave was trying to reach us from the south and east but, now that the Imperial Army had joined with the Spanish one, he was having to spend more time evading the enemy patrols than anything. The enemy army outnumbered the margrave's. It was almost ten days after our victory that we were apprised of the latest Protestant disaster. The Margrave of Baden, Georg Friedrich, had been defeated by a numerically superior force at Wimpfen, just twenty-five miles to the east of us. There were just a few survivors who reached us for the margrave had lost three quarters of his army. It also put us in a parlous position as we were now within touching distance of a vastly superior army. There was but one solution. We broke camp and fled north to join up with Christian of Brunswick at Mannheim. Our only hope of survival was the youthful Duke of Brunswick.

It was hard for Hob to understand, we had won the battle and yet we were retreating. The truth was, as Harry and I discussed when we camped, that there was no overall leader of the Protestants. On the other hand, Count Tilly had sole command of the Imperial Army and he outwitted us.

"Von Mansfield is a competent commander but he does not command men like the margrave or this Christian of Brunswick."

Ralph leaned in, "I have heard that this Christian of Brunswick is but twenty-and-five years of age. He is a boy."

I felt honour bound to defend him. I had spoken with Captain Berghof who rated his ability, "He is said to be a brave soldier and his men are good fighters."

Harry sniffed, "Well, until we can join our armies we are mouthfuls to be gobbled up by the larger forces arrayed against us. They have joined up and become the lion while we are just terriers waiting to be devoured."

It was slow going although riders sent by the two commanders kept us well informed about events. The Brunswickers were heading for Höchst and we began to hope we might join up with them at Darmstadt. The marching men were exhausted when we reached Darmstadt but relieved that we had done our part. Von Mansfield was taking no chances and we prepared to defend Darmstadt. His encounters with Tilly had shown him the worth of our enemy. He would not take him for granted. We had an officers' call where the situation was explained.

It was at that meeting that I met Sir Horace Vere. He called me over. I knew that a senior English nobleman had joined the army with his own men but I had yet to meet him. "I have been meaning to find time to talk to you, Captain James. The king thinks highly of you and sent me with my men, at his expense, to help our Protestant brethren. It is sad that we meet under these circumstances."

"I am just flattered that King James remembered me."

"You made an impression and we are the result. It is a small army that I command but I am honoured that he chose me for the task. I dare say we shall meet again, Captain James." He hurried off to join the other senior commanders for a meeting with the count.

Captain Berghof gathered his captains together. We had lost just fifty men on the march and in battle. That was a tiny number and showed the spirit that we had.

"I do not want to lose more men. Have your men scour the countryside for food. When Christian of Brunswick and his men arrive then food will be more important than gold."

Captain de Vries, who as usual stood apart, sniffed, "And as we have had only one payment, it begs the question when will we be paid next?"

Captain Berghof did not need to answer as the rest of the captains found by Edgar disliked the noble intensely and Ralph snapped, "We have been paid enough for the little fighting we have done. We fight for a cause, Captain de Vries. The payment is not the reason we fight."

"It is my reason."

There was no arguing with the man. His company apart, the rest of us spent the next two days finding food. It was where Hob came into his own. Living on the streets and by his wits had given him skills that set him apart. He knew where to find food and how to sweet-talk farmers into sharing some with us. The result was that when the rider came in from the army of Brunswick, four of our companies and the Dutch had enough food for a week.

The bugle that sounded the officers' call was ominous and we all ran to the headquarters building in the town. There were forty of us in the town hall and von Mansfield's face was ashen. "Christian of Brunswick has lost the battle of Höchst. Colonel Dodo zu Innhausen und Knyphausen is holed up in the castle but the main army has had to cross the Main. The baggage is lost." We all took that in. Harry's fears had been realised. The combined Imperial-Spanish armies had destroyed the larger half of ours. "We have to get back to Mannheim and hold the bridge over the Rhine."

De Vries said, "That is a forced march of more than thirty miles!"

Count von Mansfield was surprisingly calm, "Then we had better start now, eh? Captain Berghof, if your command would take the rearguard. I have confidence that your stout men will do their duty as they did at Mingolsheim."

"An honour, my lord."

This time the baggage was sent ahead with the cavalry. Von Mansfield did not want our baggage to go the way of the Brunswickers.

We reached the bridge over the Main in the middle of the night and we were exhausted by the time we did so. A thirty-mile march by hungry men was a feat worthy of an epic poem. It was as Captain Berghof gave us our positions that we saw that men had deserted. It was a surprise for I had thought they were all of the same mind. It was when we saw that Captain de Vries was missing and most of the desertions were from his company that it made sense.

"If I see that arrogant bastard again, I will gut him like a fish."

Harry shook his head, "Peace, Ralph, men like de Vries will get their just desserts. For my part, I am glad that they have gone. It is better that that they go now than in the heat of battle."

He was right, however, I could not help but feel guilty. I had been so keen to have as many captains as I could that I had ignored the clear flaws in de Vries. Worse was that we had lost more than a fifth of the men I had brought.

Von Mansfield rode to us when we reached the bridge, "Captain Berghof, you and your men have done sterling work already. I have two thousand men who will face the enemy south of the river. I want your companies to hold the north side of the bridge."

"Of course, my lord, and the rest of the army?"

He waved a hand in the darkness, "We will make a line along the Rhine. When Christian of Brunswick arrives we will contest this crossing."

The implication of the order was clear and Captain Berghof recognised it, "We are giving up the Palatinate?"

Von Mansfield nodded, "We have lost one whole army, that of the margrave. Our army has haemorrhaged men and we have lost the guns and baggage train of Christian of Brunswick. We are outnumbered by our enemies and the best that we can hope is that they do not try to contest this crossing."

We had to reorganise our four companies. Not all of de Vries' men had left with him and the ones that remained were spread out in the remaining four companies. We were stronger despite our depleted numbers as the ones who remained were determined to make up for the deserters.

Hob said, as we made our hovel, "What will happen to them?"

"The deserters?" He nodded. "They will probably join the enemy. The Imperial Army uses mercenaries too."

"But they will be fighting for the Catholics."

"Some soldiers, I am coming to learn, are more pragmatic than others. They seek pay and, I suppose, one cannot blame them."

"But you would not do so would you, Captain?"

I shook my head, "No, my mother's family was persecuted by Catholics and all but she were killed. I did not know them but I am of their blood and I could not sleep at night if I fought for the Catholics."

I cleaned and loaded my three wheel locks while we waited. I had begun with one and now saw the benefit of three. With holsters on my saddles, I knew that one day I could have four. That done I sharpened my sword.

The Brunswick army began to arrive by dawn. Christian of Brunswick was with his cavalry and the rearguard. We stood to and watched the dispirited army as it crossed the bridge. It was late afternoon when we heard the pop of pistols and the men south of the river loaded their guns and muskets. There was a narrow passage for the last of the Brunswickers to use. I had counted eight thousand infantrymen and two and a half thousand cavalrymen cross when we saw the rearguard of horsemen as they fought a running fight with Spanish and Imperial cavalry.

Captain Berghof shouted, "Musketeers, load." It was a desperate command for if our men needed to fire then it meant the south side of the bridge had fallen.

When the first of the cavalry rearguard clattered over the bridge the men south of the river opened fire. The enemy disappeared from view as the air was filled with musket smoke. The last man across was Christian of Brunswick and he was indeed, young. He was a young man and yet he had commanded almost eighteen thousand men.

Count von Mansfield and Sir Horace greeted him and I was close enough to hear the exchange. "We were outnumbered,

Count, I had to leave fifteen hundred men in the castle and more than a thousand fell in crossing the river. This is a dark day for the forces of the Protestant Alliance."

"We can begin again, my lord. With our armies combined…"

The young Brunswicker waved a hand behind him, "There are twenty-six thousand men pursuing us. It will take courage to hold this bridge."

"Come, my lord, leave the men at the bridge to do their duty, for you have done yours." The count and the English knight led the despondent Duke of Brunswick away.

Harry said, "Now we shall earn the Bohemian pay."

It was hard to judge how the battle across the river was going because of the smoke. When the enemy brought up their artillery however, then the guns of our defenders fell silent as they were destroyed. The wounded began to drift across and then we heard the horns and bugles as the charge was sounded. The drifting men became a flood as all order was lost. Some men, seeing the bridge congested, threw themselves into the Rhine to try to swim. The bottleneck at the bridge became a bloodbath. Men whose backs were to the enemy were slaughtered without being able to fight back.

"Musketeers, ready muskets."

Hob had taken our horses to the rear and I had my three pistols with me. Already loaded, I took two for I knew that when the last of our rearguard fell then the enemy would flood across the bridge. The first we knew was when a wall of horsemen slashed and stabbed the last survivors of the rearguard.

"Fire!" This time there was no ripple of muskets. Every musket fired at once and the wall of horsemen was shredded. Horses and men fell. It was a horrible sight. Men and horses had been struck by multiple lead balls and there were no survivors. Count Tilly and the Spanish commander Tommaso Caracciolo, Count of Roccarainola, halted. They had done all that was necessary. The Protestant Palatinate, the land east of the Rhine, was now theirs. We reloaded and waited but, by dawn, it was clear the attack was over.

A week later we received the news that King Frederick had surrendered and we would not be paid by him. We were a mercenary army without a paymaster. Sir Horace and the English troops would hold Mannheim. Captain Berghof was at a loss as to what would be our future. At the start of July, however, we were informed by a rider from the north that we were again employed by Prince Maurice. We had been ordered to march north and relieve the siege of Bergen-op-Zoom. We had a two-hundred-and-fifty-mile march back to the Netherlands. We were a despondent and dispirited army as we trekked north, knowing that we had failed.

Chapter 12

What kept us all going was the camaraderie of the men I had hired. We marched together and shared everything. In that long march back to the Netherlands we became closer. Even Captain Berghof and his men were not as close as the four companies. The loss of de Vries and the deserters had actually helped us. Having said that, the journey back was fraught with problems. We would have to pass through the Spanish Netherlands and knew not what forces awaited us. We rode and marched hard. Sometimes Hob and I would march with the men and lead our horses. It helped the horses and made us closer to the men. When we did ride it was often to scout out the roads to the sides of our main route. We did not want to be ambushed. Hob had quickly taken to riding. I think he was helped by Caesar's nature. Whatever the reason, I no longer had to keep an eye on him in case he fell. He rode with all the aplomb of a seasoned rider. He had also grown and filled out. We had taken a better and bigger jerkin from one of the dead at the bridge over the Rhine. We had also found a pair of wheel locks in the saddle of a dead Spaniard. Hob was keen to learn to use them but a march across enemy land was not the place for such lessons. He had also improved his sword skills. That was not just my doing but the other men who gave him skills and tricks learned on the field of battle. He was not yet a finished warrior but the start had been made and I was pleased. His Dutch had also improved to the point that he could converse easily with the Dutchmen alongside whom we marched.

The worst part of the march was the mood of the men. We had failed to save the Palatinate. We had been released from a contract and we had lost all the battles bar one. The fact that we had extricated ourselves well was of no matter, we were hurrying north with our tails between our legs and that did not sit well with us. There was camaraderie but we had lost and the men felt it was not their fault. What made life harder for us all was the behaviour of the other seven battalions. Regiments had been decimated and the count had reorganised us into battalions. In our case, it suited us as we were brigaded with Captain Berghof and his men. The other seven were little more than bandits and as we travelled through the Walloon country they raided and ravaged the land for food and treasure. The Walloons did not take kindly to it and many men, whom we would need in battle, were killed. We were lucky to have the Duke of Brunswick with us. The men of Brunswick were largely horsemen and they were well led. We had sixty companies of horsemen and they numbered six thousand. Along with the eleven guns we had salvaged they were our best bet to raise the siege. We hoped that the relief of the siege would take away the taste of defeat that still lingered.

The Spanish were waiting for us. As we neared the town of Fleurus the Brunswick scouts reported the presence of a large Spanish army. Although they only reported four artillery pieces and a few cavalry, our already weakened infantry would be well outnumbered. This time it was the Duke of Brunswick who took command. I think that von Mansfield had been shaken by his defeats.

I saw that they had one end of their line secured by troops in the woods. They included horsemen which meant that it would be hard to outflank that side. Captain Berghof recognised an elite Spanish regiment, the Tercio of Naples. They had been instrumental in destroying the army of the Margrave of Baden and their position in the centre of the Spanish line was one of honour. What I noticed, for the first time, was a regiment of cavalry harquebusiers. These fired a weapon longer than a pistol from horseback. The Spanish dragoons tended to dismount to fire their weapons. The harquebusiers could fire their weapons and then charge with swords. I wondered how they would be used.

As we were formed into lines I had to put those thoughts from my mind. This time I would be on foot and I sent Hob and the horses to the rear. It was clear how the battle would be fought. We would attack. We had to for Bergen-op-Zoom lay to the north of us, and if we were to relieve the siege, we had to shift the Spanish from the road. Our two wings of cavalry waited and our eleven guns opened fire. Cannons sound terrifying and make horses fearful. When we had been aboard the ship, I had seen the devastation that the cannons caused at close quarters. However, here they were fired from a distance. The balls could be seen and men could move away from the ball. If they struck, then they were devastating but the effect of eleven guns was not particularly effective. After a short barrage which caused some casualties, we were ordered forward. I marched with Harry's musketeers. We were heading for the Tercio of Naples. Von Mansfield and the Duke of Brunswick were relying on us as his best infantry to counter the best that the Spanish had to offer. The difference was that they had many more men than us and we had to rely on weaker battalions on our flanks.

This was the first time I had taken part in an attack. We moved to within musket range and then the muskets opened fire. The three enemy tercios fired first. They were mainly Spanish and Walloons and the best that the enemy had to offer. We came off worst in the initial duel. As soon as the muskets had fired and while they were reloading, the pikes marched forward to engage the enemy pikes. I went with Harry. He had a halberd, and I had my sword and pistols. I heard the Spanish and Walloon pikemen invoking the aid of God. Our men cursed them as Papists. Their aim was to steel themselves for the fight. As the wooden pikes clashed, the noise was almost as deafening as the muskets had been. The sword and buckler men clashed. The Spanish were better than the Walloons and I saw men on both sides fall. As they died I neared the front of the line. I saw a huge Spaniard take the head of one of Harry's men and, as the Englishman fell, I raised a pistol and fired. The range was less than ten paces and my ball hit his face. It destroyed it. He must have been popular for those around him sought the cause of his death and surged at me. I dropped one pistol to hang from its lanyard and raised another. It was a hurried shot but it still struck a Spaniard. This time the ball struck his shoulder, taking the man out of the battle.

It was at that moment when the Spanish cavalry charged a battalion on our flank. It was a weak one and fled. Suddenly we were all in danger of having our flanks turned. Luckily Brunswick cavalry, led by Captain Strieff, drove the Spanish from the field. Our muskets fired again as did the Spanish. Men fell but as the Spanish muskets outnumbered ours, we came off worst and when the horn sounded for us to fall back we were relieved. I was shocked at the number of bodies we had left there. I also saw that brave Captain McKay had finally fallen. He lay surrounded by a wall of dead, and one of our captains was lost.

The enemy cheered and that hurt. We had failed to break their line. As we reached our starting point I saw the cavalry preparing to charge. Captain Berghof was being tended to by a surgeon. He had a pike thrust to his knee. "Captain James, take command until I return. You can speak to both the English and the Dutch." He waved a hand at the Spanish. "We need the men ready in case the enemy tries to attack."

"I will, Captain."

I would be little more than a conduit for the captain's orders but I felt the weight of authority upon my shoulders. I had less than six hundred men to command but it was more than I had ever commanded before.

"Musketeers reload. Captain McKay's men join Captain Wilson. The order is still to hold."

I reloaded my pistols and walked over to Harry and Ralph. They had both suffered wounds. Harry's was a cut to his cheekbone. An inch higher and he would have lost an eye. Ralph had a nasty cut along his neck. He had bound it, but his collar and tunic were besmeared with blood.

"Those tercios are good. How did they get ahead of us?"

Harry answered Ralph, "They have more discipline. Our men apart, we moved more slowly than we should for men were too busy robbing and ravaging the land of the Walloons. Had they not done so then we would have had more men and reached here before the Spanish. Then we might have occupied the wood and been waiting for them."

Such were the margins between victory and defeat.

I watched as the cavalry formed up. Christian, Duke of Brunswick, had six thousand cavalry and he intended to charge them at the enemy horsemen. I had never witnessed such a charge before and it both terrified and inspired me in equal measure. The heavy horses' hooves pounded on the ground as they hurtled towards the Spanish line. The pops of the harquebuses were followed by the clash of swords on metal. The Spanish held and I saw the Duke of Brunswick lead his men back to reform. For a young man, he had great charisma. When he ordered his second charge, his men eagerly followed him and this time the Spanish horsemen were driven from the field. Our infantry and our gunners cheered as the Duke of Brunswick led his victorious men back. I saw him ride over to Count von Mansfield and they conferred.

Captain Berghof hobbled over. He had been bandaged but, clearly, he was far from mobile.

"Now that our cavalrymen have done their work perhaps we will be ordered into the attack once more."

Harry shook his head. The wound must have loosened a tooth for he spat one out, "Look at the men, Captain Berghof. They do not have an attack left in them." We looked down the line and I could see that, our battalion apart, the rest had edged a few feet further away from the Spanish. "They might stand and fight but they will not charge."

I had been watching the duke and the count speaking and saw, from the wave of the count's arm, that they were having the same conversation. "I think the count agrees."

A few moments later all was confirmed as the duke organised his men into two lines. He was going to break the enemy infantry with cavalry. The horses had charged twice already and I knew from my own horses that a third would be much slower. A slower charge would allow the enemy muskets to reap a savage harvest.

The count came over, "The Duke of Brunswick will attack the enemy and we will support him. I will march with you."

The looks exchanged between Harry and Ralph told me what they thought of the order but they were good soldiers and they marshalled their men. It was clear that Captain Berghof would not be able to advance and so he delegated, once more, the command of our battalion to me. It meant that this time I would be at the fore with the handful of sword and buckler men who had survived.

"Forward!" We followed the horses as they charged. It was the fire from the muskets in the woods that hurt us the most. As I looked down the line I saw that our battalion was now the arrowhead of our infantry attack. Instead of being a long and solid line, we were an arrow as the men on the flanks moved more slowly. The battalion that should have supported the horsemen being attacked from the woods failed to engage the enemy, and our cavalry fell back in disorder.

Christian of Brunswick was the bravest man I ever knew. He ordered another charge. I tried to follow him but there was just my battalion in support of him. The rest had hung back. We were close enough to see the savage fight that ensued. Christian of Brunswick was in the fore of the fighting. I saw the pike that struck him and knew that he was out of the battle. The arm, which he would lose once the surgeons tended to him, hung down at his side and his aides pulled him from the battle line. His cavalry followed and, suddenly, we were exposed to the firepower of three enemy tercios. The rest of our infantry was falling back, along with the cavalry. I saw disaster looming. This was like Záblatí all over again but this time I would not let that happen.

"Musketeers, on my command open fire."

The tercios were ready to advance for they saw the retreat as a sign that they had won. They began to lumber forward and that gave me hope. Their muskets had been fired already and a musketeer cannot load and move at the same time. I waited until the enemy line was just fifty paces from us before I gave the order. I saw that their rapid approach had made their lines less straight than they should have been and when I shouted, "Fire!" the volley scythed through their ranks. A few men managed to keep coming. They were the lucky ones. I held two wheel locks and when the twenty or so men ran at us with pikes, I fired. I could not miss and two men fell. I drew my sword and a dagger. The enemy attack had halted and I knew that the musketeers would need no order from me to reload. I stood with the sword and buckler men to fend off the last hurrah from the Spanish. The bucklers blocked the pikes and then swords hacked through the shafts. I had no buckler but I used my dagger, held in a hand protected by a gauntlet, to deflect the pike to the side. The momentum of the man who came at me carried him forward and I used my lunge to drive the tip of my sword into his screaming mouth.

When my captains ordered another volley, I saw that the Spanish were broken. They began to march back, pikes trailing over their shoulders to their start position.

Our men cheered and the sergeant of the sword and buckler men shouted, "Three cheers for Captain James. He is a gamecock and no mistake."

It was then that I saw the body of Ralph Carter. I had lost another captain. I had no time to mourn as the horn sounded the retreat. Count von Mansfield had taken charge. Ralph's men picked up his body and we moved back to our own lines.

The battle had raged for five hours and darkness would soon be upon us. The drum that sounded officer's call meant I had to leave the battalion and go with my two remaining captains and a limping Captain Berghof to meet with Count von Mansfield. I saw how depleted our numbers were. Other captains had fallen.

The count looked old, "We have held the field but it has cost us dear. The duke is about to lose his arm. I wish us, under cover of dark, to quit this field and march to the fortress of Breda. We will then complete the task assigned to us by Prince Maurice; we will relieve the siege at Bergen-op-Zoom."

I had never endured a night march before and I did not enjoy it. I had the advantage of a horse and I was exhausted. How the musketeers and pikemen managed to drag their heavy weapons I shall never know. It was not a march without incident. The Spanish garrison at Tongeren tried to bar our path but the Brunswicker horsemen, with a wounded leader, were in no mood for mercy and the men were swept from our path. By the time we reached Breda, we could go no further. The road from Fleurus must have been littered with discarded weapons for, our battalion apart, many men had simply discarded their weapons on the night march.

Wounds were tended but we did not linger long. Von Mansfield, now in sole charge, insisted that the army, which had shrunk to less than ten thousand, obey the command and the commission given by the prince and relieve the siege of Bergen-op-Zoom. Captain Berghof was adamant that he would obey his orders and he rode with us, although he was clearly in pain.

Spinola and his Spanish army lifted the siege at our approach. We might have been a depleted army but ten thousand men were enough to swing the balance in favour of the defenders.

It was a week later that we entered Utrecht. The Duke of Brunswick had accompanied us, his wound clearly on display and he and the count were summoned to the prince. Both were thanked for their service but dismissed. They had served Prince Maurice for just three months but the prince blamed them for the loss of the Palatinate.

The prince took it well and boldly took his depleted army into the Spanish Netherlands. He was not finished fighting the Spanish and he would spend the winter rearming his men and building up his army again. Count von Mansfield left us. He bade farewell to Captain Berghof and to me. He was a gentleman but I thought he was also unlucky. A soldier needed luck.

I was unsure of our position. We had been hired by the prince and so we stayed in the fortress. A month after the relief of the siege the four of us were summoned to meet with the prince. I was not sure that Captain Berghof would go to war again. He limped badly. Harry and Richard Wilson had recovered from their wounds but I knew the loss of the other two captains had shaken them.

This time it was the prince alone who spoke to us. He looked sad, "When I sent you with Count Mansfield, I hoped for great things. I believed that we could hold the Palatinate and then I would be able to use the count and the army of Brunswick to retake the Spanish Netherlands." He sighed, "We failed." We all waited expectantly for the sword to fall. "I will retain your companies, Captain Lawrence and Captain Wilson. You will be based here in Utrecht. You have shown great skill and I shall need those skills in the future. Captain Berghof, I would have you take your men and reinforce the garrison at Breda. We need the fortress there to be a bastion against the Spanish." He patted the chest which lay on the table. "I have here the gold that was owed you. I will pay the amount we agreed."

I saw Harry and Richard's faces light up. The gold had been promised for five companies. With deaths and desertions there were now just two and that meant more gold for everyone.

"I would speak with Captain James alone. Take your payment, gentlemen. It is richly deserved." When the door closed he smiled, "And you are wondering what is to be your future, eh?" I nodded. "You are a good soldier and I have heard nothing but glowing reports of your courage under fire. However, you have other skills that I would use. I spoke with Sir

Horace and know that King James thinks well of you and I am sending you back to England as my ambassador. The Dutch Republic needs allies. England is one. Denmark might be another. Win over King James. You will serve me well if you do so." He took out a purse and slid it over to me. "The others have been paid and so shall you. Return in six months and we will review your terms of service. Who knows, there may well be a commission for you here in the Netherlands."

I took the heavy purse and bowed my way out. Harry and Richard awaited me, "Well?"

I shook my head, "I fear I will not be serving with you. I return to England as ambassador. I shall miss your company."

Harry grasped my arm in a soldier's grip, "I would happily fight alongside you any time, James. Be careful in England. The snakes there do not wriggle but dress in courtier's clothes."

I nodded, "I have learned my lesson. Farewell."

Chapter 13

The presence of Sir Horace Vere in Mannheim showed that King James was not averse to supporting the Protestant cause, so why did Prince Maurice need me to plead his case? I could not divine the answer but I knew I had six months of employment. I had gold and I knew that I had enough coins to buy a modest home. It would not, of course, be in London for I could not afford that, but I knew that in the North Country I would be able to live with the funds I had. I looked on the positive side. This might even suit Hob. He had become a different man serving in the Palatinate. If he and Alice were meant to be together, his return meant he was able to do that.

I had paid Hob and when we reached Rotterdam, he took the opportunity of using the market there to buy presents for Mags and Alice. I went to the port. I discovered that Captain van Hooft was due in port in the next few days. He spent his time plying the seas between England and the Netherlands. I would prefer to travel with a captain I knew than risk one who might turn out to be an enemy. Don Miguel Alvarado's tentacles reached far and returning to England I knew that I was risking assassination. I was the enemy of Spain and my time in the Palatinate would only have increased their enmity.

We stayed in an inn with a stable. It lay close to the quay. Once Hob had made his purchases we spent each day looking out to sea for a sight of the ship. It was a place that smelled of the sea and that was not always a pleasant smell, for it was a changing picture as the tide rose and fell exposing weed-covered rocks. Flotsam and jetsam drifted in. Others came to view the sea; some were women looking for husbands, sweethearts and fathers, while others were sailors seeking employment. A port was a living thing. It never stayed the same. The flitting clouds changed the light and the wind brought smells and sounds from the sea. It was a place in which a man could think.

As we watched, I asked Hob about his future. "What do you mean, Captain? My future is with you unless you are dissatisfied with my work."

I shook my head, "Quite the contrary, but I could not help but notice that you and Alice were close. I thought that once my six months was up you might wish to stay in England."

"I am still young, Captain. What you say is true. Alice and I are close and I suppose she might become my wife, but I have little enough to show at the moment. Would I go back to holding horses outside the inn? Would Alice toil like a drudge serving in the inn? I do not think so. I sought to make my fortune and when I have then I might consider leaving your service. Alice is a practical young woman and she understands such things. She is saving, as am I, but we shall need many more coins if we are to attain our dreams."

As we watched in silence, I thought of my father's dream. He had dreamed of making a fortune but he had lost a fortune in gambling the way he did. Hob had begun with less but knew how to husband what little he had. Alice would be luckier than my mother. The French had taken her family and my father had lost her fortune.

We both recognised the lines of the ship as she tacked into the harbour. I now knew when a ship was laden and she was. I realised that Captain van Hooft would be busy beyond words until the cargo was landed so we waited patiently at the quay. The First Mate recognised us as he passed on his way to the Harbour Master. "I will tell the captain that you await his pleasure. He will be pleased to see you. He was worried that you might have fallen in one of the battles."

Bad news travelled fast and like all bad news was expanded beyond reality. Since being in the port we had heard that every one of the count's men had fallen at Mannheim and Darmstadt. Hob and I knew the truth but men still doubted us as we tried to correct them. It took some hours but eventually, the rotund sea captain waddled down the gangplank to greet us.

"What can I do for you, Captain James?"

"We seek passage to England."

He nodded, "Come, we will dine together. As you know I have a good cook on my ship but the food served in an inn has more variety. We can talk and decide on a price as I eat."

"The ship was laden."

"The recent battles mean that there is a good trade in arms. We carried pikes, muskets and artillery pieces."

"For the prince?"

"Not all of them. Some are for Duke Christian who is rearming his men. He is rich and he hates the Imperialists."

"And what do you carry back to England?" Hob's Dutch had improved dramatically and I saw the look of surprise on the Dutchman's face.

"Dull in comparison. Vegetables, for my little country produce more than we need…despite the war which, thankfully, is beyond our border. We also carry lace. In England, there is no war and lords and their ladies like to wear fine things."

We reached the inn of choice and as soon as we walked in the captain was welcomed. He said, "They know me here and keep a table. As soon as my ship was sighted it was reserved." He tapped his nose, "The innkeeper and I have an arrangement."

I guessed what that would be. Sea captains could smuggle things in and innkeepers, as I had learned from Edgar and Mags, were always looking for ways to keep their costs down as much as they could. I knew that the captains of the fishing boats would have a similar arrangement.

We sat at the table and a jug of ale appeared with three beakers. "As I intend to pay, Captain James, I hope that you will let me order."

"Of course."

When the waiter appeared the captain rattled off his commands so quickly that I knew he had been planning his repast for the last day. The order given and the first half of the beaker consumed, he leaned back, "So, a passage for two and horses?" I nodded, "My master said that if you sought passage then it was to be free, but horses…let us say a gilder for the horses. We sail in two days. Does that suit you?"

Time was not important. I had six months to try to persuade the king to support the Protestant cause and two more days would not hurt. I raised my beaker, "Perfect, Captain."

We had two days to fill and I used the days to explore the town. We discovered some beautiful parts of the port and some that were less so. We found the latter when we wandered too far from the beaten track. It was on the night before we were due to leave that we found ourselves in trouble. We had taken a wrong turn and the light was fading. We stopped so that I could orientate myself. It was as I did so that I heard the sound of angry voices raised. I was wise enough to know that a man did not embroil himself in the troubles of others and I was already pointing a way out when six men burst from a side alley. Two were being attacked by four. I did not want to get involved and I was about to run when I recognised one of the men. It was the Swede, Erik Hand, and, recognising him, I also saw Lars the Swede. That changed everything.

"Hob, draw your sword and watch my back." Drawing my sword and dagger I ran down the narrow street. Erik and Lars were back-to-back but they were about to be overwhelmed. I shouted, in Dutch, "Hold there."

One of the men turned but they all halted. I had bought my Swedish friends some time. "This is none of your business, dandy. Leave us lest we turn our attention to you."

I detected a Spanish accent and caught the smell of perfume. I did not slow but approached closer, "And why should I worry if a perfumed popinjay from Spain threatens me?"

Insulted, he threw himself at me. He had not seen Hob who had used my body and the shadows to remain hidden. I easily blocked the wild blow from the Spaniard with my dagger. I thrust with my sword and his reactions were slower than mine. The edge of my sword scored a hit on his leg. It was then that he spied Hob who was approaching purposefully towards him. It was now four on four and men such as the ones who had attacked Erik were not the kind to take even odds as acceptable.

He slashed his sword at me and shouted, "This is not over. Let us retire."

I wanted him to fear me the next time we met, and I knew that we would meet, so I stabbed at his thigh as he tried to disengage. My sword grated off a bone and I knew that he had a wound that would make him remember me. Erik and Lars also took advantage of the disengagement and both drew blood from the men they were fighting.

Left alone I said, "Are you hurt, Erik? Lars?" I saw that Erik now had a patch over one eye.

Erik shook his head, "We were surprised by them that is all but this was well met."

"And this is not the place to linger. Come, let us head to the quay. Hob and I are known there and we will, I hope, be safer."

Hob showed his increased skill as he took his place at the rear while I led. He kept his sword drawn and I knew we would not be surprised. It did not take us long to find our way to safer surroundings and we were able to sheathe our swords.

Erik nodded to Hob as we entered the better-lit parts of the port, "He is new."

"This is Hob, a sometimes servant but increasingly a warrior who watches my back."

Erik gave an elaborate bow, "I thank you, Master Hob."

"And I thought you were dead, killed at Záblatí."

He shook his head, "It was there I lost this eye and Galmr and Drogo fell but Lars and I survived and made our way north. We reached the Baltic and we were safe there." We had reached the quay. "I thank you for your help but I would not put your lives at risk too."

I sighed, "Erik, we are shield brothers. We fought together and Fate threw us down that street this night. You of all people know that we cannot avoid the hand of fate."

He looked around nervously, "Which inn is the safest?"

I pointed to the one where our horses were stabled, "We have rooms there."

"Then if we can find a quiet corner, I will tell you all."

The inn was relatively quiet and our coins ensured that we were accorded a quiet table away from prying ears and eyes. After downing half of his ale Erik said, "We serve the King of Denmark. He plans to come to the aid of the Protestants." He shrugged, "I would prefer a Swedish leader but the Danes are like blood, and so long as we can avenge our dead I will serve them. We were sent as spies to scout out the land of the Spanish Netherlands."

Lars nodded, "There are others, like us, scouting out the lands closer to Imperial ones. We were given this task because we speak Dutch. King Christian is the brother-in-law of your king, although since the Queen died he has not visited your land yet the two are close."

It all made sense now.

"So what will you do now?"

"The Spanish know us. Lars and I will make our way north and report to the king. Who knows, James, one day we may fight alongside each other once more."

"I hope so. If you ever get to London, seek out Edgar. He runs an inn close to the Globe Theatre in London, it is called *'The Saddle'*. He will know where and how to contact me."

"I will, for you are right and our fates are intertwined."

They did not stay long for they wished to retrieve their horses and leave Rotterdam in the night. Their plan had been to take a ship, but as no Danish ship was in port they would have to risk the roads. I felt both sad and elated when they left. Sad because they had left my life but elated because I had thought them dead already and yet they lived.

The voyage to Tilbury was peaceful and, for the Channel, remarkably benign. Hob and I were able to enjoy the deck although I do not think Caesar and Henry enjoyed the voyage. The crew learned to give the Spanish horse a wide berth. Hob's skills with horses had improved dramatically and he and my Spanish warhorse seemed to get on. He managed to calm the horse when the animal became agitated.

I felt more confident when we landed. I knew the road to Pietr's. I had decided not to impose upon him but I felt honour bound to visit with him. I decided to give my trade to Mags. For one thing, we would both be safer and, for another, my movements would be better hidden. Pietr was a known Protestant sympathiser and agent of Prince Maurice.

The streets of London were as crowded as ever but our weapons and horses helped us to make our way through the streets to Pietr's. We were, of course, known and made welcome. I left Hob to see to the horses and went to speak to the Dutchman.

"It is good to see you. When news came of the defeat, Elizabeth and I feared for you. Until you walked through my door we did not know if you were dead or alive."

I felt guilty although I am not sure that a letter would have arrived any more quickly than we had. "I am sorry that you were worried. Hob and I are well but many of those men that we hired are dead." He waved me to a seat and I took him through the highs and lows of the campaign. That there were more lows depressed me.

At the end, he nodded, "The Catholics are on top once more but we must trust in the righteousness of our cause. I will have your rooms readied."

I shook my head and told him of the attack at sea. "The Spanish know me and they will seek to hurt me. I cannot endanger you and your family."

"I have men to guard me and my home. You will be safe."

"I fear not. These men are killers and also the kind who care not about innocent bystanders. This will be better. I will see you to keep you informed of my actions but other than that I will stay away to keep you safe."

"And yet you are employed by my head of state. It does not seem right."

I decided to change the subject, "I have been away from England for some time and you have your ear to the ground. What is new?"

He brightened at that, "Buckingham and Prince Charles went to Spain to woo the Infanta but she detested Charles and the arranged marriage ended. The Duke of Buckingham and the prince are now in France speaking with Cardinal Richelieu and the French king to arrange a marriage with Henrietta Maria of France."

I could not understand Pietr's attitude, "She is Catholic and Richelieu and her father persecute the Huguenots in the Vendee." I confess that I was biased against the French. I had inherited my mother's hatred of them.

Pietr smiled, "Politics and economics, James. The King of France does not like the fact that the Spanish now seek to enlarge their Empire. They have half of Italy and half of the Netherlands. Their king has a hold over the Emperor and the King of France seeks an alliance with a strong Protestant. Richelieu and the French King are merely being pragmatic. This is good for our cause. It means that the Spanish Netherlands could be threatened from the south as well as the north."

I was not convinced but it made a sort of sense.

"Parliament is also happy that an alliance with Spain is now forgotten. Parliament is strongly Protestant. It is certain nobles that still harbour Catholic sympathies."

I did not tell him about the possible Danish involvement. I would wait until I had spoken to King James and, with Buckingham absent, this seemed like a perfect opportunity to do so.

We rode across the bridge to Southwark. In the time we had been in the Palatinate new buildings had been thrown up. There was no wall around this part of London and new building was unrestricted. We could see, as we approached, that Edgar and Mags had spent money on the inn. It stood out from the other drinking establishments. There were two boys outside and when we dismounted one said, "Shall we stable the animals for you, my lord?"

I could not help but smile. The '*my lord*' had been spoken to gain a tip. Hob said, "Who asked you to be here? These horses are valuable." He was aggressive in his tone.

The boy was not in the least put out by the words and smiled, "Master Edgar employs us but a tip is always welcome."

Edgar must have heard the voices for he emerged and grinned. It was clear that he had heard the interchange, "Hob, these are your replacements. Do not be so ungracious. Will and Hal, take the horses to the stables." He spied the bags, "You are staying here?"

"If you have rooms."

He beamed, "We will make room. Come. Alice and Mags will be filled with joy at your return."

I saw, once we were inside, that the improvements were not restricted to the exterior. The tables and chairs had been renewed and there were more sconces and lights. I spied more than just Alice and Mary as serving wenches. There were four others.

As soon as Alice saw Hob she squealed and, depositing her tray on a table, she rushed over to embrace him. There were some men drinking at a table, obviously regulars and they gave a cheer which Alice assiduously ignored.

Edgar said, "They are here for a while Alice, be more seemly." He turned to me as Alice took Hob's hand and led him towards the rooms. "How long do you stay?"

I shrugged, "I am here to visit with the king. If I get the answer my prince wishes then it will be a week or two, if not..."

He nodded, "Alice, they can use room number two." As she led Hob away, he said, "I have organised Mags's mad ways. The rooms have numbers."

"And you have spent money."

He laughed, "And now we make more. If only I had done this years ago. Why, James, it is simplicity itself to become rich."

"Do you miss soldiering?"

We had reached the stairs and began to climb, "I miss the camaraderie and the friendship but not the food, nor the hard ground as a bed. If I ride now, it is because I choose to and I do not have to endure a saddle."

We heard giggling from the room and when we opened the door, Hob lay on the bed and Alice looked like a spider about to devour her prey. "Alice, behave with propriety. You are not a doxy and you, Hob..."

Hob pushed Alice from him, "I had little say in the matter, Edgar."

"A man always has a say in the matter. Alice, they are here for a while. You need not rush at him. Tell your mother and put a sign on the best table. We shall dine with them this night." He patted my back, "It is good to have you both home, James."

As we unpacked Hob said, "Edgar is right, Alice needs to behave in a more appropriate way."

"Hob, Alice is the same girl we left, it is you who has changed. Alice is not Elizabeth. She may never be but she is still Alice."

He nodded thoughtfully. He had come home and what had greeted him was not what he had expected. Time does that to a man. It distorts his memory of what is. It gives him a picture that lives just in his mind. He had some adjustments to make.

When we descended to the dining room Mags was also delighted to see us, and I knew that she must have hired a cook for she joined us. Edgar explained, "The actors from the Globe are not here. They were hired to put on a play for some rich noble with delusions of grandeur and they are performing in the country somewhere. We still have more than enough trade but not the actors."

Mags sniffed, "They spend more on their drink than food."

"And we profit from both. All is good. Now tell us all, James. As you know, the reports we have here in England of events far away are twisted through the glass of distance."

Edgar was an old friend and I told him the tale. I spared the two ladies the gorier elements. When I mentioned Erik and Lars it delighted Edgar. He beamed, "That is the best news I have heard in a long time. I had thought them dead. It is like the story from the Bible, of the man raised from the dead. It is good that you were able to help them."

"Old friends are the most valuable, Edgar, for they have stood the test of time."

Mags put her hand on mine, "A gentleman and wise too. You will make a fine catch for a lady and do not tarry too long for you are getting no younger."

I chose to change the subject, "And speaking of marriage, I hear that Prince Charles' bride-to-be is now a French princess."

"That is true. He and the Duke of Buckingham are now in France making the arrangements." Edgar shook his head, "I do not trust that duplicitous duke. The king is now frail and, they say, ill. The duke and the king no longer share a bed."

"Edgar!"

Edgar shrugged, "That was the rumour. The fact of the matter is that Buckingham has now decided to mould the malleable Prince Charles. I fear it will not end well."

I was curious. Edgar was not an educated man but he was clever and I respected his views, "Why not?"

"Buckingham has Catholic sympathies. He failed to win a Spanish bride for Charles but a French one is still a Catholic and, despite the protestations that her religion will not change Charles, I fear it will." I waited, knowing that Edgar would elaborate. "When Captain Woodrow and I lived in London, before we came north to find men, we came across the prince. He is a shy and impressionable young man. He was never meant to be the king until his elder brother died. He has a stammer and the captain said he thought the young man sought a mentor. He could not pick a worse one than that oily dandy, Buckingham. The country is Protestant and a few nobles who wish to turn back the hands of time should not be allowed to do so."

Mags shook her head, "Come down from your pulpit, let us talk of simpler things. Hob, Alice has waited patiently for you. Her welcome showed her feelings for you. When will you do the decent thing and marry her?"

I saw that her words took Hob completely by surprise. He stared from Mags to Edgar and then to me. As much as my heart went out to the young man, I could not answer for him. This was a test of his manhood and he had to pass or fail it all by himself. He took a drink of ale and took Alice's hand, "Alice is and always has been the love of my life." Mags and Alice looked joyful. "However, Captain James and I have six months to serve Prince Maurice as his emissary in England. At the end of that time, when I am discharged by the prince, we may well be free to return to England and then I can begin my life. I shall be the caterpillar that emerges a butterfly."

No matter how poetically he phrased the words, it did not please either woman. Alice spoke, for the first time, "Hob, I am happy to marry now. Even if you leave for the Netherlands in a fortnight and are away for many months, I will wait, but I will wait as a married woman. If you do not wish to marry me then put me out of my misery. I am not without charms and there are other suitors. Thus far I have rejected them but I will not wait six more months for a decision. I am a woman now. I beg you to answer."

He looked at Edgar who nodded and then to me. I sighed and smiled. How could I, who had yet to kiss a maid, offer my advice? Hob knew more of women than did I. I saw him steel himself, "Then if you are willing to marry me knowing that I may leave again for months on end then I will marry you, for you are the love of my life and I would be wed."

His answer pleased Alice and her mother. For my part, I knew the doubts in Hob's mind and I hoped that the decision would not come back to haunt him. It meant that arrangements would have to be made quickly although I knew we had some time before we had to return to Prince Maurice. It would be a distraction from our mission but, perhaps, it would be a welcome one. The lofty lair of princes and politics did not really suit me.

Pietr would not come with me when I visited King James. It was unnecessary but I had decided to be more unpredictable. I

163

did not want my enemies to know our routine. The day after the marriage was arranged we rode to speak to Pietr. It was ostensibly to tell him of the marriage but I also wanted him to know my plans. "We will visit King James and his court, alone. I do not wish our enemies to be able to predict our movements. I did not spy any watchers, but once Alvarado knows that I am back in England there will be men. I hope to put them off the scent. I say this so that you will not be offended if I do not return regularly. When I can then I will."

"I am not offended and I admire your caution. Elizabeth and I have grown fond of you and Hob. The news of his impending marriage will delight my wife." He smiled, "She searches for a suitable bride for you whenever we entertain."

"When I am ready…"

He nodded, "You should know that the king is not a well man. Sometimes he holds court at Eltham but at others, it is Greenwich Palace."

"Where is he holding court now?"

"I believe it is Greenwich."

"And as that is south of the river we may well throw off any watchers. I will return when I may."

We left the next morning for Greenwich. It was not far along the river from Southwark. King Henry and his daughter, Queen Elizabeth, had often used the palace, travelling by river barge to do so. It was a fine palace. What I noticed immediately was that there were fewer courtiers present. The guard was changing. Nobles who wished to become richer would now seek the company of Prince Charles and most nobles knew that the real power lay with the Duke of Buckingham. The result was that when we arrived we had only a short time to wait. Sir Richard Young, one of the king's knights took us into his chamber. Before we reached the king, Sir Richard warned me, "The king is not well. His physician, Théodore de Mayerne, was with him not long ago. The interview may, perforce, be shorter than you may hope. He is keen to speak with you and the ones who wait without will be disappointed men."

Hob was left with the courtiers. When I entered, I saw a shell of a man. He gave me a wan smile and waved me to a seat, "I find it hard to look up. Let us dispense with formality so that we can speak." He waved a hand, "Sir Richard, wine."

"My lord, you know your physician said that it will do you no good to drink so much."

"Bring me wine." As the aide went off the king said, "He may be right. When I make water it is the colour of Malmsey wine, that cannot be good but what can a man do? I like wine and if I am doomed to die let me choose the manner of my own death."

Sir Richard brought wine. He poured small measures and that told me much. He did not leave us but remained close by the king's side. "Now, Captain James, I know that you do not bring me good news. All that I hear from the Continent is of disaster and battles that were lost. You are, if memory serves, a truthful young man so speak plainly. I am too old to waste time hearing diplomatic phrases. Tell me what has happened in Europe and what Prince Maurice needs from me."

"Thank you, King James." After telling him what Prince Maurice had told me I went through all that had happened. I did not mean to, but I inadvertently mentioned Alvarado.

The king might have been a heavy drinker but he had his wits about him, "You were attacked by a Spaniard? Why was I not told of this?"

"It happened before I went abroad, King James, and I did not discover the identity of the man behind the attack until our ships were attacked."

His face became angry, "I knew that the Spanish were not to be trusted. I wondered why Don Alvarado was missing from my court." He toyed with his goblet and then said, "You can tell Prince Maurice that I intend, once my health recovers, to send an army, my army, to help him defeat the Spanish. Once they are consigned to the Iberian Peninsula, we shall turn our attention to the Palatinate. Sir Horace is striving to hold there but he needs help. I would like you to discover if you can, where Don Alvarado is to be found."

"He is like all snakes, King James, skilful at hiding under rocks. England is a large place."

He gave me a smile that showed me he still had his wits, "A man like Alvarado will stand out in a small place. He will be in London and with others of a similar nature. Find him and there will be rewards for you." He turned to Sir Richard, "Give this man a hundred pounds. Loyalty should be rewarded."

"Yes, King James."

"Return when you have news. I will not be here. I tire of London. I have a home in Hertfordshire, Theobalds House, I find it more comfortable there." He gave me a sad smile, "I gave it to my wife before she died and I enjoyed good times there with King Christian of Denmark. I would rekindle their memories."

I bowed and left. Sir Richard caught up with me when I was at the horses. He handed me the purse. "What ails the king?"

"Too much drink and his physician tells me that he has kidney stones."

"I shall pray for his recovery."

"As will all true Englishmen but there are those, I fear, who will harbour ill thoughts. Fare well and I shall be at his side when you next visit."

I rode back along the river. I was quiet for I had much to think about. I had the answer Prince Maurice wanted but I was now charged with another, more dangerous task. Alice and Mags would be happy. I would be in England for some time now and that meant Alice and Hob could be married and enjoy a time as husband and wife before I returned to the Netherlands.

Chapter 14

My distraction was almost our undoing but Hob was watchful. With no conversation from me to make his attention lax, he was able to do that which I should have done. He kept watch and, as we neared Southwark, said, "Captain, we have been followed."

Inwardly I cursed myself but my voice was calm as I said, "How many?"

"At least two."

I wanted to turn around but that would have alerted them. A watcher who thought he was invisible might grow overconfident. The road to Greenwich was often used by pilgrims travelling to Canterbury. It made this a busy road. I could see how they could hide.

"Are there many travellers behind us?" I was annoyed with myself. I had not been observing the road or the travellers.

"We passed a wagon heading for the Chepe, Captain."

"Then let us prick our mounts and stretch their legs." I had observed, ahead of us, a group of pilgrims leading a sumpter. They sprawled across the road. It would look natural if we hurried to pass them. I intended to maintain the pace and hope to lose our followers. The two horses responded. They enjoyed moving at pace and whilst it was not a gallop we easily overtook the pilgrims. Ahead I saw the city to our right and knew that Southwark was less than a mile away. They might have deduced where we would be heading but any confusion would help us. As the road turned slightly around a newly constructed building, I glanced behind. I saw the followers but they were half a mile behind and I could not make out their faces. They had cowls about their heads. Their horses were poor ones. This was not Alvarado nor one of his Spanish officers. These were English cutpurses hired to follow us.

We rode directly into the stables at the inn and Hob closed the doors. We would be able to enter the inn from the yard and avoid having to re-enter the street. There were other inns and it would take the men time to find us.

The inn was a little busier. Perhaps some of the actors had returned and Edgar was occupied. We went to our chamber. I had not said much to Hob and he deserved to know all. I showed him the purse and explained what was needed by the king.

"He asks much of you, Captain. You will be putting your life in jeopardy if you hunt rats in the cesspit that is London."

"He is still my king and I am an Englishman. I owe him a duty and, besides, Alvarado is my enemy. I do not think that once he knows I am in England he will simply ignore me. He will try to kill me. In this hunt, we are both predators."

We had a small box we kept under the bed and I secreted the coins there. I would husband them. I was unsure how long Prince Maurice would employ me and I needed to make plans for life without pay.

We used the best table once more when we dined. It was close to the busiest part of the inn and if Edgar joined us, as he often did, then he would be able to observe the customers. It was a more orderly place than the one I had first visited. That was Edgar's doing for he liked order. When he found time to speak to me I told him of my task and the followers. His first reaction was one of joy, "Well, Hob, you and Alice can be wed and have time together as man and wife. Captain James has his answer for the prince and can wait the full time allowed before returning."

I could not tell from Hob's face if that pleased him or not. He merely nodded and continued to eat.

"As for these followers...I will have my men keep their eyes open for regular watchers." He shook his head, "Seeking Alvarado will not be easy."

As he took a swig from his tankard, I smiled, "Yet you know where to begin the search."

He nodded, "Aye, I do. After our last encounter with the Papists, I took to seeking out where they congregated. To the east of the Chepe, there are some inns which seek to serve the lords and those with coins to spend. There are also one or two grander houses on Throgmorton Street. Lord Montague has a large house there. He spends most of his time at his country estate in Buckinghamshire. The Spanish who seek to return this land to the Pope use the house as well as the inns close by." My face must have betrayed my thoughts for he shook his head, "If you are thinking of bearding Alvarado there then I must dissuade you. There will be many of his friends close by. The last time we encountered him it was on my land and in the streets I know. I will not risk my men north of the river."

"And you need not. King James merely wants to know where his enemies lie. All I need to do is to confirm where they congregate and then he will rid himself of his enemies. The king is as much against the Catholics as any."

Edgar nodded, "That may be but his chief minister, Buckingham, is not. You say the king is unwell, how stands Prince Charles on the matter? Tread carefully, James, for the path you travel is littered with lilia and unseen obstacles."

Hob asked, "Lilia?"

Without turning Edgar said, "Sharpened stakes placed in the bottom of ditches. They are laid there to trap the unwary."

"I will be careful, Edgar, and you are right about Hob. We will confine ourselves to Southwark while preparations for the nuptials are made. It might allay the fears of our enemies. If I do not stir from these walls they might wonder what I am up to and may even seek me at Eltham, Greenwich or Thames Street, but seeking and not finding will be to our advantage. When I go to find this nest of Spaniards I shall do so in disguise."

Edgar seemed satisfied, "Good, for here you are safe and it will please both Mags and Alice to have Hob safe and close."

It was strange for me to be unoccupied, and I did not take kindly to it. I had an active mind and I wished to use it. Edgar had no books to read and the room seemed confining. I took to sitting in the inn and nursing an ale. It was there that I met an actor from the theatre, Tom Good. He was new to London and he came each day to learn the lines of his new play. He was playing a part in the revival of Ben Johnson's play, The Alchemist. He saw me observing him and, when he discovered me to be a gentleman who could read, asked if I would help him by reading lines. I enjoyed the exercise and the reading. It became a daily routine. Tom practised in the morning and then, in the afternoon, rehearsed. In the afternoon I took to exercising in the yard. Hob and sometimes Edgar would spar with me. In the evening I watched the people in the inn. It was a routine and I resolved to keep that routine for a fortnight. That would take us to within a week of Hob's wedding. I intended to scout out the Spaniards alone. I deduced that the last week would see Hob and Edgar the busiest and my absence might not be noted.

I got on well with Tom and when we were not learning lines he told me of his life in the border country close to Wales. I learned more from Tom than he did from me. I tried to hide my profession although I suspected he knew I was a soldier. I learned how to use a modulated voice, expressions of the face and gestures of the hand. In Tom's case, they were to play a part on the stage. I intended to use those skills to play a part when I went to Throgmorton Street. Tom, for his part, seemed to like me too and he begged me to attend the first performance of the play. I agreed but felt guilty as I had my own motives. I knew that I could hide from watchers in the crowded Globe and disappear from sight more easily.

Ten days before the wedding the watchers entered the inn. My practice became my disguise for when the three men entered Tom and I were saying the lines he would speak in the play. They saw what they expected to see, two actors practising and they ignored me. It helped that my back was to the door. They went to the bar to order drinks. It was Marie who was serving. They all knew of the threat to me and when she was asked about an English soldier who served the Dutch she laughed, "A soldier? Here? The only soldiers we get are those who act as soldiers on the stage and as they have not done a history for some time, then soldiers we have none."

I was close enough to hear their words for they took a table near to ours. Tom was speaking his lines and I listened to the three men.

"He has gone to ground and no mistake."

"Perhaps he has returned to the Netherlands."

"No, Don Alvarado has men watching the Dutch merchant. When he returns, he will have to visit there. He has been there but twice. He must have found another hole in which to hide. Come, let us return to our master."

They left and Tom said, "You were somewhat distracted, James. You missed that I misspoke some lines."

"Sorry, Tom. I did not sleep well last night. Try again and I promise you my full attention."

We carried on rehearsing, and I stored the information I had gathered.

The last week before the wedding saw me with time on my hands. Tom had rehearsals morning and night and Hob and Alice were preoccupied with the wedding; I was therefore able to slip away unnoticed. I headed through the yard where I donned my cowled cloak. I wore no hat and I did not carry my good sword but I had taken Hob's old short sword which was hidden by the cloak. I did not head directly to the bridge but, instead, went along the river to The Swan Theatre. There was to be a play on that afternoon and there would be a ferry across the river. As most of the trade was from the north to the south I found a place easily enough and I was in a position to spy out any who watched me. The crowds helped me to disappear and I adopted a pronounced limp as a disguise. It was easy enough to manage as although my wound had healed, I was still aware of it. My use of the trick meant that if I used a normal gait I would appear different.

When I landed, I headed along the outside of the city wall to Ludgate Hill thereby avoiding Thames Street and Pietr's. There were men watching it. Passing the busy St Paul's I was able to hide myself in the throng. It was always a busy place and one more cloaked figure would go unnoticed. I made my way to the Cripplegate. My plan was to approach the house and the street, not from the south but from the north. I was trying to outwit men who made a living from being secretive. I passed down Broade Street and emerged in the middle of a busy Throgmorton Street. I was lucky, there was a hawker selling hot chestnuts. It was a cold day and he was doing a brisk trade. Waiting with others to buy the hot delicacy afforded me a disguise and I was able to study the houses opposite. Edgar had said that Lord Montague had the grandest house and it was clear which one that was from the two liveried guards who stood stamping their feet outside. After I had paid my halfpenny for the handful of chestnuts, I made my way slowly up the street, making out that I was a poor man savouring each of the warming nuggets. They were delicious. I sought a place where I could hide and yet watch. I found such a spot where there was a narrow street leading to Threeneedle Street. I secured a place in the doorway of what appeared to be an abandoned building. I waited.

This was like sentry duty, the main difference being that I knew who I was looking for. I sought Don Alvarado or, failing that, any Spanish-looking man. I was seeking olive skin and dark hair. Of course, that could apply to Italians but as half of Italy was Spanish the odds were that any men I found would be my enemies. The house had visitors but they all appeared to have the pale skin of Englishmen. My time fighting the Spanish had given me a good idea of the dress and manner of Spaniards. They strutted rather than walked and they enjoyed brighter colours than did we English. It therefore came as a surprise when a trio of men made their way from the direction of St Paul's. They were dressed in dark clothes. They might have entered the house unnoticed had a working man carrying planks of wood not dropped them. The three men all turned and their hands went to the pommels of their swords. I saw that they were all olive-skinned and dark-haired but, more importantly, I recognised Don Alvarado. Seeing their error they turned and hurried unchallenged through the door of the house of Lord Montague.

The confirmation of the house as a place of Spanish spies was satisfying, as was the knowledge that Alvarado was there. The information meant that I could ride to Theobalds House and tell the king. I was about to leave when another two men arrived. This time they were Englishmen and I recognised them. One of them was Sir Richard Greene and he had been at court the first time I had attended the king. There was clearly some sort of meeting taking place and I waited for another hour. In all six men arrived but I did not recognise any of them. I would know them again but it left me a problem. Did I visit the king and give him the information which seemed incomplete? As no more men arrived I left by the expedient of heading down Threeneedle Street towards the bridge. I knew that I was risking exposure by using the bridge but I had tarried too long at my watch and it was getting on to dark. Edgar and Hob would worry about me and I did not want them to put themselves in danger and seek me out.

As luck would have it I timed my crossing well. Labourers had been hired to work on some building work in the city and as it was now dark were returning to their homes south of the river.

There were many houses that accommodated large numbers. Hob had told me that sometimes they would sleep ten to a room. These workers now trudged over the bridge and I insinuated myself amongst them. I did pause at the southern end of the bridge to spy the watcher and I found him, or rather I found them both. They were lounging together close to a freshly lit brand. I saw them scanning the mob that crossed looking for an individual. I had cunningly concealed myself behind a huge labourer with a chest like a bull. I was hidden and they were not. I did not flatter myself that the two men were there purely for the purpose of spying on me. There would be other enemies of the Spanish and as many of them might frequent the theatres then it would be a good idea to mount a guard.

There was an angry reception for me when I entered the inn and the worst of the tongue-lashing I was given came from Mags. "Captain James, we have been worried beyond belief. Where have you been? What were you thinking? Anything could have happened on the street and without my Edgar or Hob to watch your back then you might have been killed. For shame!"

I knew her anger and vitriol were fuelled by concern. I smiled and spoke softly, "All of you were busy with the wedding and that is right and proper. I have a commission from the Prince of Nassau and another from the King of England. I gave my word to both men and I took their gold." I spread my arms, "I am safe and I am returned. All is well."

Edgar loomed up, "Aye, and from now on either Hob or I will watch every move you make, Captain James. You may be happy to risk your life for men who would not lose a moment's sleep at your demise, but we are your friends and would like to see you married and grow old and not die with a stiletto in the back."

An uncomfortable silence ensued until Hob said, brightly, "All the arrangements are made and we marry next week. You, Captain, would do me great honour if you would stand at my side."

I smiled, "It would be I who would be honoured. Which church?"

"The Southwark Priory now called St Saviour's. It is an old church."

173

Edgar snorted, "Aye, and they charge a pretty penny to use it for marriage too."

Mags wagged a finger at him, "Edgar…"

I said, "I would be happy to pay. Hob is as dear to me as a son and the expense should not be borne by you alone."

Edgar stood a little taller, "It is a father's duty to give a dowry and pay for the wedding and I have taken Alice to my heart. It is a kind offer, Captain, but the church and the food will be paid for by me."

"Then I shall buy a drink for each of the guests, allow me that, Edgar."

He nodded and we had made a sort of peace.

A winter wedding was unusual. Most brides chose the time of Lady's Day for marriage. My task had meant haste was all. One advantage was that on the morning of the wedding, a cold one in December, there was a heavy frost and the ground was white. It made it seem magical. We used Caesar to carry the bride to the church and with the inn locked, all those who worked at the inn marched in procession to the church which, until King Henry had dissolved the monasteries, had been the church of the priory. Inside it was magnificently apportioned and reflected the power of the Augustine monks. They were all departed now and those who used the church were from the lower orders. It inspired awe. I stood close by Hob. I was dressed in my finest apparel as was Hob. We had bought new clothes especially for the wedding and the black doublet and hose contrasted well with Alice's white dress, veil and flowers. It was all done well and I was close enough to see the love in Hob's eyes. He had entertained doubts, I knew that, but he was in love and they would be happy. I felt guilty as I realised that I would be the cause of his leaving. That was for the future and this was their day.

Caesar easily carried back the bride and groom. The inn was closed to all but the wedding guests and we had a merry celebration. I insisted on putting a gold coin on the table to buy a round of drinks and I was cheered by all those within. I had lost my own family but gained one here in London. That night I had the room to myself. Hob would share it no longer. I wondered if, when I returned to the Netherlands, it would be alone.

Chapter 15

Even had I wanted to report to the king I could not, for it was Christmas and with Buckingham and the prince returned he was celebrating with them and would not receive visitors. It was during that quiet time between the old year and the new year that I met John Felton. He was a soldier and knew Edgar. He came to visit with Edgar as he had served with him in the wars. That he and Edgar got on famously was clear.

"So, John, what brings you here? I know your family now live in London and this is a low place."

I liked John Felton who was just slightly older than me. He was an open and honest fellow and spoke his mind. He came to the point directly, "The Duke of Buckingham seeks men for an expedition to Cadiz. As High Admiral, he seeks to make war in the Spanish homeland. Drake attacked Cadiz and the duke would emulate that great Englishman. I thought to invite you to join us."

Edgar shook his head, "You are a soldier and not a sailor. No, John, after my last battle where James here saved my life I determined to give up the sword."

John accepted that and turned to me, "If you are a soldier then come with me. I can promise good pay and action."

"It is a kind offer and I would accept but I have a commission from Prince Maurice of Nassau. Until that commission is completed then I am honour-bound to serve him."

It was on the tip of my tongue to question the Duke of Buckingham's motives when Edgar did it for me.

"It seems strange to me, John, that the duke would fight so far from England. If men are being raised now and the army is to be taken by sea, then it seems to me that the Spanish will know you are coming."

"We have a fleet of over a hundred ships and there are seven thousand soldiers. I am confident."

Edgar and I exchanged a look. We both knew how good the Spanish were and they would fight even harder in Spain than they had in the Palatinate. When John left us we parted friends but I could see that he was disappointed not to have Edgar with him. I already knew of Edgar's skill and reputation but to have it confirmed by a stranger was reassuring.

It was early in January that a messenger came from Pietr. It was Johannes who worked as a bodyguard and labourer. I knew why Pietr had chosen him. He would be anonymous crossing the bridge and his arrival at our inn was not a cause for comment.

"Captain James, a message has come from the prince and my master desires conference with you."

I knew that I would not have been sent for if it was not urgent. I nodded, "Hob, saddle Caesar and I will ride to meet Pietr."

"Do you need me, Captain?"

"No, for it is broad daylight and I will not linger."

I donned my cloak and followed the Dutchman towards the bridge. I spotted the two watchers at the bridge and knew that they had recognised me. Coming back I would have to use cunning. When we reached Thames Street, Johannes took my horse and I quickly entered the house.

"The prince has recalled you. He sent a letter and impressed upon you the need to speak to the king immediately. The Spanish have surrounded Breda with a siege. The prince is trying to break through the Spanish siege lines. He needs more men if he is to succeed."

I shook my head, "I think that the king, or rather the Duke of Buckingham, has a different plan to the prince." I told him of the proposed attack on Cadiz.

Pietr knew the sea and shook his head, "It is doomed to failure, James. I beg of you to use all your skills to persuade the king."

"I will." I hesitated and then decided to tell Pietr what I had discovered and the name of Greene.

He frowned, "I know this lord and he is a staunch supporter of the Catholics. I do not like this unholy alliance. It reeks of the plot, when the king was new, to blow up Parliament with the king in it."

"Do not worry. I will ride in the next day or so to speak to the king and I will tell him my news."

I stood and he clasped my arm, "Take care, James. Your absence from our home has made Elizabeth and I sad."

"As it has me but it has kept you safe, Pietr, and that makes me happier. I am like a lodestone that attracts all manner of evil."

I left and headed back towards the bridge. I knew that the two men, perhaps more, would be watching for me. As I neared the end of the bridge I spurred Caesar. I was roundly cursed by those around me but it meant I burst from the bridge and instead of either turning right or heading straight on for the Globe I turned left on East Tooley Street and made as though I was heading for Greenwich. I knew the road having travelled there to meet the king and I knew that it soon entered the countryside with trees, shrubs and little lanes leading to small farms. The men following me would need to find horses for I had seen none close by the bridge, and by the time they had found them I hoped to have disappeared.

Within half a mile of the bridge, I saw a small road junction. The one to the left led to the river, a quay no doubt, while the other climbed through a hedgerow to a farm I could see partly hidden behind trees. I headed up the trail and then took off through an open gate. A small orchard hid me from the road and I crossed the farmer's smallholding until I reached another small track which I passed over. The track bent back to the main road and I saw a stand of alder and elder trees. I nestled Caesar behind it and waited. I began to think that they had not followed me but then I heard the sound of hooves galloping hard. I spied the two cloaked men as they hurtled down the road to Greenwich. I did not move for I heard more hooves and another three men followed. They intended me harm.

I reached the inn after following a circuitous route that avoided the bridge and allowed me to ride towards the inn from the west. I knew that they would all be worried, and I explained, as soon as I dismounted, what had happened.

"Tomorrow Hob and I will ride to Theobalds House. We could ride to Wallingford and cross there but it would add too long to our journey. We will have to use London Bridge. They will have horses but I will count on the superior quality of our mounts. The ones I saw today were nags and ready for the knacker's yard." I could see that Edgar was unhappy. "Edgar, I am a soldier. It was you and Captain Woodrow who made me one. My ship has left the port and is set on a course. What would you have me do?"

I saw him nod, "Let me and some of my men go to the bridge first. We can either stop or slow their movement."

I smiled, "Thank you, that would help."

Alice asked, "Will you return before dark? I know not how far Theobalds House lies."

I had asked already and knew the answer, "Fifteen miles. In theory, we should be back before dark but it all depends upon the king."

I knew why she asked and it did not bode well for the time when I would return to the Netherlands. Perhaps I would give Hob the chance to stay in England. He had served me well enough and I could hire a Dutch servant if I had to.

Edgar was not in the inn when we breakfasted and I realised that four of the men who normally ate with us were not eating with me as they usually did. We armed ourselves well and wrapped up against the cold January wind. Winter always seemed to last far longer than the brief summers we enjoyed. We reached the bridge when the sun had risen. The days would be short. I saw Edgar and two of his men at the bridge. He had bloodied knuckles but, of the watchers, there was no sign. I waved an acknowledgement and we headed through the city. Once we had passed the Cripplegate we made much better time for most of the traffic was heading south to the city, and two riders on good horses forced a passage through those on foot. We said little as we rode but I had words I would say on the way back. I was formulating my report for King James.

When we reached the hunting lodge that was Theobalds House there were armed liveried guards. They were Buckingham's men. There were also men wearing the livery of the Prince of Wales. We were barred from entry. I spied Richard Young and I waved to him, "Sir Richard, I beg of you, we must speak with the king. We have the news he sought."

Sir Richard looked unhappy, "I fear the king is too ill to receive visitors. He has arthritis and gout and has suffered fainting fits."

I lowered my voice, "My lord, this concerns the security of his majesty and the country."

He nodded, "Wait here and I will speak with the duke and the prince."

We were kept waiting for a good hour but eventually, a pursuivant fetched me and I left Hob with the horses. Prince Charles was seated but it was clear, even though he stood, that Buckingham was in charge. "We have no time for such distractions, Captain James. Speak your business and let us get back to the care of the king."

The look which Prince Charles gave me was one of contempt. It was as though a bad smell had entered the room and he wished it gone. I gave him the information about Alvarado and then went on to add Prince Nassau's request for men. I was unsure if I would get a second chance.

The duke shook his head, "Don Alvarado, Lord Montague and the others who conspire against the king will be dealt with…" I felt relief coursing through my body. However, it was as though a sudden cold shower of rain had descended when the duke continued, "In the fullness of time. We have other urgent matters and as for helping the Dutch…" he shook his head, "Prince Maurice has appointed poor commanders for his men and so we have decided to take charge. We will challenge the Spanish but we shall do it where it suits us, at sea, and not in the Dutch Republic." The smug look on Prince Charles' face told me that he agreed with the duke. My mission had failed. I had failed the prince and the king. I bowed and backed out. I mounted Henry and we walked our horses past the guards.

When we reached the road Hob said, "Well?"

I shook my head and told him my sorry tale. He was appalled, "But you gave him information about spies!

"They are Catholics and the Duke of Buckingham is a slippery man." We rode in silence and I then said, "Hob, if you wish to stay in England and leave my service I will understand, but I have been ordered back to the Netherlands and until my contract is over I have no choice. You do."

He said nothing for a while and then said, "I signed no contract, Captain James, but I was with you when you did. Even though Alice wishes me to stay here in England I will return with you. When the commission is over then I will return home."

I was relieved but I knew that there would be tears.

179

I did not see the watchers as we rode over the bridge but then
again they might have changed the watchers. There was little I
could do about it and so we headed, by a slightly circuitous
route, to the inn. As I had expected, our late return had worried
Alice. She fussed over Hob while I spoke to Edgar.

He shook his head, "It does not bode well that Buckingham
has power over the next king already. What will you do?"

"Tomorrow I will visit with Pietr. We will need to make
arrangements to return to the Netherlands." He glanced over at
Hob and I said, "I gave Hob the chance to stay here but he insists
upon coming."

"He is a good lad but I fear that Alice will not see it that
way."

"What happened with the watchers?"

He grinned, "We took them by surprise and gave them their
spring bath in the Thames a little earlier than they expected." He
suddenly frowned, "You will have to pass them tomorrow and I
think they will be prepared."

"I will take a ferry. I avoided them the last time."

"Good."

Hob objected at first, but I pointed out that the watchers
would be at the bridge and would not expect a man alone. As
Alice had been tearful when he had told her of his decision it was
as well that he stayed with her. I left the inn before dawn. Edgar
and two men followed me at a discreet distance. The ferries were
there already and the ferryman was grateful for the coin that took
him across the river. This time I had a shorter walk along
Thames Street to the small inlet that led to Pietr's warehouse. I
arrived as the sun was breaking to the east. Wilkinson admitted
me. He did so as he always did, grumpily, but I took no offence.
It was his way and he was protective of his master.

The family were still at breakfast but the welcome I had was a
warm one and, when my cloak and hat were taken away, I was
seated between Pietr and Elizabeth.

"You have returned quickly, James."

I nodded. I did not like to speak in front of either Elizabeth or
the child but time was pressing, "King James is ill and with
Buckingham's hand on the tiller there is little chance that
England will help the prince, I must return with bad news."

Pietr nodded and wiped his mouth, "And the weather has been so inclement of late that my ships are all at sea. I know not when they will return." I nodded and smeared butter on the freshly baked and still-warm bread. "I think that you should stay here. It will make it easier to board quickly for it might well be that a swift turnaround is needed."

I chewed and contemplated my answer. He was, of course, right, but that would not please Alice. "When do you expect your ships? I mean the earliest that one might arrive."

He folded his fingers together and contemplated the ceiling, "The first left seven days since but she needs work in a yard. I would say I do not expect a ship this week."

"Good, then that gives me seven days to put my affairs in order." It was Hob's that would be put in order, of course. "We will return at about this hour seven days from now."

They both looked relieved. I chatted with them for a while and then decided to head back across the river. The road outside was busier and I looked up and down it to check for enemies. I saw none and bidding farewell to Pietr I hurried down to the bridge. I was taking all the precautions that I could. This time, however, Don Alvarado was taking no chances. When I reached the bridge I saw four men barring my way. To the guards on the bridge, they would have looked like four men engaged in casual conversation but their eyes were on me, and in their eyes, I saw my death. I turned with the intention of returning to Pietr's but there were another four men there. While the ones on the bridge had swords, the other four had cudgels. Even had I shouted to the guards on the bridge, my life would have been ended and the eight men would have disappeared. This was like my first battle all over again and I had no choice. I turned and ran towards the Tower along Thames Street.

I took them by surprise and was aided by people trying to get across the bridge. I gained ten paces. As I ran I drew my sword and dagger. My cloak trailed behind me but I dared not loose it. I could not afford a moment's pause. I knew, from my first visit to the city, that Thames Street and Tower Street emerged into what had once been an open space. Houses were in great demand and a few had been erected closer to the tower than I think earlier kings might have liked. There were alleys between them and that gave me hope that I might be able to make my pursuers spread out.

I glanced behind and saw that it was two of the clubmen who were closest. Hulking brutes, I knew that they would have bladed weapons, too, but the cudgel would end a fight quickly as it could break limbs. When I reached the end of the street I turned sharp left as though I was heading to Tower Street and a route back to the bridge. The club men had a natural cunning and they ran to cut me off. I darted to my right, down an alley between two newly constructed buildings. There was barely enough space for one man and my shoulders brushed both buildings. When I burst from the buildings I saw the curtain wall and the massive Lion Tower ahead of me. If I turned right, I would find myself trapped by the Thames and so I would have to turn left. However, I decided to make my pursuers wary and I turned. It was a swordsman who followed me and he was wider than I was. He had to turn sideways to negotiate the alley. I stabbed him in the thigh and he stopped. Until he could be moved, I had the chance to escape. I ran along what was little more than a track. The stones had not yet been laid for a road.

Ahead of me, two men burst from another alley. I had slowed down some of my pursuers but not the other half. I had learned in my escape from the disaster of Záblatí, that hesitation cost lives. I ran at the two men. One had a club and one a sword. I did not hesitate but lunged with my sword at the swordsman. It took him by surprise and I scored a hit along his arm. The cudgel swung down at me and I slashed blindly with my dagger. I struck flesh and the man screamed. I did not linger but ran on. The two men had wounds. Three of the eight had shed blood to me but there were still five who would be anxious to take me. I had the whole of the fortress to my right. The moat effectively blocked any escape to that side and it meant all my pursuers needed to do was stop me from running to my left.

To my right, I saw the small gatehouse that led to the Lion Tower then the track became straight. Suddenly a figure loomed from my left. It was a Spanish gentleman and not a cutpurse. He must have anticipated my flight and got ahead of me. I vaguely recognised him as one of Don Alvarado's companions from Throgmorton Street. His intention was clear. He would bar my progress until his companions could join him. His sword was made of fine Toledo steel. I had fought against the Spanish enough times to be wary of such a blade and the man who wielded it. He went for the quick kill and slashed down at my head. I blocked it with my own Spanish sword, taken from the battlefield. I then used a trick taught to me by Edgar. As I lunged with my dagger I stamped at the shin of the Spaniard with my boot. The pain of the kick distracted him long enough for my dagger to slice into his side.

The pounding feet behind me warned me that I had moments left to live. I took the offensive and, slashing with my sword, danced my feet so that he was between me and the rest of his men. The Spaniard was hurt but he cursed me and said, in English, "This time you shall die!"

It was at that moment that eight liveried men burst from the gatehouse. "In the name of the king put up your weapons."

It took the men behind the Spaniard by surprise. Half obeyed and the other half fled. The Spaniard chose to end the fight and stabbed with his dagger at my middle. I still had fast reactions and I blocked it with my own dagger whilst punching at his head with the guard of my sword. He was slow to block and not only did my guard hit his head but the crosspiece drove into his eye. He screamed and then fell at my feet as the crosspiece pierced his brain.

One of the king's guards held his halberd at my throat and snarled, "You heard the sergeant, drop your weapons."

I obeyed and then heard the sergeant, "You may keep your weapons, Captain James." I looked into the eyes of my friend, Stephen Fletcher. He smiled, "Disarm the others, Walter, and take them to the guardhouse. We will let the constable deal with them."

I saw that the only ones that had been taken were two that I had wounded. After sheathing my weapons, I knelt by the dead Spaniard. He had a signet ring with a gryphon upon it. I took it for it might identify the man. I also took his purse, dagger and sword for they too might identify him.

Stephen said, "Before the captain of the guard arrives, tell me all." I trusted Stephen and told him of the King's commission and the nest of spies just up the road. He nodded and said, "When the captain comes let me speak, James."

The captain arrived with another four men, "What is the meaning of this, Sergeant?"

"We have foiled a plot against King James." He used the end of his halberd to reveal the crucifix around the neck of the dead Spaniard. "This is a papist. Captain James here is known to me. He is an ambassador from the Dutch Republic and these men tried to assassinate him."

The captain looked at me, "Is this true, Captain?"

I nodded, "I followed this man to Lord Montague's House on Throgmorton Street. I reported it to King James. I swear that I had no choice but to slay this man."

He nodded, "Take the head and place it on the bridge and have the body thrown into the river. As for the other prisoners, we will turn them over to the constable. From the looks of them, they deserve to hang too if only to make London's Streets safer." He smiled at me, "And you, Captain, how may we ensure your safety?"

I pointed to the river, "I need to cross the river."

He beamed, "Then we can help you. Sergeant, take your friend to the quay and have the royal boatmen take him across the river in the wherry."

We entered the gatehouse and passed through the Lion Tower. There we reached the quay. Stephen shouted, "Jack, I need you to take this man across the river."

"Aye, Sergeant. I will fetch my men. They are having a warm by the brazier."

"You live an exciting life, James. Did you intend to enlist my help when you came this close to the Tower?"

I shook my head, "In truth, I had forgotten that you were a royal guard now."

"Well, Lady Luck smiles on you."

I nodded as the wherry men took their place in the boat, "And not just me. I met Erik and Lars. They survived Záblatí too."

Stephen beamed, "And that is the best news I have had in a long time. Those Swedes were good soldiers." He clasped my arm, "Farewell, and stay safe."

As I was rowed across the icily cold Thames, I reflected that old friends were the best. Stephen, Edgar, Erik, Lars and I had been bonded in war and our friendship forged in blood. It would endure.

Chapter 16

Alice and Mags were busy preparing food when I returned and so I was able to speak to Hob and Edgar. I told them all. Edgar was philosophical about it, "A week gives us time to prepare Alice. She will take it hard, Hob."

"You can change your mind and stay, Hob, I will understand."

He shook his head, "I am married and I am a man. You give your word and you stand by it. This is a test of my character. She will understand." The words came out in short bursts and I knew he was upset.

Edgar shook his head, "I am new to the world of women but I doubt that is true." He turned his attention to me, "And from now on you do not stir without four of my men guarding you."

"Your men are needed here, working in the inn."

"Your life is more important than the extra coins they bring in."

"I will stay here. I have grown fond of the inn and I do not know when I will return."

The three of us gradually broke the news first to Mags and then to Alice. Mags was the more understanding. We had two days of tears and then there was the hint of a smile.

Edgar went to the bridge three days after my return and said that there were three new heads adorning it. The constable, it seemed, had executed the two wounded footpads. I knew that the others would remember me. Perhaps it was as well that I was leaving England. We also heard from Tom Good who had heard it from one of the theatregoers, that men had been arrested at Lord Montague's home. I did not know who ordered it, but I was glad. At least the nest was cleansed. They would build another but until it was built then they would not be able to conjure mischief. Talking to Tom Good about his play, The Alchemist, made me think of Don Alvarado as such a man. He dealt in a dark world and used unholy methods to achieve his ends. England was Protestant and nothing that the Spanish or their supporters would do could change that.

Johannes arrived seven days after I had visited with Pietr. He gave me the news that Captain van Hooft's ship had been seen in the estuary. The tides meant he would not arrive until the following day. It gave all of us, but especially Hob and Alice, an extra night together. They made the most of it. Mags, Edgar and I dined well in a cosy corner of the inn. I realised that the two of them had replaced my parents. They were not the same by any means but they cared for me and wanted the best for my life. I knew I was lucky to have found them. We left as soon as the sun rose. Spring was less than a month away when the days and nights would be of equal length. Edgar and his men came with us leaving a tearful Alice being comforted by her mother.

I spied the heads as we crossed the bridge. They were a grisly reminder of how close I had come to an early death. We did not go to Pietr's house but to the warehouse at Bylingsgate. It was downstream of the bridge and was the one used by Pietr's ships. Of Captain Van Hooft and his ship, there was no sign but the labourers were there along with the merchant.

"He will be along soon and it will be a swift turnaround. The storms have cost us money." He handed me a parchment, "This is for the prince." He also handed me a basket, "This is from Elizabeth and will give you some treats for the voyage."

I nodded to Hob who had been given a similar basket by Mags, "We will dine well, Pietr."

"Ship Ho!"

I saw the familiar shape of *'The Maid of Utrecht'* as she tacked her way through the tinier ships that plied the Thames. Pietr chuckled, "Christian will not be happy to have so many little boats in his way."

I nodded to the boxes waiting to be loaded, "What is the cargo?"

He sighed, "Just what you would expect, James, weapons. War costs people but the ones who do not suffer are the ones who make the weapons of war. The price is rising as this war continues."

The ship had to turn about and was not helped by the small boats that seemed to think that they ruled the river. It was a red-faced Captain van Hooft who waved at us, "We will have to be quick on the turnaround." He saw the horses and his face fell. "Horses?"

"They will be no trouble, Captain, they have sailed before."

He saw me for the first time and his scowl turned to a smile, "I did not recognise them. It will not be a problem." He turned to the First Mate, "Get the cargo unloaded and prepare the sling."

I shouted, "We will walk them up the gangplank, Captain. It will be easier."

He waved his acknowledgement. This would be a test for Hob and me. We left the saddles on the animals and secreted in our doublets the apples that would tempt them up the gangplank. Had the gangplank not been a wide one, thanks to a generous tumblehome, then we would have used the sling. As it was the crane attached to the sling was now used to load the crates and boxes aboard. As they were hoisted, I took out an apple and coaxed Henry towards the ship. It was a good apple and as he crunched a chunk out of it, I moved the apple so he stepped onto the gangplank and moved up it. Caesar was just as compliant. If nothing else it showed me that we had trained the horses well. Once aboard we took off their saddles and attached the animals to the rings on the steerboard side of the ship. Hob had decided to sleep on the deck with the horses and that meant we did not need to try to get them into the Stygian darkness of the hold. It also meant cleaning the deck was easier than cleaning the hold.

Pietr came aboard with the two baskets while a crew member carried our bags. Edgar had procured two leather bags and I knew not whence he acquired them but they were well made and had, like the satchel given to me by Prince Maurice, a waxed lining. He was vague about his acquisition. All that he said was that their owners would no longer need them. Hob took them to my cabin and I clasped Pietr's hand.

"This may be a short visit to your homeland, Pietr. It could be that the prince no longer has need of me."

"And if you do return then seek me out. You are an enterprising young man, and I can find employment for one with your wits."

"I am just a soldier."

"No, James, you are more than that."

Captain van Hooft shouted, "Time to shove off!"

It was a command for Pietr, and the merchant stepped from the ship. Even as he stepped onto the stone quay the gangplank was retrieved and the ropes securing us to the land were thrown aboard. With just the topsails to catch the breeze, we headed downstream. The tide was on the turn and the current would carry us around the meandering bends of the Thames to the sea. When Pietr and the Tower disappeared from sight, I joined Hob by the horses.

"Another adventure, Hob."

He nodded, "And yet I am a different person than the one who first looked with wonder at the world. I have fought and I have killed, I am a married man and have known a woman. I am no longer Hob."

A thought occurred to me, "What is your second name, Hob?"

He shrugged, "I know not. When the priest wed us I took Edgar's second name, Smithson. The priest did not mind."

I reflected that it was as though Hob had been reborn when Edgar had arrived at the inn. What would his life have been like if Edgar had not returned?

The voyage was long and it was a cold one. The winds did not cooperate but the horses seemed to prefer being on deck and the lack of strong winds, whilst slowing us down, made for a smoother voyage. We reached Rotterdam later than the captain would have wished but he was a sailor and philosophical about such things. We mounted our horses and rode to Utrecht. Captain van Hooft had told us that Prince Maurice had still to relieve the siege of Breda and did not even know if the prince was there. We headed to the place I knew we would find information.

When we reached Utrecht we were greeted by the commander of the garrison, Colonel Berghof. He had been in command of Breda when we had left, a lifetime ago. His wound stopped him from being an active soldier but he could still command the garrison. Hob went with the servant to the chamber allocated to us while I spoke with the colonel. I felt as though he was an old friend.

"The siege is not going well, Captain James. Spinola is a good commander. He has been a mercenary leader for some time and has the beating of Count von Mansfield."

"And the prince?"

There was hesitation and then he said, "You should know that the prince is unwell. He has a complaint. His doctors think he drinks too much and his liver is failing. The result is that he cannot give his full attention to the relief of the siege. His brother, Prince Frederick Henry has taken command of the rest of the Republican army and he is at The Hague. Perhaps you should visit with him."

I shook my head, "My commission was from Prince Maurice and he is the man to whom I will report."

While we ate, I learned that the English army, led by Sir Horace Vere, had also been badly handled and the Duke of Buckingham had recalled the soldiers that had survived. It told me that the balance of power in England was shifting.

We left for Breda in the company of a column of carabineers sent to reinforce Prince Maurice's army. Their captain, Cornelis de Gortter, was a pleasant young officer and as this was his first command he happily chatted to me as we rode south. He was keen to learn about the battles in which I had fought. I did not want to dishearten him as most of the battles had ended in failure. I gave him hope at the end of the list of disasters when I said that his men, armed with the harquebus and wearing buff coats, might succeed where others had failed.

The Spanish were masters of siege. They had completely surrounded the fortress and protected their siege works with defences. As they controlled the land to the south of Breda and had water as an ally, it was difficult for the prince to break them down. The Spanish were, quite simply, wearing down the defenders inside Breda. Cornelis and I reported to Prince Maurice. I was shocked at his appearance. His skin was yellow, a clear sign of problems with his liver. His eyes were bloodshot and he seemed to me to be a weary man. He greeted the captain warmly, "Your men will be more than welcome, Captain, find your tents and I shall see you in the morning at the officer's call. Perhaps the fresh blood you bring will invigorate the men. This is a pestilential place in which to fight. We fight not only the Spanish but disease too. I would speak alone with Captain James."

Left alone I was waved to a seat. I took the letter from Pietr from my satchel and handed it to him. His hands shook as he broke the seal and he peered myopically at the writing. When he had finished he dropped it despondently on the camp table he was using.

"The letter tells me all but I pray, give me your own version of the situation."

I sighed, "King James is ill and the Duke of Buckingham is the effective ruler of England. He sees the sea as his opportunity to gain glory with a victory over the Spanish. England will fight the Spanish but on Buckingham's terms. I do not think that the Dutch Republic can expect more support than she already enjoys. I have failed."

He shook his head, "I threw you, as a small pebble, into the pond and you did have an effect. General Vere would not have come if you had not made overtures to King James. No, my friend, the money I invested in you was well spent. The problem we have is that the Spanish have too many men for us to defeat and with the Palatinate in Imperial hands we are ever threatened from that direction."

"And now what do I do? I have taken your gold and I will serve you still."

"I will use you as a soldier. We have the remnants of the companies who remained from the disastrous campaign in Germany. Captain Lawrence commands them. Join his men."

His words, if not his health, brightened me. If I were to fight then there was nowhere better than alongside Harry Lawrence. Hob waited outside for me.

"We seek Harry Lawrence, Hob. We are to become soldiers again."

"That should be easy enough, Captain. Listen for the English voices and their songs." He was right, the companies we had brought from England, Ralph's and Harry's, had a vast repertoire of English songs, some lyrical but most bawdy, and they had kept us entertained. Captain de Vries had, of course, disapproved but even the Scottish soldiers had enjoyed them. We passed many Dutch camps and a couple of German ones before we heard the English voices. That it was the camp we sought became clear when we identified the words of the song.

I called, "Ware the camp," as a warning before we entered. The singing stopped and, even though I had spoken in English, men's hands went to weapons. As soon as we were recognised the frowns turned to smiles. Hob had always been popular and men crowded around him.

191

Harry came over to me with an outstretched arm, "I wondered if you would return. It is good to have you here. Do you fight with us?"

"I do. I failed to persuade the king to commit the army to help the Dutch."

After tying our horses to the horse lines I went with Harry to sit on the half barrels used as seats. "How is England?"

I still had some of the food and ale given to me by Mags and Pietr. I shared some good English cheese and the last of the ale with Harry as I told him of the king's illness. When I had finished he said, "So you think that the king is not long for this world?"

I shrugged, "No matter what happens, he is too ill to rule the country and so it is the Duke of Buckingham who holds the reins."

"And Prince Charles? What of him? We hear he is to marry a French princess."

"So it seems. It is hard for me to judge but I think that, like his father, he is too much in the sway of Buckingham. When Buckingham was away with the prince in Spain I found the king to be more receptive. It was almost as though Buckingham had a spell he used to control King James. I know that King James wanted to send English soldiers to fight for Prince Maurice but now…"

We ate the cheese in silence. I wiped my hands on my cloak as I studied the faces in the camp. "These are all that remain?"

He nodded and emptied his coistrel, "Aye, I am the last captain and these one hundred men are all that remains of the men who left London a lifetime ago. Some came to us from other companies. General Vere, when he failed to breach the line, shed men and some joined us."

"Where is the general now?"

"He is in the Hague conferring with Prince Maurice's brother, Prince Frederick Henry. He went to report on Prince Maurice's health. Many of the Dutch believe that Prince Maurice is too ill to fight here. I agree with them."

"How goes the fighting?"

"This is low-lying land and the dykes have been breached so that the only way we can attack the Spanish is over causeways. It does not suit musketeers. I am not sure it suits pikemen. Good old-fashioned archers and billmen would, in my view, have greater success than we enjoy here. This is not a level battlefield. Prince Maurice cannot think of new ways to attack. I hear he sent for more cavalry."

"He did, we rode in with a regiment of them."

Harry laughed but it was a sardonic laugh, "And that is a waste. What can they do? Their horses will take up valuable land that we could use for our camps. It is crowded enough as it is and dysentery is rife."

"You say it is hopeless then?"

He shrugged, "We are paid and, most of the time, fed. That means there is hope, of a sort." He looked up as Hob approached, "Did you bring tents?" I shook my head. "Then you must share. Hob, take Captain James' gear to my tent. It is the one with the standards close by. As for you…"

Hob grinned, "Do not worry about me, Captain, I have been offered shelter already."

As he left Harry said, "He is a golden nugget, James. Keep him safe. His smiling face is worth a dozen men."

"I know, Harry, I know."

Daylight did not bring hope but depression. Men picked their way around the camp from islands of solid ground to other dry areas. There appeared to be more water than grass. We were lucky in that our three horses were the only ones occupying our camp and they had enough grass. What Captain Cornelis would find I could not conceive. Harry went to the officer's call and I organised my bedding and weapons. I cleaned and loaded my pistols. Hob brought the whetstone and sharpened our blades. When Harry returned his face was as black as thunder.

"Prince Maurice has decided to launch an attack on the Spanish lines using the cavalry. We are held in reserve to exploit the victory." He shook his head and waved over the boy drummer. "Sound the drum, Ned, we march to watch others fight."

I knew why Harry was despondent. Prince Maurice was desperately clutching at straws. The attack was hasty and ill-conceived. He was trying to win quickly. The Spanish would know that an attack was to begin and they would be ready to face it.

The artillery pieces had already been dragged into position and they began the bombardment of the enemy redoubts. The Spanish had made them well. We were formed up into three blocks of musketeers and pikemen. Hob and I stood with the pikemen. We would act as sword and buckler men if we were forced into a fight. As Captain Cornelis and his carabineers formed up we waited. When the smoke from the bombardment had cleared, the trumpets sounded and the horsemen charged. The Spanish waited until the horsemen were less than one hundred paces from them and then they opened fire and their own artillery belched forth. Neither side used large ordnance. Most of the guns were three or four-pounders, but loaded with smaller balls and fired at such close range meant that they scythed through horses and buff coats alike. The captain and some of the luckier ones actually made the Spanish lines and they fired their harquebuses. That they killed some Spanish was clear even from our distant lines but there were too few who made it for it to be called a success. Captain Cornelis brought his survivors back. We cheered, not the success for there was none, but the courage they had displayed. The cheers from the Spanish lines were the signal that they had won. We tramped back to our lines.

I never saw Prince Maurice again. After the abortive attack had failed we just kept watch. A rumour spread around the camp that Prince Frederick Henry and Sir Horace Vere were on their way from the Hague but the news that ran around the camp was that Prince Maurice had died. His ailment had finally taken him. I was sad about the death for I had liked Prince Maurice but I also wondered about my own position. What would happen to me?

The arrival of the new Stadtholder and the six thousand men brought by Sir Horace Vere gave all the camp hope. Sir Horace had shown that he was able to hold his own against the Spanish and he had with him his kinsman, Robert de Vere, the Earl of Oxford. As we were the only English mercenary company left, Harry was summoned to the meeting with Prince Frederick Henry, General Vere and the earl. Harry took me as his aide.

Prince Frederick Henry was younger than his brother but I soon learned that he had more military skill. However, he had little time for mercenaries, and made that clear from the first, "My brother invested heavily in mercenaries and, in my view, it was ill-spent gold." He looked at me, "Captain James, the Dutch Republic thanks you for your work. You have another two months of employment, after that your services will no longer be needed. You, Captain Lawrence, have three months to serve. Unless General Vere requires your services then you will no longer be needed."

Sir Horace was a good soldier and he smiled, "I am sure that I will need two good officers such as these gentlemen. I shall find employment for them, my lord."

That done, the prince showed his skill. He outlined a plan that would involve the general's six thousand men attacking before dawn. We would be attacking the same redoubt where Captain Cornelis had failed but we would not have to endure the artillery fire. It was a good plan. We had a week to prepare for the attack and that, too, was good. The Earl of Oxford and his pikemen would lead the attack. They were paid for by the earl and were all good soldiers. The general attended to every aspect of the attack and all of us knew exactly what was needed of us. Our company would follow the earl and exploit any breaches that he made. I had wanted to leave Hob at the camp but he was having none of it. He had shared tents with the other soldiers since our arrival and felt part of the company. Harry and I knew that he was not yet skilled enough but he would not be dissuaded. I ordered him to watch my back knowing that was the best way to keep him safe.

Our plans to sleep during the day before the attack came to nothing for there was too much excitement in our camp. This would be an English attack and, as such, there was national pride at stake. I managed what Edgar called a nap during the afternoon but it was not enough. We heard the distant bells from the churches in the Spanish Netherlands and it told us it was Lauds. We rose and prepared for war. I had my buff coat and Hob his leather jerkin. We formed up in the darkness and it seemed inconceivable to me that the Spanish defenders would not hear us. However, when the Earl of Oxford began his march across the causeway, there was silence ahead of us. The narrow causeway forced us to march just four abreast. Once we neared the redoubt then we could make a wider formation, but if they had guns manned then their balls could sweep through our files and render our attack ineffective. I breathed a sigh of relief when we reached the flatter and slightly drier ground before the redoubt. The sun was just appearing from the east when a Spanish sentry sounded the alarm.

The Earl of Oxford was a calm man and his command seemed more like a request than an order, "Forward."

His three hundred pikemen, however, were well-trained and they moved forward as one. Harry allowed a small gap and then shouted, "Forward!" He marched at the head of our smaller formation. Jack of Yarm carried the company standard and Ned the drummer boy bravely beat out the rhythm that would keep the men in step. With Hob behind me and my pistols in my hand, we followed the pikemen.

The ripple of muskets told us that the Spanish now knew they were under attack but it was not the barrage the horsemen had endured in their attack. Some men fell but far too few to slow our attack. The pikes clambered over the redoubt and there was a cheer as they fell upon the defenders. Order went as the pikes sparred with enemies armed only with swords and muskets, now used as clubs. From the Spanish lines, we heard the trumpets sound as General Spinola ordered men to plug the breach.

We reached the redoubt as men poured from the Spanish rear to reinforce the redoubt. Harry shouted, "Form a line." He knew that a wall of pikes might hold the enemy until General Vere could bring up the rest of our men. We had a toe hold and that was all. It helped that we were all English and our voices identified friend from foe. Our pikemen kept a straight line and I held my two pistols aimed at the backs of the earl's pikemen. As the fighting spread, the line ahead thinned and when the pikeman before me was skewered by a Spanish sword I prepared to fire. The Spanish sword and buckler man had seen my raised pistols and he ran at me with his shield held before him. I just reacted and fired both pistols, not at his head or chest but at his unprotected knees. It was, quite literally, a low blow but I knew the worth of these Spanish armed with sword and shield. The lead balls sent at a range of no more than six feet tore through flesh, bone and cartilage. He fell, screaming at my feet, a barrier to those trying to get at me. I dropped my pistols and drew my sword. I slashed at the first man who came at me and was rewarded when the end sliced across his nose and his cheek. I was aware that the sword and buckler man was not dead and he was trying to raise his sword to hack at my leg. I plunged my sword into his throat and then, as I stepped back, grabbed his shield. I had never used one but I reasoned it would be more protection than my dagger.

The Spanish had been reinforced and we now faced pikemen as well as sword and buckler men. Our musketeers kept up a desultory rate of fire but there were too few of them and the weapons took too long to load. They were most effective when used in a volley. Here, they kept peppering the men who closed with our pikemen. The pike that drove at my face would have been a mortal blow had I not managed to flick up the shield and deflect it over my shoulder. Hob was quick thinking and he used his short sword to hack through the haft of the pike, rendering it almost useless as a weapon. The man wore a breastplate and as those behind impelled him forward I rammed my sword into his throat. He fell, gurgling his life away at my feet.

It was then that Jack of Yarm fell. Once more Hob showed not only his courage but his quick wits. Before the standard could be grabbed by the eager Spanish swordsman who had just slain the luckless standard bearer, Hob had grabbed the standard and I had punched the Spaniard in the side of the head with the shield. He reeled and allowed me to chop sideways towards his neck.

"Keep behind me, Hob, you have shown more than enough courage for one day." As he stepped back I saw the body of Ned the drummer boy. He too had been slain. We had paid a high price already for this piece of the Spanish redoubt.

"Reform the pikes!" Both the captain and the earl bellowed out the same order within seconds of each other. I found myself next to Dick and Peter. Their pikes protected my sides and I was their protector from swords.

The Spanish were pouring men into the breach we had made. I thought that with seven thousand men we might have held but

General Spinola had more men in reserve. If we had attacked at a number of places we might have enjoyed success, but disease and low morale meant that we were the only attack that Prince Frederick Henry could mount. We would either succeed or the battle and the siege would end in failure.

The Spanish brought up their own musketeers but our company, now reinforced by General Vere's men, began to pour volley after volley into them. Our men had the advantage that their muskets were on their stands already and the Spanish had to set theirs up. It was then that Spinola sent in his lancers. Encased in armour, they charged at the earl's pikemen. The pikes were brave but outclassed and they fell back. It was clear that the enemy had more men to use and while we had musketeers and pikemen, they had cavalry and artillery which they dragged into position.

It was General Vere who gave the order, although we all knew it was coming, "Spike the enemy guns and fall back."

We had with us engineers who carried hammers and spikes. They simply drove the metal spikes into the touch holes of the cannons. A good engineer might be able to repair the damage but it would take time. When the sergeant of engineers shouted, "All clear!" we began the march back.

It was not easy. We had to keep a wall of pikes facing the enemy. The Earl of Oxford's men had passed through our pikemen for they had been mauled by the Spanish and it meant that when we reached the causeway it was our company that stood four abreast and marched backwards. It was fortunate that we had spiked their guns for otherwise we would have been slaughtered. As it was the lancers came at us. They rode large horses and could only manage to be two abreast. It gave us a chance. The four of us at the fore had swords but the pikes of the others gave us a protective canopy. As the lances of the two leading riders came at us our pikemen parried and blocked. We slashed at their horses. One of the horses was cut and, rearing, fell with its metal rider into the water. Harry managed to stab the other horse in the throat and that too fell. With the causeway blocked we managed to make it back to our lines. We were cheered by the rest of the army. The mercenaries had shown that they were the equal of the Spanish. It felt like a failure but, as the

Spanish had lost far more men, Prince Fredrick regarded it as a victory.

It was not. Three weeks later the garrison was forced to surrender and they were marched out. We joined them on the long road back to The Hague.

It was when we were just thirty miles from The Hague, that we received the news that King James had died. We had a new king and the two men who promoted me were now dead. My future died with the prince and the king who had died just a month apart. Fate was taking a hand and it was not in my favour.

N

Griff 2023

50 Miles

Chapter 17

General Vere and his brother the Earl of Oxford were also returning to England. The earl's men would be returning with him. Thanks to my service at Breda I was offered a berth on one of the ships commandeered to carry the English contingent home. I knew that Captain van Hooft would have taken us but I did not know where his ships were and, to be honest, Hob and I just wanted to get home. Hob was keen to be reunited with his bride and I felt like a useless extra part. Prince Frederick Henry had honoured his brother's promise and both we and Harry were paid off. Harry and his company would remain in the Netherlands, confident that they could find more work. I took the money and gave Hob his share. We both had leather satchels attached to our saddles and we secreted the gold there. I had been paid more than Hob and I was now a rich man. I did not have the fortune my father had lost, but the money in my saddlebags and that which I had left at Edgar's inn was more than a common man might earn in three lifetimes.

As we waited to board the English ship, I said, "Now you are free from the promise you made. When you return home choose your own life. You have coins in your purse and whilst not a wealthy man, you and Alice have more than enough to make a start."

He smiled, "And the start we shall make is to be a married couple. Our time since we wed has been short and we had the spectre of war hanging over us." I nodded. Hob was wise for one so young. "And you, Captain James, what will you do?"

"It has been years since I left my home in the north to follow Captain Woodrow and Edgar. Perhaps I will visit there."

At the back of my mind hung the spectre that was Don Alvarado. He was not yet dead. He had gone to ground and lurked somewhere, no doubt with mischief on his mind, and I had no idea where he was. If I disappeared into the vastness that was England, he might not know where I was. I clung to the hope.

The two of us had a berth on one of the smaller ships. We did not travel with the general and his brother. I did not mind for I felt closer to the pikemen who were on the cog. It also meant that our horses were the only ones aboard the ship. We sailed, not to London but Southampton. The voyage would not have the meandering Thames to contend with and English ships had used it since the time of the Black Prince. I was happy about that. If Don Alvarado had watchers they would be on the Thames and not Southampton.

This was late spring and the sea was lively but with that liveliness came winds that whisked us west quickly. By the time we docked, the earl and his kinsmen had already left. They hastened to London to be at the funeral of King James. I was more cynical than I had been. The funeral was the opportunity to be seen by the new king and, perhaps, gain some honours from such a meeting. The two were returning as heroes from a campaign where the taking of one redoubt at Breda was a single victory. In General Vere's case it brought him the title 1st Baron Vere of Tilbury. I did not begrudge him the title for he had earned it, but he had earned it with the blood of many men. A drummer boy and a standard bearer were but two examples of the price that had been paid.

The death of a king was news and all the way to London we heard, as we watered our horses or enjoyed food and ale, of the effect the death had on the people. The new king was not yet married and the rumours of the Duke of Buckingham's influence had many Protestants worried. The impending marriage to Princess Henrietta was also a cause of conversation. Whilst it was not unusual for English princes and kings to marry French princesses, this would be the first since King Henry had left the Catholic church.

For the first time, we were able to approach the inn from the south. When we came down the Thames we had to cross London Bridge and there our movements could be observed. Cloaked and cowled, even though it was May, we were anonymous. It was after dark when we reached the inn and we walked our horses for the last half mile. It was my decision for I erred on the side of caution. With our horses flanking us we were invisible. When we reached the inn we took our animals into the yard and the stable. Edgar now had an ostler and Garth recognised us, "Captain James, Hob. This is a surprise and there's no error. Your wife will be pleased to see you." Just then there was a raucous roar from inside the inn. Garth shook his head, "Today was the first day for the new play at the Globe and the actors are celebrating as though the king himself was in the audience. Edgar and Mags will reap the financial reward. The actors are drinking Malmsey!"

We entered the inn and Mags and Alice were in the kitchen. Hob's welcome was overwhelming. Mags gave me a hug, "You are home from the wars safe and we thank God." She pulled back, "Home for good?"

Alice and Hob were still smothering the other in kisses and I said, quietly, "Our contract is ended and Hob has no need to go to war."

"And you?"

I shrugged, "I don't know."

She stroked my hair, "James, you are getting no younger and you have no wife. How old are you now?"

I sighed, "By my reckoning twenty-seven summers."

She shook her head, "Edgar was the same. You need to leave your mark on this world, James. You have gold enough. Seek a bride."

I laughed and gave her a sad smile, "I know not where to start."

"Nonsense, you were brought up a gentleman and you can speak languages. You have manners and you are polite. You will soon find a bride."

"No, Mags, for I live outside the circle where such brides are to be found. Edgar and Hob were lucky but I fear that my luck is restricted to the battlefield. The fact that I am still alive is my luck."

Just then Edgar came in, "We need more food the actors are…James, by all that is Holy you are a sight for sore eyes."

I smiled and clasped his outstretched arm, "You are busy. I will put my bags in the room I use and join you later, if I may?"

"Of course."

"And my room?"

Mags squeezed me, "We keep your room for you, James, you are one of the family and we have enough rooms to cater for our clientele. It is and always will be, your room."

I took my bags and slipped up the back stairs. Alice and Hob had preceded me. I was just unpacking when Mary, one of the serving girls, came up with a hot stone for the bed. "It has not been used since last you were here, Captain, and will need to be aired."

They were kind people and were like my own family now. This would be a perfect place to live except that it was London and for me London represented danger. I took off my riding boots and donned the softer shoes I wore indoors. There was a jug and bowl of water and I freshened my face. As I hung my sword and baldric from the door I wondered if I would need it again, and then realised just as quickly that, while I might not be a soldier any more, I had enemies in England and I needed protection. So long as I stayed in London then there would be danger and that danger would not be for me alone. Hob, Alice, Mags and Edgar, not to mention Pietr and his family would all be in danger through association with me. Even as I rose to leave the chamber, I knew that my sojourn in the inn would be brief. I would visit with Pietr and his family, just to let them know I was alive and then I would head north. Robert Manning had been my father's friend and was, so I hoped, still a friend to me. If nothing else I might find solace in the familiar world in which I had grown up.

I had tarried so long that by the time I descended, the inn was half empty. The actors had spent their money and staggered home. They lived squalid lives and most wasted what gold they earned. To me, they seemed like moths that sought the flame of fame but flew too close and then burned themselves out. Tom Good was the exception. He was still there but, unlike those around him, had drunk sparingly and still had his wits. Edgar was busy serving ale and so I stopped by Tom's table.

"James, returned from the wars whole, I see?"

I nodded, "And you, Tom, are garnering the glory of the accolades from your audiences."

He laughed, "Aye, they like me well enough. I have decided, James, to begin my own company. Here I work for another and the plays are restricted to the summer months. I will seek to take a company and use one of the indoor theatres north of the river. The audiences are smaller but the rewards are more regular and greater. I now have a good repertoire of plays from Shakespeare to Johnson and Webster. I know how to entertain."

"Then I wish you well." I leaned in, "I too will leave this side of the river, but I will head home to the north and spend some time there."

"You tire of London?"

"I do. It suits you but I do not like the bustle and the crowds. I yearn for a simpler life."

He nodded and put his arm under his sleeping companion, "And I will take this one back now with me. He is my comedian. I can handle the dramatic roles but William here is a master at comedy...when he is sober. Between us, we will captivate our audiences."

That was the last time I saw Tom Good. I hoped he realised his dream but just talking to him made my own dream seem clearer.

Edgar saw that I had finished and waved me to his table. There were just a handful left in the inn and the serving wenches could deal with them. The other men who handled the drunks were now doing as Edgar did and were enjoying their own ale and supper. Mary brought us over two ales and two platters of food. It was the last of the stew that they had sold in the inn. As such it was filling. The bread was no longer fresh but as the last meal I had eaten had been a pie on the road from Southampton, it was filling and what I needed.

As we ate, I told Edgar of the siege at Breda and the death of Prince Maurice. "He was a good man but I am not sure he was a good general."

I nodded my agreement, "It may be that he was outclassed. Tilly and Spinola are good generals. I fear that the Catholics will win. I have yet to see a Protestant leader who is as good. Christian of Brunswick was the best but he lost his arm and I fear, the confidence of his men. A good leader needs his men to believe in him."

Edgar laughed, "Is this the same callow youth who followed us north on the road to war? You have grown wise."

I decided to be honest with Edgar. He deserved honesty. "I will not be staying long, Edgar, I intend to return to the house where you found me. I need to find myself again. I do not know what the future holds but I cannot see it here in the fog that is London."

He nodded, "I can see that and what you do not know, James, is that Hob's seed has taken. While you were away, we learned that Alice is with child. Mags is delighted for she is to be a grandmother."

"Hob will not want to leave."

"No, and I shall make him a partner in the inn. He has natural wits and you have brought him on. We are grateful for that."

"I just did what you and Captain Woodrow did for me."

"When will you leave?"

"I will visit the Dutch merchant tomorrow. I owe him much and then I will leave here within a few days."

He nodded, "There will be tears."

"I need to go as soon as I can for the longer I am here the more likely it is that Don Alvarado will learn of my presence and I would not bring harm to this family."

"Since the house was raided I have not heard of him, but you are right to be cautious. He will be waiting beneath some rock or other. I will follow you tomorrow and spy on the spies."

I was relieved.

The next day, cloaked and cowled, I walked to Thames Street. A horse marked me out and walking I was able to join the flow of people crossing the bridge. I kept my cowl over my head and averted my gaze. Edgar would do the watching. Once at Pietr's house, I knew that Edgar would find somewhere to secrete himself. Wilkinson gave me his normal welcome, that is to say, he glared down his nose at me as though some unpleasant smell had arrived.

"I will inform the master that you have arrived unannounced once more."

I smiled. He would never change.

Pietr came to greet me and his smile was in direct contrast to Wilkinson's scowl, "It is good to see you. Come, I have a new wine I would like you to try."

Once in his office, he poured me a goblet of a heady red wine. I sipped and smiled. Raising the goblet I said, "To Prince Maurice. He was a good man and I hope his soul is safe in heaven."

"To Prince Maurice." He drank more deeply than I did. "I fear that his brother will not be as generous to me."

"Your business will suffer?"

He shook his head, "To be honest, I gave the prince better rates out of patriotic fervour. I am still a patriot but if his brother does not wish to avail himself of my ships, I will make more profit. My family will not suffer. And you?"

"I came here today to tell you that I am heading back to the north. I need to find James Bretherton once more."

"I shall miss you. I have lived vicariously through your adventures. Each time he docks, Captain van Hooft regales me with the tale of you fighting the privateers." He chuckled, "As though I have not heard it ten times before. It is a good story." He refilled his goblet, "How will I contact you? Elizabeth and I are both fond of you. Distance may be between us but old friends are not to be abandoned."

"Edgar has *'The Saddle'* in Southwark and he knows where I am to be found. He is a man, like you, that I trust."

Pietr insisted that I stay for lunch so that I could bid farewell to Elizabeth and she wept as I left. I did not see Edgar but I knew that he followed me. When he entered the inn he shook his head, "There seemed not to be any who took an interest in you, James, but stay within this inn until you leave."

That night we celebrated not only the return of Hob and I, but also the prospect of a child and, it must be said, my impending departure. I did not know just how fond Alice was of me but she kept slipping her arm through mine to tell me that she hoped the unborn child would be a boy so that they could name him James in honour of me. I had thought she would be glad to see the back of me as I had whisked Hob off to war more times than enough. I realised then that I did not understand women.

I left two days later. Hob insisted that I took Caesar. "He is your horse and he will not enjoy being stabled. My days of riding a horse to war are gone, Captain. I shall miss my adventures with you but I have a new adventure of my own; a family."

Mags packed me some food and was as tearful as though it was her own child who was leaving. Edgar said, "I know where you will be staying, James. If you need anything then send word.

Distance will not dull the friendship we share. We are sad to see you leave but I know that you have to go. Go with God."

I left the inn and this time did not cross London Bridge. Instead, I headed west to the ferry across the river close to Westminster Abbey. There were not as many ferrymen there but I would be outside the walls of London and could make good time to the long road that headed north. I had not seen any watchers but this was not the time to take the risk. For the first time in a long time, I rode alone and I felt lonely. This was my future, a life without anyone to watch my back.

Chapter 18

I had never ridden the Great North Road; I had left the north by sea and this road built by the Romans was a new one to me. I had the route for Edgar had drawn me a map. He had even identified some safer inns along the way. As he had told me, it had been some time since he had travelled the road but it was a start. I had been told to head for Walthame Cross some sixteen miles from where I began my journey. I knew it was not a great distance, but Edgar had pointed out that to find another inn where I could find safe shelter would add twenty miles to my journey. He had made the same journey himself and I took his advice. He assured me that the Four Swannes was a good inn. There was an Eleanor Cross in the town. Erected by King Edward to honour the route of his wife's coffin, many people followed the crosses as a sort of pilgrimage.

As I waited for the ferry, I studied the others crossing the river. None looked threatening and no one approached me to make conversation. That suited me. I wanted my own company. The ferry added an hour to my journey and I was glad that I had heeded the advice of Edgar. The roads leading through London to the Great North Road were also thronged. There had been many nobles who had attended the funeral of King James at Westminster Abbey and I had to weave my two horses through the crowds. I was glad when we finally left the people and their animals behind and I could let my horses open their legs. I was not worried about tiring them out. I could change horses and make good time.

I reached the town in the late afternoon. Edgar had been correct. If I had tried to push on I would have had to ride along the road in the dark. I would have been a tempting target to any footpad or brigand. I was lucky in that the inn had stalls for my two horses and a room, albeit a small one, for me. I chose a small table in the corner and ate a fine meal. As I did, I studied the map and the instructions from Edgar. The next inn was in the village of Papworth. There was no choice here. The village had just one inn and it was small. Edgar had been concerned about its inclusion in my itinerary as he had only stayed there once. I decided that I would be wary. If I thought there was danger, I would push on and find a farmer who might let me use his barn. The Great North Road drew brigands and bandits like a candle draws moths.

The inn was quiet and the innkeeper himself came over to clear my table. "You are a soldier, I see."

I nodded, "Aye, returned from the wars in the Netherlands."

He tapped his leg. I noticed he had limped, "I was a soldier, a billman." He shook his head, "I was right glad to give up the bill and take up innkeeping. I landed on my feet when I met my wife, for this was the inn of her father. After soldiering I found the life of an innkeeper easy."

Left alone with the last of my beer to finish, I reflected that he and Edgar had similar experiences. Could I be an innkeeper? As I downed my beer I laughed at my own ludicrous thoughts. Edgar had Mags to teach him how to run an inn and I knew nothing. I would have to wait until something presented itself to me.

When I left, the next morning, I saw more people than I had on the road leading to the village. Edgar's warning to keep my eyes open paid off when I spied a furtive fellow watching me. He clearly did not want me to see him and ducked into an alley when our eyes met. I headed north on the road built more than a thousand years earlier and known to the Romans as Ermine Street. I decided to push my horses. It might have been a coincidence but I was not prepared to take any chances. If someone was following me then my two horses were my best guarantee of evading them. The man I had seen was on foot. If he was working with others then it would take time to find them and pursue me. I rode hard. I still had some of the food given to me by Mags and there was always grazing and water in the villages through which I passed. I galloped through Papworth and its solitary inn. I watered the horses in Huntingdon and bought a pie from a baker. I wanted as much distance as I could between me and the furtive fellow. When night approached, I spied a track leading off from the main road. I took a chance. I rode along it and saw, at the end, a farm. There was no spiral of smoke and, as I neared it, I saw that part of the roof had fallen in. It was deserted. There would be no welcoming bed for me but, at least, I would have somewhere for the horses and I might be able to find a room that had walls and a piece of the roof.

I dismounted and let my horses drink from the water trough which had clearly seen better days. I drew my sword and pushed open the door which hung from one leather hinge. A sudden movement from my left made me start but it was a bird or a bat. Whatever it was it flew, and that meant it was not human. The house had been deserted for some time. It looked as though someone had ransacked it already for anything that was worth taking. The cross I spied, in what had been the main room, gave me an indication of who the owners had been. It was the sign of a Catholic home. The story became clearer. This was the work of locals who resented the Catholics. What had happened to the family was unclear. I quickly discovered that the house was derelict but there was one small room at the back that had a roof. I fetched the horses and tethered them to a broken beam. I used the saddle and horse blankets to make a bed for myself and ate a cold supper washed down by some ale. I slept knowing that my horses would alert me to any danger.

A bird that had come to the house to forage for insects woke me. The sun had risen and I was still whole. I saddled my horses and led them to the trough. After they had drunk, I let them graze on the long grass that had sprouted. I ate the last of my supplies. I would need to buy more this day. As the horses munched I studied the crude map. The best-laid plans concocted by Edgar were now like leaves blown from autumn trees. I had to start again. I could have turned around and gone back to London but that would not have eased my problem. By my calculations, I had seventy miles before I reached Lincoln. It was a royal town and as safe a place as I could find. Before then I would have to sleep rough. I looked for places where I might buy food. I would need oats for my horses. If they became weak then I was doomed. I chose Peterborough as the place where I would buy supplies. It had a market and Lord Burghley was lord of the manor. I had met the man once before at the court of King James and I could always find some way of seeking sanctuary with him.

I reached Peterborough not long after the hour of sext. The inns were busy and I ignored them. Instead, I bought oats for the horses, a round of cheese, some bread and a pie. I felt vulnerable as I walked around the most crowded place I had seen since London. I felt as though every eye was upon me. It was with a great sense of relief that I left and pushed on north, glancing behind me to see if I was followed. I saw no obvious signs of pursuit.

I pressed on until I came to the village of West Deeping not long before dark. I was viewed suspiciously by the men in the centre of the village. I waved at them but kept going. Darkness enveloped me and I saw no sign of a refuge. I had no choice but to enter the woods to the east of me. I made sure that I entered at a place where I would not make a mark and then turned back on myself. I walked the horses until I found a clearing and a puddle left from recent rain. They could drink and I had oats for them. I tethered them and put nosebags on them. That done, I walked back to empty my bowels. It was fortunate that I walked some distance from my horses for I had just finished when I heard the horses on the road. The road was less than thirty paces from the place I had chosen and I waited close to a tree.

The horses stopped and an English voice said, "Those men said a rider with two horses came up this road, my lord, why do we stop here? We can catch him."

A chill gripped my heart when I heard heavily accented English spoken. The speaker was Spanish. "This English mercenary is a cunning man. I have waited long enough to have vengeance on the man who killed my brother. I will not rush into anything. There is a house to the west of the road. You two go there and ask if they have seen him. Juan and I will wait here."

That told me there were four of them. Which man had I killed? I had killed many Spaniards, but most had been in battle. As I waited, listening in the dark, I came up with just a handful. The men in Throgmorton Street, the ones at the bridge and the privateer. I had been right to be cautious.

After a short time, the two men returned, "They said they had not seen anyone and we saw no hoofprints."

"Then we push on to Lincoln. He bought food in Peterborough, and he will need more."

"My lord, where is he going?"

"I know not but it is clear he is heading north. I heard a rumour that he came from the North Country. We will follow him until he is taken."

"My lord, that could take weeks."

"And what else is there? Until the word comes from Spain then we have to wait anyway. I will have this mercenary and take his head."

I waited until the horses had moved off before I risked returning to my horses. I was safe enough for the night but I could not use Lincoln. It was too dark to use the map but I knew I would have to leave the Great North Road. My enemies were ahead of me and they would be waiting.

The map showed me that my only chance to avoid Lincoln was by using Newark. Newark was known to have catholic sympathisers. That meant danger but, perversely, might mean that my Spanish pursuer would not think to look there. I intended to push hard and buy supplies in Newark before rejoining the road north of Lincoln. I reached Newark at noon, and after watering my horses, bought what I needed before leaving quickly. There were many people in the market town. While that afforded me some anonymity the fact that I had two horses marked me out. It could not be helped.

I found another wood after dark, having travelled fifteen more miles from Newark. But for the oats, my horses would be in a poor condition. I was glad that they had been so pampered at '*The Saddle*'. When I rejoined the road to York I did so cautiously. I peered up and down the road and, seeing no riders, risked riding on the road. I was looking for four riders. When I heard hooves galloping from the south, in the late afternoon on one of the loneliest sections of road I had encountered, my instincts made me peer behind. It was just two riders but they were galloping hard and I was suspicious. My pistols were in holsters on my saddle. Since the encounter with the Spaniard, I had kept them loaded. I might need to use them. If I had kept riding hard then it would have made the two riders suspicious and so I not only slowed but stopped, as though one of my horses was injured.

The two men were cloaked and were clearly soldiers. As soon as one of them spoke I recognised his voice. It was one of the Englishmen who had been with the Spaniards.

They each had a pistol but they were in holsters. The nearest rider said, "You are Captain James Bretherton?"

Where the idea came from I have no idea but I spoke in Dutch and said that I was Christian van Hooft. I had confused them. The other man said, "It is not the man."

The first man was suspicious, however, and said, "Two horses and the description is the one his lordship gave us. It costs us nothing to take him back to Don Alvarado for questioning."

I now knew who was hunting me and I knew my fate. I would be possibly tortured and definitely killed. I had to be as ruthless as the men who were hunting me. The man's words signed their death warrant. I had my hands on my pistols and I drew and fired in one motion. I killed one man outright. My ball took his head. The other was hit in the shoulder. He slipped from his horse and was dragged by the stirrup. When his head hit the wall that was adjacent to the road, I knew he was dead.

I could not afford to answer questions so I put the two bodies on the backs of their horses and led them north. Darkness would soon be upon me and I sought a refuge. Desperate times call for desperate measures and when I found the ford on the Trent, just as night fell, I led the horses down to it. Sheltering in the bank I took the bodies from the backs of the horses. I took everything from them that might identify them and then slipped their bodies into the water. The current took them. By morning they would be many miles away from here. I put their pistols and swords on Caesar and then took the saddles from the backs of the two horses. I hid them as best as I could in a stand of trees and then I took all four horses across the ford. It was good that I had done this with Caesar before now. My two warhorses dragged the other two. Once clear of the water, I took the first road I could that led north. I passed very few villages and I kept going until I found a recently harvested field of barley. I let go of the two horses which happily grazed on the stubble. They would be found and either the finder would be an honest man who would report their finding or, more likely, he would take them as a gift. Either way, we were ten miles from where I had hidden their saddles. I was more concerned with hiding from Don Alvarado. I knew just how persistent he could be.

My problem was that I had to get back on the Great North Road for the smaller roads were slowing me down. I rode hard to reach the road and made it after dark. It was a lonely section of road and my horses were tired. I found a sheltered spot between a stand of trees and after seeing to my horses and giving them almost all of the oats, I wrapped myself in my cloak and had a fitful night of sleep resting against the bole of a tree. My restless horses woke me before dawn and I saddled them and mounted quickly. As dawn broke I saw the sign that told me Selby was just three miles away. There I could find food but there was also the danger that my foes were ahead of me. Don Alvarado could have hired more men. I could not assume that there were just two waiting for me. I still hoped that I had left them behind me on the road. I had disappeared and in that disappearance would lie doubt in their minds.

Before King Henry had dissolved the monasteries there had been an abbey. Some of the buildings still remained but the village was not as busy as it had been before the Reformation. This was an agricultural area and I bought more oats for my horses as well as some early apples. I dined in an inn where I ate hot food and drank good ale. This was like being on campaign again and a good soldier would fill his boots when he could. I knew, from the mile counters, that I had less than fifteen miles before I reached York. Whilst that was still far from the place I called home, it would be close enough for me to try to make it in one day, if I could reach York. I had loaded my pistols when I rested by the tree and with three pistols in my holsters and a sharpened sword I was ready for any threat.

The threat, when it came, was not to me. I was nearing Riccall, a tiny village not far from Selby when, as the road descended towards an abandoned dwelling, I heard raised voices from ahead. The road twisted around a stand of trees hiding whatever the problem was but I prepared myself by releasing the pistols from their holsters. The simple leather loop was just designed to stop the weapons from falling out when galloping. I moved Caesar, the horse I was riding, onto the grass verge to make the hooves of both horses less noisy.

I heard the voices before I saw the people, "You have horses and you have money. We are poor people. If you are a Christian then it is your duty to share with us. Dismount and hand over what you have. We do not want to hurt you but we shall."

Dropping my reins and using my knees to direct Caesar, I came around the bend and saw four men standing, holding short swords. There was a man, I took him to be a preacher from his dress, and a young woman, riding side saddle. They rode hackneys. I did not slow and I used my voice to command although the two pistols I held were commanding enough. "Disperse and let these travellers pass."

The larger of the men was belligerent. I recognised his type. There had been a couple like him in Captain de Vries' company. They were bullies and as such could be dealt with. "What have we here? A dandy with a couple of pistols. I think, boys that we all shall have a horse soon."

I had kept moving and I was less than ten feet from the man. More importantly, I had placed Caesar between the footpads and the two travellers. I aimed the pistols at the bully and the man next to him, "My friend, I am not a dandy but I am a soldier. I have fought in the Dutch wars and I hit that at which I aim. I have two pistols loaded and ready to fire. If you move then you and your companion will die. I have a third pistol and believe me I know how to draw and fire. That will leave the last man left to face me and my sword." The fourth foot pad was a youth of sixteen or so. I smiled, "So, son, do you think that you can fence as well as me?" I raised the pistols and kicked Caesar so that he moved forward to put the guns, whose barrels must have looked like cannons, closer to the bully and his companion. His companion and the youth were the first to bolt.

"I will not die here, come, Jack, let us return home."

The two ran leaving the bully and the last man. "Now, that leaves two of you and I have two pistols."

The bully suddenly lunged at me with his sword. My pistol cracked and smoke obscured him. When it cleared his sword lay on the ground and he was clutching his mangled hand. Levelling my other pistol at the last man I said, "Now go and take your lives as a gift."

"Bastard!" The bully spat out the words but his companion was already staunching the bleeding. The unwounded man wrapped a cloth around the wound and they took off after the other two. I holstered the pistol I had fired but kept the other aimed at the fleeing men. When I was sure they had gone, I dismounted and picked up the short sword.

The two people I had rescued had been silent but as I dismounted the man said, "We are in your debt..."

"Captain James Bretherton. You are welcome. This is a dangerous road and a better watch should be kept."

"Aye, you are right. I am Reverend Robert Neville, and this is my daughter, Charlotte. We are going to my new parish in York. I can see by your buff coat that you are a soldier and we are grateful for your intervention."

"I am heading for York too, but I fear that I cannot ride far with you."

The woman, for I saw now that she was not a girl, said, "I pray you, why not? There may be more like these on the road."

"Let us say, Mistress Neville, that I have enemies on the road too. Besides, if I ride ahead of you, I can clear the road of any danger. Riccall is just ahead. I will ride there with you."

She smiled and, in that smile, I saw beauty I had not seen since my mother had died, "You are an honourable man, but I would still prefer your company, for it seems to me that you know how to handle danger."

"That I do, but I would not bring that danger to another."

The reverend said, "He is right, daughter, and the chances of other footpads are now slimmer. The man in the inn in Selby had warned us of a group of footpads. Now that they have been chased away we should be safe."

I mounted and rode so that the woman was between me and her father. "Your parish is in York?"

"Yes, St Helens, just north of the river. And your home is...?"

"It was in Piercebridge but my parents died some years ago. I am returning from the wars to find some peace."

"Amen to that, all men deserve peace. If you do not mind me saying so, you are young to be a captain and to have experience of war."

"Believe me there are younger men than I who are generals and have more skill. The Duke of Brunswick is younger than I am and yet he commanded well against the Spanish."

"The Papists are still a threat I fear."

"And you Mistress Neville, what are your hopes?"

"I shall keep house for my father."

There was an awkward silence that was only filled when the reverend said, "My daughter was engaged to be married but the young man to whom she was engaged fell from his horse whilst trying to leap a fence. He broke his neck."

"I am sorry, Mistress."

She gave a sad smile, "Geoffrey was a wild one. I had hoped that his wild days were behind him but he wished for one last adventure before we were wed and he raced his friends." She sighed and put her hand to her mouth.

"When I was offered this parish, more than two hundred miles away, it seemed a perfect opportunity to put the past behind us."

"And yet footpads who prey on the innocent were waiting. I wish I could stay with you but I would not bring my danger to your life."

We reached Riccall and the pistol shot had alerted the villagers who were gathered in knots talking when we clattered into the village.

"Did you hear a gunshot?"

I patted my holster, "That was me. These travellers were set upon by four footpads and I discharged my weapon at them. One was wounded."

The headman nodded, "That would be Ralph and his gang. The Sherriff should do something about them."

I dismounted to let my horses drink at the trough, "Are you not men? You know who these men are and yet you allow them to cause distress to honest folk. For shame."

The headman said, "Ralph was a soldier."

"Well, he is now a soldier with an injured hand. Perhaps now he might be cowed." He nodded, "How far to the next place of safety for these people?"

"Fulford is just a few miles up the road and York is only eight miles away."

I nodded, "Then you should be safe."

While the horses drank I reloaded my pistol. I saw Charlotte Neville watching me. "Do you think you shall need it again, Captain James?"

"If I do not reload it then I shall be sure to." Once done I mounted, "If I have the chance then when I am settled into my home I should like to call on you."

The reverend beamed, "It would be an honour and I, for one, should like to hear of your adventures. I am sure that they would be illuminating."

"Farewell."

I left the village, but I confess that I wondered if I should have stayed with them. There was something about Charlotte Neville that stirred something within me. I could not identify what it was and that disturbed me. I had just eight miles to go and York seemed to me a haven. There was a Sherriff there and I felt sure that I would be safe. I let my horses gallop along the empty road. My mind was distracted. I had allowed the chance meeting to enter my head and that is never a good thing. After the tiny hamlet of Naburn with just three houses, the road drew close to the river. I did not even notice the trees for I was already anticipating a night in an inn and hot food. My mind was still wrestling with the memory of Charlotte Neville when the harquebus opened fire.

My life was saved by a couple of things. One, the harquebusier had been too hasty. He should have waited until I was closer and secondly, the flash from the gun alerted me so that I was already drawing a pistol and slipping to my right. The ball hit my left arm and the buff coat took some of the force. I had seen the flash and I tried, as best as I could, to steer Caesar towards it. To one who was not a soldier, it would have seemed like madness to head towards danger but I knew how long such a weapon took to load. I saw the man frantically reloading and I raised my pistol to fire into his face. The ball hit the harquebus and drove some of the metal into his eyes; it was a mortal wound. It was then that Don Alvarado fired his wheel lock and he hit my left leg. He was close enough so that the ball went through the buff coat and, with a wounded arm already, I found myself slipping from Caesar's back. I kicked my foot from my stirrup and hit the ground hard. My right shoulder screamed in pain.

Instinct took over and I rose as quickly as I could to my feet. I was drawing my sword already when Don Alvarado lunged at me with his sword. I was unable to totally block the blow and he scored a hit on my right arm. I felt the blood flow.

The Spanish noble saw my wounds and a wolfish grin appeared on his face, "You have the luck of the devil but that luck has run out. I swore, when my brother died at London Bridge, that one day I would end your life. It has cost me three men but it is worth it to see you now, crippled and helpless. You have no innkeeper to help you now. I will cut you to pieces and leave your …"

I did not discover what he would be leaving for I took my chance as he gloated and, while I still had some strength, lunged at his middle. He had no buff coat and he was already anticipating my death. He failed to block the strike and my sword entered his left side. I saw the blood on my blade. I did not make the mistake of wasting my breath. Instead, I watched his sword. I had learned to be a swordsman but this Spanish noble would have been trained from youth to fight with a blade. I could not afford to underestimate him.

"Protestant scum!" He was angry and he charged at me. I blocked each blow with my sword. I was aware that I was losing blood and that, eventually, it would weaken me and I would die.

My problem was that I had a left leg that I could not rely upon and a wound to my left arm that prevented me from drawing my dagger. He had no such restriction and he drew his own dagger. The movement made blood spurt from his wound and gave me hope. I slashed my sword at his face and he was forced to raise his two blades to block it. More blood spurted from his wound. I was close enough so that our faces were just a foot apart and I used an Edgar trick. I headbutted him. He was not expecting it and his nose broke. Such a wound makes eyes water and I brought my sword across his body. I hit his left arm and his dagger clattered to the ground but the effort had made my own wounds bleed more. When he lunged at me with his sword I was not quick enough to block the blow, and his sword entered my already wounded left thigh. I gritted my teeth as he drew back for the coup de grace. He had planned on toying with me but he now knew he had to end this fight as quickly as possible. I used a last trick. I could not rely on my left leg but my right was still whole. As he lunged at me I spun on my good leg. My left leg screamed in pain as I swung it around but when my sword slashed, it was across his unprotected back. The razor-sharp blade drove through his fine clothes and into his flesh. My momentum and the weight of the stroke broke his backbone. He fell at my feet. I watched his blood as it poured from his body and was then aware that my own blood was puddling with it. Everything became dark. It was as though black clouds had appeared but there was no rain; instead, I found myself falling into a black hole from which there was no escape.

Chapter 19

Charlotte Neville

When we watched the soldier who had saved us ride up the road, I felt sad. How could it be that I had just met the man and yet he had enchanted me? As we picked our way along the road I rationalised that he had saved us and that was the reason for the strange feelings. Perhaps our lives had not been in danger but we could have lost everything. Was this just gratitude that I felt? It had been six months since Geoffrey had died. In that time, I had prepared myself for life as a spinster who cared for her father. I had resigned myself to life as a housekeeper, but meeting Captain James had stirred longings in me.

The gunshots and the smoke that came from the north made us both stop. Had the footpads returned or had Captain James, as he had feared, suffered an attack? Just then I heard hooves on the road and turning saw the headman from Riccall and his son riding two weary-looking sumpters. They carried swords.

"We heard the pistols. If this is Ralph and his men I will hang them myself! You two wait here and my son and I will investigate."

My voice surprised even myself, "No, my father and I will come with you. You are two alone. Perhaps our presence might frighten them off."

My father smiled, "My daughter is right. We owe the Captain. We will ride behind you."

We came upon the four horses and the three bodies. The horses had wandered to the grass verge and were munching away. The headman shook his head, "That is not Ralph, but I fear that the captain is dead. Peter, collect the horses, we will put them on the backs of their horses and take them to York. This business is for the Sherriff."

I leapt from the back of my horse and raced to the captain. There was so much blood that I was sure the headman was right but when I touched his neck I felt movement. "He is alive!" I tore open his doublet and, removing it, saw the wound made by what looked like a ball. I ripped the neckcloth from one of the dead men and pressed it close to the wound.

My father joined me, "She is right. Let us bind the wounds and get him to a surgeon."

The headman shook his head, "He has lost so much blood already…"

My voice was angrier than I intended, "Then every second we wait loses him more. Tear the cloth from the dead and my father and I will staunch the bleeding." We found all the wounds and I realised that none of them was life-threatening. Had we not arrived when we had then he might have bled out but our arrival meant that he had a chance of life. My father forced some brandy taken from one of the saddlebags of the two men who had clearly attacked him, into his mouth. I did not like it but we had to drape his body over the saddle of his larger horse, the one without a saddle. Letting the headman and his son lead the others, my father and I rode with the wounded man between us.

When we reached Fulford we had luck. There was a vet there who had just visited a farmer to attend to a horse and he was able to stitch and cleanse the wounds. He shook his head, "I am not a surgeon. He needs better care than I can give him."

My father paid the vet and we hurried to York. We spied Mickelgate, the main entrance to the city from the south. Once we reached the gate into the city the headman pointed, "There is a church there, St Mary's. I believe that as it is close to the former abbey they will have doctors."

One of the town watch said, "Aye, they have one there and he served in the wars. He can tend to wounds."

The headman said, "Take the captain there and I will report this sorry affair to the Sherriff."

The church was not far from the gate and the noise of our hooves brought a priest from within. My father said, "I am Reverend Neville and this brave man was attacked on the road. He needs attention."

The priest nodded, "I have experience of wounds. Fetch him within." We helped to carry him into the kitchen of the house close to the church. We laid him on the table.

My father said, "We can leave him now, daughter. He is in good hands. We must hasten to my new parish."

I could not believe his words. "Father, is this the act of the Good Samaritan? This man saved us and we, in turn, are saving him. I will not stir until he speaks and this doctor says that he will live."

I had shocked my father. He had never heard me stand up to him and even I wondered at my own reaction. He nodded, "I leave her in your hands, my friend."

"This is God's house and she will be safe here." He smiled, "Besides, I can use another pair of hands."

After he had gone I took off my riding cloak. The doctor washed his hands and pointed to the bowl. "If you are to help then wash your hands in this bowl of vinegar. We have much to do and I hope that you are not squeamish. There will be blood."

I shook my head, "I do not know if I am squeamish but I shall do my best."

The doctor stripped the captain down to his undergarments. It was then I saw the extent of his wounds. "It is good that he is unconscious. The body helps us. I will have to work fast; whoever sewed him up stemmed the bleeding but I do not know what remains in the wound."

I steeled myself not to faint. I did not look at the blood and the bones I could see beneath the flesh, but instead I studied the young man's face. He was handsome. I had thought Geoffrey was handsome but, in comparison, he was a boy and here was a man.

The doctor began to pick around at the arm, "This is the worst wound for it was a bigger ball. Whoever stitched him removed the ball but I will have to open the stitches to see if any foreign bodies have been driven into the wound. They can make the blood poisoned and kill. Hold his arm. He is unconscious but his body may move involuntarily."

I put my hands above and below the wound. As the doctor used a pair of tweezers to pull out pieces of lead and cloth I felt the arm try to move. I found myself smiling. He was alive. The other serious wound was the ball to his leg and, surprisingly, the sword thrust seemed to cause the doctor the least trouble. It took some hours but eventually, he was healed and bound.

The doctor put his hand on my arm, "You have courage. I know of many men who would not have faced what you did."

"I did not even think about the blood. I just knew that I had to be strong, for this man saved us and then put his own life in jeopardy so that we would not risk further attack. That is true courage. Steeling myself not to faint is nothing in comparison."

"Wait here. I will fetch the curate and the verger. We shall carry him somewhere he can be more comfortable."

I had no idea where the curate and verger were to be found for the two were away for a long time. Left alone with the wounded man I stroked and straightened his hair. I found my hand touching his face and I wondered at my own boldness. I took his hands and placed them at his waist and as I did so one of his hands squeezed a little. I thought he might be awakening but his eyes remained closed. I kept hold of his hand.

"Captain James, what brought you into our lives I know not, but I am glad that we met. Helping the doctor gave me a purpose I had not felt before. I pray that you live through this night so that I can tell you when you are awake."

The doctor said, from behind me, "He shall live." He nodded to the two men with him and they gently lifted the captain and carried him into what looked to be a living room. "The curate and I share a room and it is up the stairs. We will let him sleep here on this couch before the fire. One of us will watch him."

I shook my head, "I will watch, doctor. There is a chair there and when he wakes I would have him see me first." I suddenly realised how that sounded. "Does that sound foolish?"

"No, you are a kind woman and if you do not mind then stay by all means." He turned, "Verger, find somewhere for the three horses. Absalon, fetch food and drink for the young lady and a platter for the man for when he wakes." The two left and the doctor banked up the fire.

I was curious, "The man at the gate said that you were a doctor. How is it that you live in a house by a church?"

"This is my parish. I was a soldier once and tended to my comrades' wounds. If you had come to me with anything other than a wound I might have struggled. I gave up the sword and took up the cross. I see in this young man another warrior. He has a good sword that has seen martial service. I shall be interested in his tale."

"All that I know is that he is Captain James Bretherton of Piercebridge and he has recently returned from the Dutch wars."

Just then the verger came back, "I have unsaddled the horses and fetched in his weapons and clothes. I also found these in his saddlebags. I thought it best to keep them close to him." He took out two leather bags, both were heavy. He opened one and I saw gold and silver within.

The doctor said, "Perhaps that was why he was attacked. There is a fortune there. Thank you, verger, it will be safe with us."

I must have dozed off for when I woke the fire was dying. I refreshed it with kindling and drank some of the drink the doctor had left. As I turned around I saw that the captain's eyes were open.

I hurried to his side, "You live!"

He smiled and croaked, "Then I am not in heaven?"

I took the cup the doctor had left and cradling his head in my right arm poured a little into his mouth. "No, Captain James, but you almost were. A doctor has saved you."

He frowned, "Why are you here?"

"You wish me to leave?"

"No, it is just that… where is your father? You should not have to tend to me."

I laughed. The man clearly did not know women. "I am here because I choose to be. You saved us and I am repaying the kindness. Now sleep. The doctor said it was the best medicine. I will wait here at your side and when the doctor confirms that all is well then I shall leave and go to my father."

"Then I hope he says I am still ill for I would have you at my side for as long as possible."

There must have been some medicine in the drink for before I could reply the captain had drifted off to sleep. Stroking his hair I said, "And I would stay here too, Captain James, for you have a hold over me and I know not why."

I was asleep when the doctor returned and he woke me. I saw that the captain was sitting up and was being fed broth by a young woman, "This is my cook, Maria." The cook smiled as she patiently spooned the broth into the wounded man. "We did not wish to wake you."

"I am just glad that you are able to eat." I was aware that I still wore the clothes in which I had travelled. They were besmeared and spattered with blood. I stood, "I had better get to my father. Do you know where the parish of St Helens is?"

The doctor said, "The verger will show you." The captain tried to rise. "You are going nowhere, Captain James."

"Will I see you again?"

I cocked my head to one side, "Do you wish to?"

"Of course."

"Then I will return when I look less like someone who has been dragged through a hedgerow backwards."

"You look perfect to me."

I shook my head, "Doctor, you had better examine his eyes for I fear there is something wrong with them."

The verger led me to the Ouse Bridge and then into the busy part of York. It was not far from the house my father and I had been given. The church was a small one but it would suit my father. He beamed when he saw me and gave me a tour of the house. Like the one in which I had stayed the previous night, it was small and my room was little better than a broom cupboard. It would suffice.

"And how is the young man?"

"He lives and for that, I thank the doctor and, of course, God."

My father had a look of concern on his face, "Daughter, I fear that you are smitten with this soldier and I counsel you against it. The feelings you have are not the foundation for a life together. You lost Geoffrey and I think that it has coloured your judgement. This is a passing fancy. It is a dream from which you shall wake. Immerse yourself in the parish and you will forget him."

My father meant well but he was wrong and I knew it. The captain and I had bonded. I felt more for him already than I had ever felt for Geoffrey. I had grown up living close to Geoffrey and our parents had decided that we were a couple. I had just accepted it for Geoffrey had been a personable young man. What I felt for the captain made me blush.

"I will go to the market and buy food. I take it the cupboard is bare?"

"It is." He handed me a purse. It was not a heavy one, "Choose wisely, Charlotte, for we have to cut our cloth appropriately."

I found a basket in the kitchen and with a cloak about me I went to the markets and shops. My mind was distracted but the act of shopping forced me to think of matters other than Captain James. When I returned home, not long before noon, there was a liveried soldier there with the horses from the fight.

As I approached they turned and my father said, "This is my daughter, Charlotte, she tended to the young man who was attacked."

The soldier bowed, "The Sherriff has placed the heads of the two dead men on the gates at Monk's Bar. He has fined the dead men for their attack but he thinks that their belongings, including the horses, should be shared by the three who were most inconvenienced."

I frowned, "What about the men from Riccall?"

"They have been compensated for their time." He turned back to my father, "Can I leave the division to you, Reverend Neville?"

"You can." After the soldier had gone my father was almost joyous, "We have a bounty from God. This is most unexpected and welcome."

"Father, it came from Captain James."

"Just so and we will see that he has his share."

As much as I wanted to return to the captain I knew that I owed it to my father to sort out the house. He would have to prepare the first sermon, for Sunday was just two days away. The result was that despite my need and desire to return to the patient I worked until dark, and knew it would be the next day before I could travel back to the other church. I rose early and made breakfast. I left as soon as I could and hurried to the wounded soldier.

Chapter 20

When Charlotte left me I felt an emptiness. Was this what Hob had felt for Alice? Edgar for Mags? Had my father felt this way when he had met my mother? I was confused for this seemed so sudden. Her words, when she had left me, gave me hope but I wondered if I was reading too much into them.

The doctor entered with more broth. "You are recovering well, Captain James." He smiled, "Perhaps it is the young lady's ministrations, eh?"

"Doctor, you are a truthful man, I believe, and a man of God. Answer me truly, do you believe there is hope that such an angel as Charlotte Neville could consider a future with me?"

He paused mid-spoonful and said, "I am a man of God and a soldier. I understand you more than the ways of women but what I saw, from the moment you two arrived, was that she was smitten by you. Love between a man and a woman is an unknown for me, but when I saw her watching you it was not the watching of one who nurses but that of someone seeking hope. If you want the advice of a confirmed bachelor, then pursue her."

That pleased me, "And when can I rise?"

"First you need to pass water and empty your bowels. When that is done you may dress and walk about. I confess that your presence here makes life hard but I do not want you to think you have to leave. Two days of walking should see you ready to leave. You are heading for Piercebridge, I believe?"

"That was my plan but…"

"Take it from an old soldier. Keep to your original plan. The distance will help you to make the right decision about Charlotte Neville."

I made water that night and the next morning emptied my bowels. The two functions delighted the doctor who allowed me to dress. I walked around the church grounds in the fresh air. He gave me a stick but it was not needed. The wound to my leg had been a clean one and I was able to put weight on it. The worst of my wounds was the ball that had struck my arm. When I returned indoors the doctor examined me and said, "You will need to return to me in ten days time to have the stitches removed."

"Then I can leave?"

"I said two days of walking. You have had one. If tomorrow is successful then you leave the next day."

I knew I would go to visit Charlotte on the third day. I would prepare for the meeting as though I was readying for an attack on a redoubt. I would leave nothing to chance. That night I laid out the clothes I would wear and cleaned my boots. The simple acts, allied to the walking I had done, tired me out and I slept on the couch like a baby.

The doctor, curate and I had risen and were at breakfast when there was a knock at the door. It was Charlotte. When the doctor brought her in and I rose she beamed, "You can walk. God be praised." She smiled at the doctor, "And you too, doctor."

"I of all people know that God gave me my skill. Sit."

There were just four chairs in the tiny kitchen and my knees touched Charlotte's. I blushed. She too felt the knee but did not move it. Instead, she told us of the Sherriff's decision. "So, you must come, before you leave, to visit with my father and then receive your share of the unexpected bounty."

"That will be tomorrow."

Her face fell, "You leave tomorrow?"

"I have imposed enough on the good doctor, and if I am to begin a new life I need to start as soon as possible. When I lay bleeding on that road I thought my life was over. God has given it back to me and I must start anew."

Her voice was small as she said, "Alone."

I put my hand on hers, "I hope not."

I know not about the rest of the world, the Antony and Cleopatras, the Troilus and Cressidas. I had heard of literary romances from Tom Good, but when I put my hand on hers and she put her other on mine, it felt as though love had descended and filled that humble room.

The doctor smiled, "This is meant to be."

We chattered away like magpies oblivious to the fact that the curate and the doctor left us. It was only when the woman who cooked for the doctor, Maria, came to clear the table that we knew.

"Would you care to walk about the grounds? It is a pleasant church and the doctor says I need to walk."

"Do not do too much. I would not have you undo the doctor's good work."

"As I said to the doctor, this is the first day of a new life. I must embrace the future."

She was emboldened by my touching of her hand and said, "And what is that future, Captain James? Do you go back to being a soldier?"

"I do not think so. When I left London, my intention was to return to the home of the man who took me in when my father lost all and to seek his advice."

"And that has changed?"

"You know it has for you came into my life and that has changed things."

Her hand reached out to touch mine, "How so?"

"I would not have you leave it."

Her fingers squeezed mine, "Nor me but what do we do about it?"

There was a stone table close to the lych gate. It was where they placed the coffins before entering the churchyard. We sat there. "I would have you as my wife but I am a practical man. If you are to be my wife then I need a home to take you to. It will not be in York. Could you leave your father's side?"

"When Geoffrey died I had no hope and I clung to my father like a lost sailor to jetsam. He does not need me and since I have met you, I have come to dread a life cleaning house and smiling at parishioners. If that was a proposal, then I accept. As for a home? I would live in a tent if it meant I could live with you."

"No, I may not be as rich as once I thought I would be, before the Virginia debacle, but we can have a home."

"Then wherever that is will please me."

I raised her hand and kissed the back of it, "You know that tomorrow I shall leave and may be away for a week or more, but I swear that I will return."

"My life ended when Geoffrey died but I was reborn when I nursed you. We are both reborn. I can wait."

"Good."

"Do not forget that you have items and animals to collect from my father's house."

"Then on the morrow, I shall come to speak to the two of you on my way north."

Just then the bells of the Minster tolled sext. She stood, "I have been away for some hours and I left without warning my father. I must leave but I will see you tomorrow?"

I stood, "You will."

Standing on her toes she kissed me on the lips. I felt transported. When I opened my eyes she was giggling, "What a wanton I am but I think that God smiles on this. How could he do other for this was meant to be." She turned and headed back to St Helens' Church.

The curate had been tending the graves, unseen, and as he rose he smiled, "She is right, Captain and even I can see that." He pointed at the graves. "These are the graves of my parents. They died in an outbreak of the plague. I know that they were happy together and when they died they were reunited. They had just twelve years of marriage. I hope that you and the lady have longer but whatever time you have, use it well for life is parlous, is it not?"

"Aye, the doctor and I both know that. We have seen life snuffed out like a candle."

The doctor did not wish to take it but I insisted that he accept the gold guilder for his care of me. "Use it for the poor, or the church, I care not but I owe you my life and, while I believe that it is worth more than a one guilder, I will sleep happier knowing that a debt is paid."

The verger gave me instructions and I rode Henry and led Caesar through York, across the Ouse Bridge to the church of St Helens that lay in a busy section of streets. I steeled myself as I stiffly dismounted. My leg had complained when I had mounted and it did so when I dismounted but it had not caused me pain when I rode. I took that to be a good thing.

I had barely knocked on the door when a beaming Charlotte opened it, "My father is within."

I took off my hat and ducked below the low lintel. The Reverend Neville was in his office, writing the sermon he would deliver on his first Sunday. He stood and smiled, "It is good to see you whole, Captain. You are here for what is rightfully yours?"

232

I said, "Partly, but also to ask for that which is now yours and would be mine."

He frowned, "You speak in riddles, Captain."

"I would marry your daughter, Reverend Neville, and I seek your permission."

His frown turned to a smile, "I may be an old man, Captain James, but even I have the eyes to see the change that you have wrought on my daughter. I pray that this is not the whirlwind of a summer storm that will leave devastation in its wake, but thus far you have shown yourself to be an honourable man."

"And I give my word, as an officer and a gentleman, that nothing is more important to me than the welfare and well-being of Charlotte."

He stood and proffered a hand, "Then you have my permission." He sat and took out two purses from his drawer, "The Sherriff sent these, the proceeds from the sale of the goods of the murderers. There are also two horses." He pushed one of the purses towards me, "You know horses better than I do. I will let you choose the one you take."

I shook my head, "Charlotte will need a horse to return to the home I shall buy. I will let my bride-to-be make that choice."

He laughed, "A good start and I can see that you are a wise man."

As much as I wished to linger, I knew I had to leave. Reverend Neville said that he would read out the banns so that whenever I returned, we could be married. I passed the Minster and left by the Marygate as I headed north to Piercebridge. My fine plans to ride the sixty miles were dashed by my wounds. I feared I might burst the stitches and was forced to stop in Northallerton to stay in an inn. The result was that I reached Roger Manning's home the next day by noon. He was with his son, Peter. The boy had grown and Roger was fencing with him. Peter was now a youth and I saw that he had skills. I had started to teach those skills and his father had honed them. Would he go to war too?

When my horses clattered into the yard they both stopped and turned. The delight on Roger's face was clear to see. I stiffly dismounted and he raced over to embrace me. "The warrior returns." I could not help but wince at his grip and he stepped back, frowning, "You are wounded?"

I nodded, "And I have tales to tell. Would it be too much of an imposition to ask for shelter for a few days?"

"Of course not. We are delighted and you shall stay as long as you wish. Your return has brought joy to me and to Peter."

"Your wife?"

He shook his head, "Caroline succumbed to a winter chill two years since and did not recover. There are just the two of us now."

I was sad because Caroline had been a kind woman. It made my decision to marry all the more urgent. A man never knew how long he would have on this earth.

"Come, Peter, take James' horses to the stables." He put his arm around me. "All these years and not a letter. We knew not if you lived or died."

His chastisement was justified. I could have written. I am not sure how long the letters might have taken to reach him but if I had sent them from London...Hindsight is a wonderful thing and you see all the things that you could have done and yet did not.

Roger's house was huge and there was plenty of room for me. He was still a successful farmer. He never made a fortune but he was frugal with what he did spend. My father, in contrast, had enjoyed a fortune and wasted it. I changed from my travelling clothes and joined the two of them in the cosy parlour I remembered from my time in his home. Peter, too, had changed and I saw that he was, indeed, a fine young man. He had grown.

Alice, the housekeeper, squealed when she entered the room with the wine, "You are back, Master James, and a man grown. God be praised."

Roger smiled, "Master James is staying for a day or so, Alice."

The wine poured, Roger sat back in his leather armchair, "While you changed, I had the cook begin a fine meal for us. We have some hours before we dine. Begin your story where you left us and omit nothing. There are no ladies here to have their sensibilities hurt by your words."

I did so, realising that Charlotte would need to hear all before we wed. I owed it to her. After hearing of some of the things I had done she might not approve. I told the tale chronologically and I avoided making criticisms of the leaders I had served. I saw their eyes widen when I spoke of King James. That was the one point that Roger interrupted me as he stood to top up our goblets, "Hobnobbing with kings and princes. Your father would have enjoyed that."

I nodded, "But not my mother."

"Not your mother, you are right. I pray you to continue and forgive the interruption."

When I came to Don Alvarado and the chase up the Great North Road I found myself speaking more quickly. I was almost out of breath when I reached the part where I nearly died. I did not gloss over the meeting with Charlotte and my infatuation. It was key to my tale. I timed my ending to perfection for the housekeeper came in to tell us that food was ready. We went to the dining room.

We said Grace and the food was served. We did the food justice by not speaking. When the platters were cleared Roger asked, "And so you wish to marry this angel of mercy who tended to you?"

"I do."

"You know that your motives may come from gratitude."

I had considered that and I nodded, "I can see how another might think so but here," I tapped my chest, "I know that she is the one for me."

It was almost as though Roger had set me a test and I had passed for he beamed, "And your future? You will live in York?"

"I would live here in this village. I had thought to live closer to where I was born, but the memory would be too hard to bear for that house now belongs to Sir Giles Wyndham. I was happy here and I would live here. The question is, can I afford it?"

"The price is not a problem. I have a row of cottages that I own for those who work on my land. Two are empty but they are not palatial."

Peter piped up, "You could build. We have land, Father, and he could build a house here."

"A good idea but he brings a bride here, Peter. Take a cottage, James, and see how your bride fares. There is a quarry nearby with good stone and there is a piece of land close to the river that would make an excellent dwelling."

"Thank you, Roger, you have given me more than I deserve."

"You are as dear to me as Peter. Your father was my best friend and I saw his faults. I have always felt guilt that I did not do more to dissuade him from the perilous path he trod."

I nodded and drank the wine.

There was silence and then he said, "But it does not provide you with occupation. We have danced around your profession, James, but it seems to me that you are a soldier. All that you have told us points to your skill. You are not just a soldier but a leader. You are ill-suited to a time of peace."

He was right. I was not the type of man to sit idly by doing nothing.

When he gave me a solution I did not like it. "Sir Giles Wyndham is Lord Lieutenant of the County. He is also distantly related to you. He has the militia to train." He shook his head, "Sir Giles has no idea how to do it."

"But Sir Giles…"

"Will be impressed by your association with King James and Prince Maurice and you are distantly related. I will speak with him. If nothing else you could train the militia."

It was not an ideal job for it would only be for one day each month but it would be something and that might give me the chance to think of what I might want to do. When I had come north I had not begun to think of an occupation. I was just running away to hide, I suppose. Meeting Charlotte changed all of that. I had her and a future family to think of.

The first task, the next day, was to choose which of the two cottages I wished. One was slightly larger than the other and I took that one. They were furnished but I could see that I would need a better bed. I paid the carpenter in the village to make me one. Roger then rode to speak to Sir Giles. Surprisingly the man I had detested when he had visited my home seemed keen and I was invited, along with Roger, to dine with him. Perhaps time had mellowed him or changed me but I did not find him so pompous. He spoke kindly of my parents and seemed keen for me to be his captain of militia.

He smiled, "God chose not to give me sons. I always envied your father and Roger here for they sired two fine sons. I have daughters who have married well but chosen to live as far away from here as they can. Now that my wife has passed on I have dedicated my life to this land. I think that you would do well and my militia would be the equal of any." He smiled, "And you are a relative, albeit a distant one. You seem to have inherited our ancestor's martial skills and not your father's foolishness. Perhaps this was meant to be."

I was flattered and accepted. However, I still had a nagging doubt that people were just doing me favours and I did not like that. My time with Prince Maurice and my service to the king had made me see a life with purpose. The captaincy of the militia did not seem the same.

I returned, as promised, to York to speak to Charlotte and her father. I rode alone and I confess that, when I entered the house I was fearful. What if Charlotte had come to her senses and changed her mind? The welcome I received allayed my fears. She could not wait to be married and to join me. Her father, too, seemed a happier man. He had hired a housekeeper for the parish was a wealthier one than he had expected. I spent two days with Charlotte and her father making all the arrangements for the wedding and planning, with Charlotte, what we needed to buy for the cottage. I was able to describe the cottage well and it was clear to me that I was like a babe in the woods for I had not thought of all the things that Charlotte listed. "Bedding, pots, platters, cutlery, curtains…" the list went on so long that my face fell. She smiled, "Do not worry, James, for I can buy all that we need here but you shall need to find us a wagon to transport it and I would like to visit the house before we are wed. I do not wish to have all the work to do when we are just married."

I now had my own list of work and when I left, I had a clearer idea in my head of what I would need to do. I arranged to return in a fortnight. Charlotte assured me that all would be ready by then. It was a different James Bretherton that rode up the road to Piercebridge than the one that had left. One life had ended and a new one had begun.

Epilogue

The return to our new home after the wedding was joyous. I had employed many of the villagers to help me prepare and when we arrived we were welcomed like royalty. It helped that Charlotte had the kindliest way of speaking to everyone. She made them all feel special. Roger entertained us the first night and then we headed for our new cottage. That it was small did not seem to matter for it was our first home. I did not know if this would be our only home for, having seen the plot of land, I had already decided that we would build a new home there. That was for the future. First, I had to learn how to be a husband and then begin to earn the money that Sir Giles had given me. I would no longer be a soldier but a trainer of men. I was excited. In many ways I had much to thank Don Alvarado for. If he had not decided to try to kill me then I would never have met Charlotte and might never have considered being a captain of militia. Who knows? I might have returned to serve the King of Denmark as a mercenary fighting in the war against the Papists.

The End

Glossary

Haliwerfolc – the men of the saint (Cuthbert)
Knacker's yard – horse abattoir
Muskettengabel – a rest for a musket
Secrete – a small helmet hidden beneath a cap or hat
Serpentine – the match holder for the lighted fuse on a matchlock
Swetebags – bags containing herbs and concealed beneath
clothes to take away the stink of sweat
Walthame Cross – Waltham Cross

Canonical Hours

Matins (nighttime)
Lauds (early morning)
Prime (first hour of daylight)
Terce (third hour)
Sext (noon)
Nones (ninth hour)
Vespers (sunset evening)
Compline (end of the day)

Historical Background

This series will be about the war between the Catholics and the Protestants in the early seventeenth century. It was a bloody war that devastated huge tracts of Europe. Between 5 and 9 million soldiers and civilians died in the 20-year conflict. The Spanish and Imperial troops were first faced by mercenaries, the Dutch and the Bohemians. Once the Danish and Swedes became involved then the conflict spread. James Bretherton is an amalgam of the mercenary leaders who fought in Europe. Despite being mercenaries, they all believed in their cause. These were not the condottiere who just fought for pay. I have used real battles and events as my structure. I have not glossed over the battles nor made then unduly heroic. They were not. I write about war from the perspective of the soldiers and not the generals.

Southwark Cathedral only became The Cathedral and Collegiate Church of St Saviour and St Mary Overie in 1905. Before that, it was a parish church serving those who lived close to London Bridge.

Books used in the research:
The English Civil War - Peter Gaunt
The Thirty Years' War 1618-1648 - Richard Bonney
Imperial Armies of the Thirty Years War Infantry and Artillery - Brnardic and Pavlovic
Imperial Armies of the Thirty Years War Cavalry - Brnardic and Pavlovic
The Army of Gustavus Adolphus 1 Infantry - Brzezinski and Hook
The Army of Gustavus Adolphus 2 Cavalry - Brzezinski and Hook
The English Civil War Armies - Young and Roffe
Lutzen 1632 - Brzezinski and Turner
The English Civil Wars - Blair Worden
The Tower of London - Lapper and Parnell
Dutch armies of the 80 Years War 1568-1648 Cavalry and Artillery - Groot and Embleton

Dutch armies of the 80 Years War 1568-1648 Infantry - Groot and Embleton

Other books by Griff Hosker

If you enjoyed reading this book, then why not read another one by the author?

Ancient History

The Sword of Cartimandua Series
(Germania and Britannia 50 A.D. – 128 A.D.)
Ulpius Felix- Roman Warrior (prequel)
The Sword of Cartimandua
The Horse Warriors
Invasion Caledonia
Roman Retreat
Revolt of the Red Witch
Druid's Gold
Trajan's Hunters
The Last Frontier
Hero of Rome
Roman Hawk
Roman Treachery
Roman Wall
Roman Courage

The Wolf Warrior series
(Britain in the late 6th Century)
Saxon Dawn
Saxon Revenge
Saxon England
Saxon Blood
Saxon Slayer
Saxon Slaughter
Saxon Bane
Saxon Fall: Rise of the Warlord
Saxon Throne

Horse and Pistol

Saxon Sword

Medieval History

The Dragon Heart Series
Viking Slave *
Viking Warrior *
Viking Jarl *
Viking Kingdom *
Viking Wolf *
Viking War
Viking Sword
Viking Wrath
Viking Raid
Viking Legend
Viking Vengeance
Viking Dragon
Viking Treasure
Viking Enemy
Viking Witch
Viking Blood
Viking Weregeld
Viking Storm
Viking Warband
Viking Shadow
Viking Legacy
Viking Clan
Viking Bravery

The Norman Genesis Series
Hrolf the Viking *
Horseman *
The Battle for a Home *
Revenge of the Franks *
The Land of the Northmen
Ragnvald Hrolfsson

Horse and Pistol

Brothers in Blood
Lord of Rouen
Drekar in the Seine
Duke of Normandy
The Duke and the King

Danelaw
(England and Denmark in the 11th Century)
Dragon Sword *
Oathsword *
Bloodsword *
Danish Sword
The Sword of Cnut

New World Series
Blood on the Blade *
Across the Seas *
The Savage Wilderness *
The Bear and the Wolf *
Erik The Navigator *
Erik's Clan *
The Last Viking

The Vengeance Trail *

The Conquest Series
(Normandy and England 1050-1100)
Hastings
Conquest

The Aelfraed Series
(Britain and Byzantium 1050 A.D. - 1085 A.D.)
Housecarl *
Outlaw *
Varangian *

244

The Reconquista Chronicles
Castilian Knight *
El Campeador *
The Lord of Valencia *

**The Anarchy Series England
1120-1180**
English Knight *
Knight of the Empress *
Northern Knight *
Baron of the North *
Earl *
King Henry's Champion *
The King is Dead *
Warlord of the North
Enemy at the Gate
The Fallen Crown
Warlord's War
Kingmaker
Henry II
Crusader
The Welsh Marches
Irish War
Poisonous Plots
The Princes' Revolt
Earl Marshal
The Perfect Knight

**Border Knight
1182-1300**
Sword for Hire *
Return of the Knight *
Baron's War *
Magna Carta *
Welsh Wars *
Henry III *

The Bloody Border *
Baron's Crusade
Sentinel of the North
War in the West
Debt of Honour
The Blood of the Warlord
The Fettered King
de Montfort's Crown

Sir John Hawkwood Series
France and Italy 1339- 1387
Crécy: The Age of the Archer *
Man At Arms *
The White Company *
Leader of Men *
Tuscan Warlord *
Condottiere

Lord Edward's Archer
Lord Edward's Archer *
King in Waiting *
An Archer's Crusade *
Targets of Treachery *
The Great Cause *
Wallace's War *
The Hunt

Struggle for a Crown
1360- 1485
Blood on the Crown *
To Murder a King *
The Throne *
King Henry IV *
The Road to Agincourt *
St Crispin's Day *
The Battle for France *

Horse and Pistol

The Last Knight *
Queen's Knight *

Tales from the Sword I
(Short stories from the Medieval period)

Tudor Warrior series
England and Scotland in the late 15th and early 16th
century
Tudor Warrior *
Tudor Spy *
Flodden

Conquistador
England and America in the 16th Century
Conquistador *
The English Adventurer *

English Mercenary
The 30 Years War and the English Civil War
Horse and Pistol

Modern History

The Napoleonic Horseman Series
Chasseur à Cheval
Napoleon's Guard
British Light Dragoon
Soldier Spy
1808: The Road to Coruña
Talavera
The Lines of Torres Vedras
Bloody Badajoz
The Road to France
Waterloo

Horse and Pistol

The Lucky Jack American Civil War series
Rebel Raiders
Confederate Rangers
The Road to Gettysburg

Soldier of the Queen series
Soldier of the Queen
Redcoat's Rifle
Omdurman

The British Ace Series
1914
1915 Fokker Scourge
1916 Angels over the Somme
1917 Eagles Fall
1918 We will remember them
From Arctic Snow to Desert Sand
Wings over Persia

Combined Operations series
1940-1945
Commando *
Raider *
Behind Enemy Lines
Dieppe
Toehold in Europe
Sword Beach
Breakout
The Battle for Antwerp
King Tiger
Beyond the Rhine
Korea
Korean Winter

Tales from the Sword II
(Short stories from the Modern period)

248

Books marked thus *, are also available in the audio
format.
For more information on all of the books then please visit
the author's website at www.griffhosker.com where there is
a link to contact him or visit his Facebook page:
GriffHosker at Sword Books or follow him on Twitter:
@HoskerGriff or Sword (@swordbooksltd)

Printed in Great Britain
by Amazon

39177746R00139